THE PURSUIT

OF AGENT M

THE PURSUIT OF AGENT M

DEWITT COPP

CUTTING EDGE

ISBN-13: 978-1-957868-04-2

For Peter

This author and the poet wish to thank Hardwick Nevin for the use of his poetry
in the book.

Published by
Cutting Edge Books
PO Box 8212
Calabasas, CA 91372
www.cuttingedgebooks.com

CHAPTER ONE

Night fell. In its swift, heavy falling, a few small grains of time were added to Mark Costain's nearly exhausted supply. Since the road, he had been running, and they had been running after him.

The terrain was too rough and thickly wooded for pursuit by car. The rain-bloated mat of clouds, blanketing grayly above the trees, eliminated the use of aircraft. And so, through the late afternoon, it had been his physical powers against theirs; he fleeing for his life, they to end it. In the upland timber, which terminated against the sheer cliff wall, night brought a temporary delay to the inevitable climax.

Costain, unknowing, stumbling upward through the limbo twilight amidst the towering, wet trees, tripped and fell, rolling down a shallow bank, coming to rest on his back, the rain pecking impartially at his face. Some flickering ember of strength urged him to regain his feet, but the darkness snuffed it out. He must lie still! ... He must concentrate on how to draw air into his lungs without burning them up. It was impossible! ... Someone had stuffed him full of burning cotton, and air, instead of putting out the fire, was making it bum more fiercely. He opened his mouth wide, desperately hoping enough raindrops would fall in it to dampen the blaze. The effort made him retch, his body jerking convulsively, ugly, wrenching sounds torn out of his throat.

The seizure finally spent itself and with its slow passage, awareness returned and brought realization. He was lying where he had fallen, his body soaked, trembling. He was one long hurt inside and out.

There was no knowing how far he had run. It didn't seem anyone could have run so far. Now there was this very solid darkness, the rain, and a cold, rising wind. On it came torn snatches of indistinguishable words, and with them the final, frightening fact exploded in his clearing mind. They were after him! Sweet Jesus, it had finally come to this! …

He jerked to a sitting position, hand grasping instinctively at the automatic pistol in his jacket pocket. On hands and knees, he scrambled quickly up the bank of the small depression. He could see nothing but the vague black silhouettes of trees, dimly fused into the impenetrable night. Eyes and ears straining, body tensed, heart pumping hard again, he crouched motionless.

The voices had stopped. For all he knew, they might be all about him! They were just lying there, waiting for him to move! He had to get out of here!

Panic flared through him. Run!

The calm, inner reason of Costain's hard mind quickly doused the blaze. "Stay where you are! What you can't see, they can't see."

He lay down carefully on the edge of the gully and thought about his next move, listening for sounds of approach, sounds of voices.

Over the years he had developed the habit of silent inner debate, in which the more aggressive side of his nature argued with his more cautious self.

"I can't stay here."

"No, but if you move, they'll hear you."

"Not if I'm careful."

"You're in no shape to try mountain climbing."

"I'm in no shape to sit here and wait till it's light so they can shoot me when I try."

"How far is the mountain?"

"I don't know. It seemed close ... I think."

"You're surrounded here. Probably they have men on the mountain."

"I'll have to try and get by them."

"They've got you, Costain. They've got you good."

"Be still! Shut up! Sit here and die!" And then more calmly, "Which way is the mountain?"

"You were running toward it at the last."

"Yes. And these voices seemed to come from out there."

"The land slopes up, doesn't it? Find how it slopes."

"Yes. I'll find it. All right, let's go ... Quietly!"

It took Costain the better part of an hour to reach the cliffs. The upward slope of the land gave him his direction. Moving painstakingly, using obstructions he could distinguish close ahead, he kept his course relatively straight.

Each time he set his foot down, he did it like a man walking on broken glass, tentatively, gingerly. After every step, he stopped and listened. It made his progress tortuously slow, nerve-racking.

The wind had become stronger, and the urgent sounds it produced amongst the trees helped to cover the noise of his step-by-step passage. But, Costain reasoned, if the wind was an aid to him, it was also an aid to his pursuers.

In one respect the rain helped, too, its heavy, relentless fall soaking the leaf carpet. But wind and rain together also had a strong adverse effect, working to sap the remaining strength of his thinly clad body.

The desire to run began to overpower him, the checkrein on his reason to weaken. Half a dozen times he took bulky objects to be men and nearly fired at them. When a portion of a tree branch fell crashing behind him, he spun about with a choked cry of fear. His body shook from more than cold, but the cold made him want to run, too.

Then, all at once, he knew there were no more trees in front of him, and in three careful strides he had come up against the cliff wall. He leaned against its smooth, wet side, breathing wearily, feeling as though he had run all the way.

Pocketing the pistol, Costain raised his hands above his head and felt for a hold. There was none, not even a thin crack. He moved several cautious steps to the left, keeping his arms raised, feeling; a blind man feeling. He moved to the right and repeated the search. It was no good. He lowered his arms and stood motionless, head cocked, thinking, remembering.

During the long chase, his intent had been to reach the mountains. They had not tried to cut him off from this; instead, they had effectively steered him to this particular spot. They'd known when he came up against these cliffs the chase would be over.

Despair engulfed him. His shoulders sagged, his back bent. He stood with his forehead pressed against the cold, unyielding rock wall, eyes closed, the rain falling on his neck exploring icily down his spine.

"Done!" the word echoed with hollow finality.

"Have to try and get through them."

"Useless! Just what they're waiting for."

"Haven't come after me. Why?"

"Why should they? … When it's light."

"Have to find a way up the mountain."

"There is no way."

"Try again."

He tried again, carefully lengthening his exploration, not knowing in how small an area they had him trapped. He found no way up. No place for a hand hold. No place for a toe hold. Nothing but slabs of smooth rock, forming an impregnable barrier.

Had he really expected to escape?

Suppose he did get over the mountains. They'd be waiting for him on the other side.

He would stand at bay in the October dawn, and they would kill him. In this manner, at this time, and after so long. It was all to be expected. Here in the woodland he would fall and his blood would stain the leaves a brighter hue than frost-painted maples.

He raised his head and suddenly knew that a few feet away something else was standing against the cliff wall. He was ready to shoot when he realized it was a pine tree.

He moved to its protective bulk and thought it odd how trees sometimes grew literally out of rock. The lower portion of the trunk was pressed tightly against the cliff base. At head level no more than six inches separated wood and stone. Looking upward he could see that the conifer's lower branches extended in a rough fan-shape from the tree's three open sides. There was no telling how tall the pine stood, but in reaching around its trunk he could barely touch his fingers. He stood a moment, staring up, blinking his eyes against the rain, feeling a faint twinge of hope stirring.

"Climb it."

"What for? It'll take you nowhere."

"Try it!"

"Ridiculous!"

"If it grows up close to the cliff all the way … there might be a ledge."

"Waste of time."

"Find out!"

"Straws in the wind."

"Climb!"

The lowest branch was too high for Costain to reach, but by using the cliff as a back support and shinnying, he got up to it easily enough. He rose carefully on the wet limb, holding on to the trunk with one hand, letting his breathing settle down. Even from this vantage point, there was no telling how high the tree rose. He would have to climb higher.

He went slowly, his already soaked body freshly showered by rain-sodden branches, the smell of pine needles sharp in his nostrils. Very gradually the distance grew between the tree and the cliff. With each added degree of height, he paused and examined the rock for sign of ledge or fissure. Its surface remained unchanged.

The tree was a big, high one. He could tell that now, but as the trunk began to thin, its sway increased under his weight and the wind's force. The branches grew smaller, bending and cracking under him. Water cascaded off his head and shoulders, running frigidly down his back and chest.

He set his jaw against the discomfort. Weariness and defeat climbed with him, warring despairingly against his efforts. He drove himself upward, until he felt it unsafe to go higher. Holding on with his legs around the trunk, an arm locked over a branch, he arched the upper half of his body away from the tree to see if he could detect the top.

He shut his mind to the swaying and the nasty cracking noises, concentrating on the meaning of what he saw, or thought he saw, trying to peer through the deceptive sky muck.

He was leaning away from the branchless side of the tree, and yet above, it seemed there was a branch extending toward the cliff, its end not in sight. Reaching out his arm and letting his weight go as far as he dared, he could just barely touch stone.

He resumed his former position, pressed against the trunk, trying to assimilate this new discovery. If the branch above did go inward, then there must be a ledge or some sort of indentation in the rock. From here he could not be sure this was so, but it seemed so. It might be his eyes desperately putting imagery in his mind that did not exist. But if it did exist, and there was a ledge there, would the bending trunk take his weight at that elevation, and if it would, could he possibly get himself from the tree onto the cliff? Either he went higher and chanced it, or he went down. If he fell, death would only come that much sooner.

He took a deep breath and began to inch his way up. How far must he go? Five feet … Six. How high was he? Did it matter?

The branches were too small now to take his weight, and he had to push and worm his way on the relatively clear side of the tree. He could feel it bending! Giving! Cracking!

Costain swung his head out and saw that he'd misjudged the height of the extended limb. It was still out of reach, but he had been right! There was a ledge some distance below it. He could see its rim! There was nothing he could use for purchase, no way he could leap up to get his hands on it! He had to manage from where he clung.

The trunk's increasing bow was punctuated by agonized ripping sounds above the buffeting wind. It bent on an angle toward the cliff, and in that he saw his only chance. His design had been to try and keep his weight away from the arching. Now he put all his bulk into it. As the tree bent swiftly to the breaking point, Costain twisted his body around, and still holding on with his legs, thrust his arms up at the ledge rim. His right hand made contact and held. His left struck flat stone. He gave a last convulsive thrust with his legs and sought furiously to find a hold for his left hand. It caught, but in letting go the tree, the shock of his full weight on hands and shoulders nearly jerked him free. His fingers dug into the wet rock. They were slipping as he hung on the cliff face, the wind pummeling at his dangling frame. He brought his feet up and got them on stone. Then arms, legs, toes, every worn sinew in him went into the attempt. And somehow he was lying on flat rock, his breath sobbing in great gulps.

When his breathing began to steady, he raised his head and took stock of his hard-won perch. He estimated the shelf to be a good four feet wide where he lay. It was backed by another cliff wall that rose vertically into the night. Only exploration would tell how far his resting place bordered it.

Rising on hands and knees, he began to crawl cautiously to his left. The ledge quickly narrowed under him, and he halted, lying down on his stomach and reaching out to feel what his eyes could only vaguely discern. The ledge ended abruptly, blocked by a bulge in the rock. It was no good that way.

Back to his original starting point, he planned to investigate in the opposite direction.

"If it thins out, I'll have to stand."

"If you don't slip getting up, the wind will blow you right off."

"God, if it peters out like this other side."

"Why wouldn't it?"

"Suppose I just stayed here, lay flat in close. Would they figure I was up here?"

"Don't underestimate them. When it's light, they'll discover the tree. They'll know. A helicopter would spot you easily."

"All right, then it's this or nothing."

"It'll add up to nothing."

"I'll try this one on foot."

"On foot or on horseback, you'll bust your—!"

Standing, Costain turned and faced the cliff, spreading his arms out to embrace its cold, unfriendly surface. The wind quartered gustily at him, a cruel lever, trying to pry him loose. He gathered himself for the exploration and began a delicate side step, spread-eagled, his fingers attempting to cling and hold where there was nothing to hold.

Why not stop this! Let go and fall backwards! ... It would be so simple. What use in continuing this vain running? ... This wretched, painful, ordeal! There was no escape!

"Doomed!" thundered the wind against the rock.

"Doomed!" splattered the rain in an insidious minor key.

"Costain! ... Costain!" An angry chorus of voices jeered at him. The night was full of ghosts! ... The man he'd killed.

They were waiting for him to fall, eager for him, eager to smash his body and carry it broken and bleeding down to the everlasting blackness.

He very nearly did fall, not from a misstep or by supernatural interference, but because his reaching left hand, instead of pressing against stone was suddenly pressing against nothing! The precarious, thin line of balance was thrown out of control. He felt his body twist, powerless to prevent its fatal motion! For an instant he struggled, scrabbling at the cliff, fighting to regain his equilibrium.

When he got it, he stood transfixed, pressing his body in a frenzy to the escarpment. He knew that his last reserves of strength were about gone, but he knew, too, there must be a vertical cut where his hand had failed to make contact. It was hard to force himself to move now. His advance was measured in inches. A small side step, a slight shifting of hands and body to match it, hands that were now placed on either side of his head.

The ledge grew thinner. He couldn't look down to see how thin, but the edge of his heels were no longer on it. Then he had reached the fissure, his left hand touching its rim. He put his hand out as far as he could reach to see if he could bridge the opening. He could not. Another small step and he knew he could go no farther on the ledge. But this time his searching hand had found the far side of the cut. The inner portion was veined and indented. He could get a good grip on it. He set his hand as high and as far as he could stretch. Then on tiptoe, he tight-roped the last foot of the ledge right into the cliff itself, and for a sickening instant, only his straining left arm kept him from falling, his toes fighting to gain support on the sheer rock. Then his right hand shot out to anchor on the opposite side of the gap, and he jerked his feet up to plant them in the cleft, one on top of the other. He pulled himself higher, not halting until he was able to fit his whole body into the cut, resting his back against one wall, his feet braced against the other.

For a short time he remained in that position, arms and legs quivering with reaction, his head sunk on his chest. After a while, he lifted it and took stock of his surroundings. The couloir in which he was perched appeared to ascend in a long "V" and he knew enough about rock formations to believe that it would open onto cliff top.

For the first part of the ascension, he was able to use his back as he'd done in climbing the tree. When the cut continued to broaden, he went up legs spread, finding holds on each side. And finally, near the surface, going up one side altogether. It was easier than the tree, and not one half the ghastliness of the ledge. In rising to the final top, an unreasoning elation gripped him. He felt like a man who has risen out of a black well of infinite depth. He felt hope rising with him.

Really he had not escaped. There was still the mountain ahead; a mountain whose height he did not know, whose condition he could only guess. He had to cross it, ridiculously clothed, physically exhausted and half frozen. He had to cross it to face new terror, new traps. It was over 150 kilometers to the Austrian border. But in this small, bitterly-contested victory, he saw a change in his luck, and so it brought a change in his spirit. If he had luck, he had something. It was the only thing left now.

Standing on level ground again, patches of swirling cloud swept about him. In climbing higher he would be engulfed in it. His sense of direction would depend entirely on feel. He went away from the rim considering this new obstacle and came to a steep, barren slope. It was not another sheer wall, and he could mount it if his strength held. Costain knew he was a physically strong, extremely fit individual, but he would have given much to have possessed the stamina of twenty-eight as opposed to his thirty-eight years.

He blew on his numbed, swollen fingers and thrust them into his jacket pockets, hoping to restore a semblance of warmth to them. He stamped his feet, his leg muscles aching and cramped. To stay here was to grow colder. Whatever remained of the night he must use to put as much distance between himself and those who awaited the dawn below.

If scaling the cliffs had been a nightmare, the hours that followed turned into an incalculable hell. The rain congealed to sleet. The wind matured to a gale. Shale and rock and lichen growth surrendered to snow. The snow did to his lower body what the wind, and cloud, and sleet did to the upper half of him. Stupefied awareness began to deteriorate into periods of delirium. In such a mental state he became at one point a kind of disembodied spectator, observing again his own sudden downfall.

There had been no warning. The knock on the door might have been anyone coming to pay a Sunday afternoon call. He saw himself open the apartment door and knew that the sight of Hans Goltz would momentarily throw him off balance.

As the Assistant Engineering Director of Research and Development for Czechoslovakia's Aero-Morava, working in the highly critical and secret field of rocket and missile design, Costain was thoroughly familiar with Hans Goltz, the special security officer assigned to the plant. For other reasons, he had judged that he knew far more about Goltz than Goltz would ever know about him. Now, in that shocked instant of recognition, the thought flashed that he was wrong. He'd committed the fatal mistake of underestimating his man.

The tall bony security officer with his great beak of a nose, dominating his thin expressionless face, gestured with his hand and Costain automatically stepped aside to let him enter.

By the time he'd shut the door, Costain was again in control of his thoughts. Goltz was alone, or appeared to be. "Well, this is a surprise," he said, trying to make a dry joke of it.

"Sit down," Goltz replied, indicating the chair.

"Something has happened?" Costain felt a cold wind sweeping him.

"Yes," Goltz nodded shortly. "Something has happened. I've found you out … Mister *Costain*."

Costain frowned and blinked at his unwelcome caller. "I beg your pardon?" he heard his voice from a great distance. It was more than ten years since anyone had called him by his right name. For all that time he had been Mark Vorak. He saw Goltz' right hand come out of his coat pocket, holding the big, black automatic pistol.

"Sit down." The order came again.

Costain obeyed silently.

"Now then, the play acting is over. I know you're not even a Czech, you're an American spy, and you've done your dirty work since Aero-Morava was founded ten years ago. You've been very clever, but not clever enough for someone like myself. I know all about you. I, Hans Goltz, have found you out for what you are." This last was the only indication of the security policeman's consummate ego.

Costain shook his head, struggling to get his thoughts in line, "You must be out of your mind," he said with a mixture of shock and annoyance, "You know I'm an aeronautical engineer, you fool! And a damned important one. You have no right to come here and try to intimidate me with some insane accusation!"

"You're an engineer, all right," Goltz agreed. "But you're an engineer who has been stealing the secrets you've helped to develop. Stealing them and sending them to your filthy imperialist masters." His tone didn't rise or fall. It all came out with deadly matter-of-factness.

Costain's mind raced. He was caught. This was the day that he knew had been bound to come, but he had never fully accepted that it would come … particularly of late … somehow he'd made a slip. Somehow this careful ferret had gotten onto him. Now he had one last card to play, and if it didn't throw doubt into his captor's convictions, there was no hope in further talk.

Disdainfully, Costain stood up. "You're right, I am a spy," he said, "but not for whom you think." He smiled frostily. "I wonder if you know Jan Radek, our noted Minister of Internal Security, as well as I do?" He didn't let Goltz reply, but went on quickly and emphatically. "I know him on a first name basis. Did your burrowing tell you that, policeman? I was placed here by Jan Radek not just because of my engineering ability, but because he wanted a man he could trust who could report to him on the activities of others in the company. So you see," he said it sarcastically, "you and I are in the same business, Goltz. Don't make an ass of yourself and destroy a promising career."

Costain could feel the perspiration trickling down his sides, could feel the trembling in the backs of his legs. If Goltz knew the details of how Jan had hired him just before the Communist take-over, knew the nature of their friendship, he would then know that Jan Radek, like Mark Costain, had long been leading the dangerous double life. To catch a Costain would only be a link in the chain, and a warning to others. To catch a Radek would be to expose the entire apparatus, to wipe out lives and years of work.

Goltz gave a vigorous thrust of his hand against Costain's chest, and he went back a step, his legs hitting the chair, sitting down again.

"You'll remain seated until I tell you to stand. I know all about your reports to the Ministry. They were what first aroused my suspicions about you. Oh, I spent long nights of study on some of them, my friend. Long nights. Your so-called reports were nothing but a cover to send out secret information about what was being developed in your department."

"Sure," Costain nodded, knowing that if he was going to act, it would have to be soon, "sure, I sent them to Jan Radek, who passed them on to the President of the United States."

"You sent your reports to the Ministry, and someone there who is in league with you passed them on. You're going to tell me who that person is."

"You mean you're not clever enough to find out?" Thank God, it was only this bad! Radek was not suspected … yet!

"Since I've solved this case all by myself, I've seen no reason to involve others," Goltz admitted candidly, and Costain held back the sigh of relief. "When I have all the details you will give me, I shall place the case in my superior's hands. Now, get up," the gun waved in signal. "We'll go where we have better surroundings in which you can talk."

Costain had made up his mind that when he was told to stand, he would attack, attack knowing he had only a small chance. But either way, he would not be forced to betray anyone. Ten long, lonely years, and the grand masquerade was over. The "long termer" had been flushed into the open.

Now!

Being a disembodied observer helped him to see the swift brutal climax. He had gone off the chair in a head-long dive. One hand reaching for his enemy's throat, the other for the wrist that held the gun.

If he had underestimated the cleverness of Goltz, it was Goltz who underestimated his ability to act with such speed and precision. The spindly man, taken off guard, never had a chance against the physical power of Costain.

They hit the floor with a room-shaking crash, Costain on top of his adversary. Goltz, half stunned, scrabbled vainly to bring his weapon to bear. Costain literally tore the gun from its owner's grasp, and reversing it, struck viciously ... and struck twice more.

When he arose, breathing deeply, his whole body shaking, he realized that he had killed Goltz. He had to get out of here! ... Get his car and head for the border ... Get the hell out fast! As much as his own safety, there was the information about the latest break-through. It was of more importance than everything he'd sent out over the years.

Goltz had said he played this alone, but had he come here alone?

Costain hurried to the window and looked out carefully. He saw the two strong-arm boys, that the security policeman usually kept in tow, staring up at him. They were standing on the sidewalk beside the official car. In another couple of minutes they'd be investigating their chief's delay.

Costain went out into the hall and down the corridor to the window that faced on the fire escape. He opened the window and the cold hit him.

God it was cold! ... Where was he? ... The fire escape? ... No, that went down, he was going up ... Up! ... forever up! They'd caught him and killed him, and he had been sentenced to go forever up!

Costain, unknowing, crossed the mountain peak, and like a man drunk and mindless, went staggering and stumbling over the lee side. His momentum carried him forward. On the steep reverse slope, he fell and went rolling in an uncontrolled glissade, coming to a stop at the base of the slope. The stubborn instinct of a knocked-out fighter put him on his feet again, a swaying grotesque figure, whitely covered. Dumbly, he made several tries at trying to climb back up the way he'd come. On the third try, he slipped and skidded around to face a more level expanse. Costain walked along it stiffly, a weaving automaton. He had no knowledge of his actions, nothing to stay his walking off its edge. He was completely oblivious to the fact that his body was tumbling through space, hurtling down and down.

CHAPTER TWO

The sheepherder's dog found Costain, lying a few feet clear of the snow line. The dog sniffed the battered, prostrate body warily, then looked down the slope to where the old man sat resting. He barked twice, and the old man arose and came slowly up toward him in the clear, sharp, early morning light.

The view he left was spectacular, the flank of the mountain dropping in a series of vallied plateaus to the russet, fog-patched plains. "Like giant steps," the old man was thinking when the dog called him.

Ordinarily, he would not have come this high on the mountain, but in the storm several ewes and their new lambs had been frightened from the protection of the pasture. Since first light, he and the dog had been searching for the foolish animals. Today he would move the herd to the lower valley while the weather remained good. The autumn storms had arrived, and he must have the sheep off the high ground before they became too severe.

The old man remained calm and thoughtful on seeing what the dog had found. It was an unexpected thing, but not enough to ruffle him. He sighed a little sadly, noticing the clothing the man wore. "It is certain," he said to the dog, "this one is not a climber of mountains by choice."

Before he knelt to examine the body, he took in the snow field. His faded brown eyes with their craggy brows and sunbursts of wrinkles saw the swath the man had cut through the snow. It was apparent he had fallen from the cliff, and his body had rolled down the slope to this point.

The old man made a clicking sound with his tongue as he knelt. The dog moved next to him, whining softly. His master rolled Costain onto his back with great care.

There was an ugly gash on Costain's temple, running back into the hair. The entire side of his face was blood-matted. The old man shook his head and put a tough, gnarled hand under the wet jacket. He did not expect to find a heartbeat and knew his first surprise that day when he did.

His eyes went to the cliff again. "To have fallen all that distance. It must be at least a hundred feet ... and he lives." He looked at the dog. "He lives. I must determine how badly he is injured."

The old man experienced his second surprise when he could find no broken bones. Except for the wound on the head, except for badly torn, swollen hands and knees, he could detect no serious hurt.

"He is not so unlucky," the old man nodded thoughtfully. "The snow saved him in his fall, and his rolling saved him from the snow. This is in the nature of a miracle."

The dog wagged his tail and panted in agreement, his breath making cloud puffs in the freshly scrubbed October air.

The old man, who'd lived all his life on or close to the mountain, saw the hand of God in many acts. He saw it now because the stranger who lay before him was still alive. And he saw himself chosen as an instrument of aid. He was not concerned with reasons or consequences. His own reasoning transcended the affairs of men. It was meant that he come here. He would do what he could. He rose stiffly off his knees and squatted on his haunches, wiping his nose with the back of his hand, sniffing deeply. He scratched the dog's head, thinking of what to do.

"He's too big for me to carry. He would break all my bones ... If I could get him on his feet and he could walk a little—You want to carry him?" The dog stared straight ahead and acted as though he hadn't heard the question.

"No, I don't blame you. All right then. You will go and find the foolish ones and bring them back. I shall take this one down. I would like to get the herd lower today, but it may not be possible because of what we have here. It is as God wills. Go now. Go. Bring them back."

The dog trotted off on his appointed task, and the old man tried to revive Costain with snow, without success. Because there was no blood running from ears or nose, he did not believe that the skull was broken, but there was no doubt it was badly bruised.

He ended up by dragging the unconscious man down the rocky incline. He did it slowly, grasping Costain under the arms, moving him only a few yards at a time. In a short space, he was sweat-covered and breathing hard. Truly, this was a big man, like a great log! To try and drag him all the distance to the shelter would be too much. It would be better to take him to the cave he had seen in the ravine. He would take him there because of the distance and for more serious reasons. A man did not carry a weapon, such as this one had in his jacket, without cause. A man did not travel these mountains so dressed for sport. If others were looking for him, better he be hidden until his purpose became clear.

From his unrestricted vantage point, the old man could detect no movement below, nor had anyone appeared on the cliffs that rose to the summit. Still, it was to be expected that someone would come. Everything said that to him, and it was a question whether they would be skilled enough to discover the marks the injured man had made in the snow. He was being careful to leave no trail over these rocks. Every time he set Costain down, he would backtrack and remove signs left by dragging heels. Only dogs would be able to find this man now. If they brought dogs, he could do nothing more. If he was indeed obeying the will of God, as he believed himself to be doing, then it was to save this one, or to be caught in punishment for his many sins. Either way, by the blessed Virgin, this one was making him pay! His back was already broken and his arms and legs were full of stone. The air cut sorely in his chest, and his breath came in quick, heavy gasps. The place he had chosen seemed a very great distance.

After much exertion, the old man got Costain hidden in the jumbled rockfall. The cave was actually a separation between two tilted slabs of granite. The enclosure was so protected by adjacent configurations that it was a good place for concealment. Only by walking up to the opening would anyone be able to see Costain's unconscious form.

Sighing his tiredness and relief, the old man quickly checked to see that there no apparent signs leading to the hiding place. Now that the thing was done, he felt a desire to be gone. He went down the remainder of the slope almost at a run and didn't slow his pace until he reached the timber. By the time he left the woodland and entered the gently sloped intervals where the herd was pastured, he'd regained his breath and his composure.

The sheep were grazing peacefully. A chorus of tremulous "baa—baas!" greeted his approach. He spoke to them, threading through their ranks to the shelter. The day was growing warm, cloudless and hazy. The weather should hold through the day. The dog was not back yet, but he would return when his job was done.

The old man knelt down on his blanket, taking the skin bag from the peg. He uncorked it and, tilting his head, milked a stream of wine into his mouth.

He gulped the amber juice with thirsty enjoyment. And when he set the bag aside, he felt his strength coming back.

"Ahhh! That is indeed better for one such as me." He brushed the dribblings from his mat of gray-black beard and palmed the sweat from his brow. It was then he heard the sound, a strange buzzing, clanking noise. The sheep heard it, too, and began to mill nervously, their bleating swelling. He went out amongst them, his voice assuring, his eyes squinting for a sight of the unfamiliar sound.

It came over the tops of the trees, a buglike machine with turning blades and a flat glass bulb in which there were two men. He had seen such a machine once before when in the town, but he stared up at it in openmouthed awe.

His surprise was eclipsed swiftly by fear and then transformed into rage when he saw the machine was dropping down toward him, and that its attendant sight and sound was bringing terror to the sheep. They would stampede, and there would be nothing he could do to halt them! He waved frantically at the settling machine, shouting for it to go away. The swirling main body of the herd broke, charging for the far end of the pasture and the thick woodland.

"Devils! Fools! Dung-eaters!" He screamed at the descending helicopter, running toward it, shaking his stick. To destroy his sheep by this monstrous stupidity! His helplessness was a wild thing.

It was the dog who saved the herd from possible self-destruction and definite dissolution.

The old man did not actually see him race out of the timber and charge the flank of the stampeding herd. He did not know the dog was there until he sensed the animals were turning in their flight. Then he swung about and watched his companion and friend use his amazing dexterity and intelligence to drive the tightly packed mass away from the trees and mold it into a churning, rotating wheel of milling, struggling animals.

The men in the helicopter had realized the disastrous effect of their approach and swiftly skidded their machine to the opposite end of the pasture, where they made their landing.

His voice quaking with shock and emotional gratitude, the old man called his thanks to the dog. The sheep were quieting slowly, but their nervousness was such that a very small thing could trigger them again. The dog darted about, nipping at those still trying to break away. The air was choked with plaintive cries, a bedlam of complaint. He spoke above it soothingly, moving amongst the flock. Out of the corner of his eye, he saw the two men of the machine approaching and waved them back.

After a moment of debate, they stopped and waited. One of them shouted, "We want to talk to you!"

He muttered an obscene reply and ignored them. When he felt it safe, he moved slowly toward his unwelcome visitors, some of the sheep moving with him. He had his anger under control, but it was still there.

The two stood watching him closely. They wore coveralls and round peaked hats. Each had a silver badge on his left breast, and around their waists there were black gun belts supporting bolstered revolvers. They were young and fit, and the short, square-faced one, apologetic.

"Sorry, Grandpa," he said with a twisted grin. "Didn't mean to scare your sheep."

The old man eyed them coldly before he replied. This one would be all right. The other with the scar he didn't like. "What is it you want with me?" There was no subservience in his harsh voice, nor in his manner.

"We're looking for a man," the Short One replied.

The old man knew that he must not seem too alert. He stared blankly, stupidly. "I am here alone … with the dog."

"Have you seen anyone?"

"Only you. You have nearly cost me my whole herd." He stamped his stick on the ground in censure. The thought of it fanned his anger.

"You keep a civil tongue in your head," Scarface ordered flatly. "You don't own these sheep."

"I am responsible for them. I tend them," he said with spirit. "In that, they are mine."

"Well, just calm down," the other said placatingly. "What's your name, Grandpa? How long have you been here?"

Scarface took a notebook from his pocket, ready to write the information down. He glared at them, a dirty, ignorant, old man. "How long have I been where?"

"Here. In this place … this pasture," the short questioner explained, letting his glance sweep the area.

He told them and made them ask for his name again before he would give it, then started to turn away as though the conversation were at an end.

Scarface barked angrily, and the old man, secretly enjoying himself, faced about.

"You've seen no one today?" The friendliness was gone from the Short One's keen eyes.

He shook his head.

"We're police, you know that?"

He stared at their badges. "I have seen police before," he said.

"The man we're after is a murderer, an enemy of the state. If you were to help him, it would be too bad for you."

"Why should I help such a man?" He shrugged. "I know no murderers."

"We know he's around here somewhere." Scarface jabbed his finger at the old man with rude authority. "He won't escape, and you won't either if you're lying."

The old man sighed and pulled at his beard. "Why don't you go hunt for him? … Away from my sheep."

His reply further irked Scarface. "I think we should take him in for questioning." He snapped his notebook shut.

The short policeman didn't favor the suggestion with an answer. He had his eyes on the shelter. "Go have a look in there," he said.

The dog came up, surveying the intruders. He was panting from his labors.

The short policeman squatted down and put out his hand for the dog to sniff, talking to him. He patted the dog's head. Without looking up, he began speaking to the old man. "This criminal we're after is very dangerous. He would kill you if he saw you. There is a big reward for his capture. If you should catch sight of him, or any sign of him, get away from here fast. Get off the mountain and tell them in the town. We'll be in the vicinity. We'll be watching for you."

The old man knew that the dog-petter was giving him a friendly warning. "Even if I did see this man you seek, I couldn't leave the sheep for long."

"This fellow will watch the sheep." The policeman stood up, his tight smile back. "I have a better idea. If you see anything suspicious, build a fire. We'll see it from the air."

"I always build a fire at night."

"I am talking about during the day."

"This—this criminal … how do you know he's here?"

"We know," the policeman nodded seriously. "We've got a large searching party covering the other side of the mountain. If they don't find him, they'll be coming over this way."

The old man felt his heart jerk. He spat disgustedly and then swung his gaze to the sheep. "Will they bring dogs?"

"Yes, they have dogs."

"Please!" Now his whole being was full of anxiety. "Don't—don't let them bring dogs here! They—they! It would be a terrible thing!"

The policeman nodded understandingly. "Yes, they probably would raise hell, wouldn't they? They're trained especially for hunting." He patted the worried sheepherder on the back. "We'll have them keep the dogs out of your pasture, so long as they find no scent."

"But they'll scent my sheep!"

"They'll be leashed. Don't worry about it."

The old man blubbered his fears until Scarface returned from searching the shelter. "Shall we take him along?" he asked nastily.

"Did you find anything?"

"Nah."

"Let's go."

"What about him?"

"What about him?" The policeman in command eyed his larger associate with contempt.

Scarface bridled, "The old bastard's probably lying. You can't trust this type, I know. I—"

"We're looking for a murderer, not a shepherd," the Short One cut him off. "S'long, Grandpa," he smiled fleetingly at the old man. "Remember what I said, watch yourself."

The old man sat on a rock and soothed the skittery sheep with the soft, sad notes of his wooden flute. The police in their flying machine were gone, although intermittently he could hear the sound of their aerial hunting, and once he caught sight of the helicopter sliding along above the tree tops. It seemed to him they were moving back and forth across the flank of the mountain, going down its side step by step. He thought of what he had learned, and he considered the things he might do. He was lacking in respect for those of the police, and so it had always been, even in the old days. It was essentially that he lacked respect for all authority, and since boyhood the manifestation of it had been reflected in the police. They were not protectors in his mind. They, were givers of orders and frighteners of the weak. He had heard their orders, but seldom did they frighten him.

True, they could come in their buzzing machine to disturb his sheep and anger him, and bring him trouble. They could come with their wild dogs and guns and find the one who had killed and kill him in turn. The question was, could he prevent it? To go now to where the fugitive was hidden would be dangerous. The men in the air would see him doing this. Even if they didn't, to bring the hurt one here to the pasture now would be even worse. Was there a safer hiding place, a place where dogs could not track?

The old man grunted, lowering his flute. "I know of no hiding places," he said to the sheep. "I have no need to hide … In the middle of the sea would be a good place." The water made him think of the torrent rushing down the mountain, but it was too far away, and even so, a hurt man would be no match for its strength.

What, then?

He began to play again. He could take the herd to the lower pasture as planned. It would be better for them, and it would indeed be better for him. But to leave in this fashion? Was it not strange that he had been directed to this man, only to abandon him?

Certainly he was not a respecter of killers, no more than of the police. He knew there were reasons that forced men to this serious crime. The punishment for it, however, must come from God.

It might be that he was to be punished, too. The police had warned that the man might kill him. The image of death did not trouble him, and so how could it be that? No, it must be as he first thought. He would stay and see what unfolded. By tomorrow it should be answered, and he could move the herd down then.

The old man pocketed his flute and arose. A few of his charges protested. "I am hungry," he told them. He went toward the shelter, a tough, square-set old man, vigorous and strong despite his age. His long life on the mountain had molded his thoughts and beliefs to match the simplicity of his surroundings. He was removed from men and their causes. He had compassion. He understood human weakness. He recognized only the strength of his God.

He sat in front of the shelter, letting the sun warm him, sharing his rough fare with the dog. He was patiently waiting for what must come, and when it did it was completely unexpected. He had been upset once this day and made more angry than was his custom. Now he was upset again, and this time it was not anger that possessed him but fear.

The dog knew first. He suddenly stopped teasing for more to eat and turned about, his hackles rising, a low growl of warning coming from deep in his throat. The old man looked toward the trees across the pasture and saw a figure emerge from them, staggering blindly.

Merciful Christ, it was the fugitive!

He arose with a hoarse cry, waving at Costain to go back. The hurt man gave no sign of hearing. He wove a few steps farther and fell on his hands and knees. The old man ran toward him, calling out, and saw him get to his feet and advance a few more yards before he fell again. The dog reached him where he lay and began circling, teeth bared, growling, ready to strike.

The old man came up winded and shaken. He silenced the dog sharply, ordering him back. Costain, his eyes glazed with pain, braced himself on one arm and fumbled for the gun in his jacket pocket.

The old man shook his stick at him, shouting, "You fool! Why didn't you stay where I put you! Now look what you've done!"

The fugitive didn't comprehend. "Try to stop me," he snarled. "I'll kill you!"

"You won't kill anyone any more!" the old man barked, raising his stick. "Let the weapon be!"

The wounded man didn't obey because he saw wisdom in the command, but because the little strength he had ran out of him, and he collapsed on his side. The gash on his head was bleeding again, streaking his face. The dog crouched, low-bellied, close by, rumbling threats.

"Why couldn't you have stayed where I put you!" the old man repeated, his voice full of querulous dismay.

"You ... put ... me!" Each word was a hurt sob of bewilderment. "You!" The old man had never seen such dark blue eyes; that they had difficulty in focusing and were filled with naked animal desperation made their intensity that much more pronounced.

"They are coming with their dogs," he said bitterly. "They will follow your track here."

"You ... put me ... in that cave!" Costain seemed unable to let it go. He pushed himself to a sitting position and sat, head hanging down, breath coming with difficulty.

"If the flying machine had seen you—" The old man raised his head, listening intently. He neither heard nor saw any sign of the helicopter. "Lie still!" he ordered, and ran back toward the shelter. The wine he brought in a wooden cup revived the unwanted visitor, and in a few moments he was able to help Costain to the shelter.

The old man covered Costain with his blanket and poncho and put a rough bandage on his head. Then, with the dog, he hurriedly moved a portion of the herd back and forth across the wounded man's track. When he had done it sufficiently, he drove the sheep into the timber, spreading them out and moving them all the way to where the trees ended and the rockfield began. He didn't dare go beyond. If he were to be seen in such a place, it would bring suspicion to their minds.

He thought the sheep would cover the hunted man's scent, but he couldn't be sure, and when he reached the pasture once more, he'd decided he would start the herd for the lower valley at once. With luck and speed, they would reach it by dark. He didn't like to desert the wounded man, but what else could he do? By his own blundering, the man had made any other course of the utmost danger. The hunters would come. Even without dogs they would come, for their line of search must cover the entire mountain side. There was no place to hide this man now. He would leave him in the shelter.

Far distant, a dog's yap whirled him about. He stared up at the mountain top, and there, above it, he saw the hand of God. He saw it in a small white cloud, crowning the irregular dome of the summit, a cloud no bigger than a minute. He had seen this cloud often enough and knew its meaning. Snow! Within the hour there would be snow. Yes, the wind had shifted. It would quickly bleed the warmth from the air. The snow would fall in flat, wet flakes, perhaps as far as halfway down the mountain. It would fall thickly, not lasting long, but long enough to cover all traces of the fleeing one.

The old man felt a surge of joy wipe away the sweat of fear. Whenever God spoke to him, it was so. Sight of the cloud calmed him and gave him back his confidence.

The cloud said, "Stay. I shall help you." He knew why he had been so undecided about moving the sheep today. Usually, it was of no moment to make such a decision. Now it had been made for him. Tomorrow, not today.

The snow would not last. It was of a special nature, its purpose clear to him. He watched the cloud swell and spread until it curtained the mountain top and hid the tiny figures that moved over it.

The snow would slow the search. It would make things very uncomfortable for the police, although it was probable they were trained climbers, and prepared. Still, the snow would have the pasture covered by the time the hunters came to it. He would build a fire, and some of them would come and warm themselves at it gratefully.

He grinned at the magnitude of his daring. Well, fire or no fire, he could not keep them away, and wouldn't it be better to make them feel well toward him? It would not be pleasing to the fugitive, but he could see no other way.

He listened a moment for the sound of the flying machine, and when he didn't hear it, he went into the shelter.

"If the police find me here, you'll get yourself in trouble," Costain greeted him, his voice quietly normal.

"I know all about the police." The old man blinked his eyes, getting them accustomed to the change in light. "Are you hungry?"

"Thirsty."

"I'll give you some water ... How's your head?"

"The bandage helps. Why are you helping me?"

The old man brought a cup of water and helped Costain raise himself so he could drink.

Costain drained the cup noisily and sank back with a sigh. "Why?" he asked again.

"You want more?"

"If you have plenty ... Yes, thanks ... The police are following me, you know?"

"I know. Don't talk so much. Save your strength. They will be here again."

When the old man returned with the water, he saw cold suspicion in Costain's expressive eyes. "No," he replied to the unasked question. "Would I have troubled to hide you in the rocks? First they came in their flying machine that looks like a bug. Now others are coming down the mountain."

"Then I've got to go." Costain made a weak motion to pull himself up.

The old man gestured with his hand. "You're unable to go anywhere."

He handed the cup to Costain and watched him drain it in several swallows.

"They'll find me here," the fugitive sighed.

"No, I have a plan. It will be hard for you, but they'll not find you. It will snow soon."

"Look, who the devil are you? Why all this for me? Do you know why they want me?"

"They said you might kill me." There was a hint of mockery in the old man's rasping reply.

"They're right, I might." It was said seriously, not because there was truth in it but to impress.

The old man chuckled, "Not now, Mr. Killer, not now."

Costain lay back with a resigned exhale of breath. The old man saw him wince his eyes against the pain in his head.

"Where are you going to hide me?"

"Right under their noses." The old man grinned puckishly, wiping his nose with thumb and forefinger.

As the old man knew it would be, the pasture valley was snow-covered, and the air filled with a deluge of flat, wet flakes by the time four of the hunters emerged out of the late afternoon murk and converged on his fire.

He had built the fire in front of the shelter, and the weary men who warmed themselves at it were indeed grateful for its existence. Chilled, and disgruntled by their lack of success, they had built up a personal hate for the criminal.

"God, I hope the bastard fell down a hole!"

"I am glad you didn't bring your dogs here." The old man was all concern for his sheep. He kept one eye on a sizable group that huddled near a rock outcropping, the dog holding them in check.

The hunters ignored him.

"It'll be dark before we get down," the corporal said.

"Dark! Hah! It'll be the middle of the shittering night!" The tall trooper spat.

"My feet are frozen already!" The trooper next to him stamped his feet and extended first one and then the other to the fire. "They should call it off until it clears. How can we find him in this? I don't think he came this way ... He wasn't dressed for climbing ... He doubled back ... Probably way the hell and gone to Bratislava by now."

"God, I'd like to get my hands on him!" The corporal's gloved hands beat together against the cold and the hope of accomplishing the wish.

"If you had brought your dogs," the old man persisted, "they would have attacked my sheep."

"Screw your sheep, Grandpa. We heard all about your bloody sheep."

"Those goddam dogs couldn't find a rabbit in a bath tub!" The tall trooper sighed, hefting his rifle.

"We've got to go," the corporal announced. "The others will get far ahead."

"What difference does it make? He could hide anywhere," the fourth man spoke for the first time.

"He could freeze his balls off, too," the third trooper said, "which I hope he's already done, even though I personally would like to shoot them off."

"Where is the bad man from?" the old man asked. "Opava?"

"East, from Estrava," the sanguinary trooper grunted.

"Grandpa," the corporal said, "if you're smart you'll get out of here when the snow stops."

"Tomorrow." The old man stirred the fire with his stick, sending a stream of sparks rocketing upward. Suddenly, he was not relaxed any more. The sheep were drifting away from the rocks. When the dog circled to hold them at one point, they gently flooded away at another. He called to the dog sharply. It was a mistake for the corporal caught the concern in his command.

"What's the matter, Grandpa?"

"Nothing. Nothing. It's better they stay in one place," he said quickly. "It's really nothing." Because the pack was not overly large—and he cursed himself for this now—and there was only the dog to keep it from moving, it was a great deal of something! The sheep didn't have to shift but a few yards. It was obvious they wanted to. They had become aware of what they concealed, and it bothered them. The old man went to help the dog, swearing under his breath. Another few minutes and the darkness would be such that it wouldn't matter. He checked the movement of the animals coming toward him. They halted reluctantly, voicing their disagreement.

The corporal startled him. "Why don't you let them roam?"

The old man didn't turn as he heard the policeman's approach. Helplessly, he saw that he could not check the shifting animals. To get vigorous with them would only be to attract more attention. Their movement was not that great or that far.

Merciful Virgin! He could see the feet and lower legs of the fugitive where he lay half covered in snow at the foot of the rocks!

"In this snow it's not good!" The words came out almost as though he were in pain, shrilly and with too much force. He instinctively turned to face the corporal, knowing he must draw the policeman away. In the soiled light, he couldn't tell if the man's look was one of suspicion or curiosity. If he knew anything about sheep, it must be the former because the attention brought to this small part of the herd should certainly have also been directed to the larger, more distant portions of it. He explained earnestly, "These are ewes. They have just been lambed. It makes them nervous. Anything can arouse their fear." He managed a sly grin. "Even policemen without dogs. I keep them close."

Rigidly, the old man marched back to the fire, hoping the corporal would follow.

The policeman didn't move. He stood silently watching the sheep.

The dog, intelligent as he was, could not realize that a slight drift in the pack's location could be of any great importance. The old man saw him relax his efforts, sitting on his back legs, keeping a calm eye on his charges.

"What are you thinking about," the tall trooper called to the corporal, "lamb stew?"

The corporal didn't reply. His gaze appeared focused on one point. In helpless horror the old man saw him start walking toward the jumbled mound of rocks where the wounded man lay.

Costain was not fully conscious. He lay in an in-between zone where the tides of knowing and unknowing played a gentle game of give-and-take. He was aware that the sheep had moved because their going brought change. They took away warmth and let in light. Warmth he wanted, needed ... Light was an enemy. It hurt. He thought of calling the sheep back like you would a dog ... It seemed there was a dog ... a dog and an old man. He drifted into nothingness on the thought of it and returned with a question: what was he doing lying here in this mass of white cold? He was being covered by it ... buried in it. Dead and buried ... That was it, he was dead ... No, that was not it. He could not be dead. All reports of hell spoke of opposite temperatures, very hot ... very, very hot. It was a joke. He went away laughing at it and came back to an awareness of light. A round, reddish light winking at him. No, not winking, wiggling, dancing. By God, it was a fire! That was all he needed, a fire! If he couldn't stand up, he'd crawl to it.

The light of the fire was blotted out. Vanished. Maybe he was dreaming. Going blind? No, it wasn't that. He could see something—snow, and then he could see the reason the fire was gone, even if he couldn't quite grasp its significance. There was a man walking toward him, who'd blocked out the fire.

Clarity hit Costain with the same icy thrust as a trickle of melting snow that ran down his neck and under his shirt to finger rigidly across his chest above his heart. He knew, and momentarily the shock of it make him powerless to move. He was caught!

The corporal halted to one side of the rocks. Costain could no longer see him. He knew the policeman was very near. He thought he could hear him breathing.

God, if only the gun was in his hand instead of in his pocket! He gathered himself. He had to make one attempt to reach it! Had to! Was not going to die like this!

In that jagged instant before he made his move, a sound feathered against his ears. It was followed by a seemingly unrelated sensation and then explained by a smell. The explanation checked him.

The sound was a splattering hiss, not unmusical. The sensation was of tiny drops of hot liquid tickling the calf of his right leg through the thin dusting of snow that stockinged it where the pants were torn. The smell was strongly sour and pungent. The man who stood so close was relieving himself on the rocks, and the urine was splattering on Costain's leg.

The old man couldn't bring himself to look at the corporal when he returned to the fire. He couldn't look at any of them. To their repeated warnings and admonishments to take his sheep off the heights as soon as it cleared, he nodded, and muttered, and bowed, and kept his hands tucked under his armpits for a warmth he did not really need.

When they departed, disappearing into the snow-choked evening, he went into the shelter and calmed his nerves and thirst with a long drink from the wineskin.

The breath went out of him in a long, wailing sigh. He choked on it and began to laugh. Then he couldn't stop the laughter. It seized and shook him until he was weak and dizzy with it, and there were tears on his cheeks. He was still laughing when he went to assist Costain.

Even the wounded man saw the joke in it. He croaked weakly through chattering teeth as the old man brushed the snow off and then helped him back to the warmth of fire and shelter.

CHAPTER THREE

Shortly after nine in the evening, the wind shifted around and began blowing gaping holes in the overcast. The snow was shut off nearly as abruptly as a closed faucet.

From where he lay, the fire at the open face of the shelter prevented Costain from observing the sudden change in the weather, but he could hear the wind pummeling gustily at the logs beside his head. By squinting his eyes at a crack in the wall, he saw a star framed in a cloud rip and knew the sky was clearing.

Earlier, he'd eaten his first meal in over twenty-four hours. The hot meat, wild mushrooms and thick slabs of strong cheese, washed down with a plentiful supply of wine, did much to restore strength and balance to his mind and body.

It was only when he moved suddenly that the dull ache in his head became a sharp blade, knifing inward, stabbing him into jagged dizziness.

He wished the old man would come back, before he fell asleep. They had to talk … There'd been little talk. At first, he'd been too weak and cold from lying in the snow to care, then too hungry at the sight and smell of food to have any other thoughts, and now finally, when he was ready, the old man had to go off and take care of his sheep. He must do something to keep awake. Thinking would only put him to sleep. Costain reached his hand down under the blanket and felt the bulk of the gun in his pocket. He took it out, examining it in the half-light. He extracted the clip and opened the chamber and was holding it up sighting when the old man came back.

"Bang, bang," he said, stamping the snow off his feet, blowing on his stubby fingers.

"The snow's stopped?" Costain placed the automatic on his chest.

"Yes. Can't you see?"

"Not with the light from the fire."

The old man looked and grunted. "Unless the wind turns about again, it will be a clear morning."

"Is that apt to happen, I mean the wind shifting?"

"This time of year, who knows?" He shrugged. "You can't tell."

Costain watched the old man sit down cross-legged and take the wineskin from its peg. "How are the sheep?"

"Well enough." He poured some wine into a cup and took several swallows, then filled the cup again. "You would like some?"

Costain started to shake his head, then caught himself and smiled faintly. "Not now, thanks."

The old man looked over the rim of his cup at the gun resting on his guest's chest. "That is a formidable weapon you have."

"Yes." Costain held it up. There was something viciously attractive in its silhouette.

"A weapon of precision." He finished the wine in the cup and picked up the skin and shook it. The liquid sloshed pleasantly, and the old man poured himself another drink. "You are formidable, too," he said, toasting with his cup.

"No, not really." Costain returned the clip to the barrel. It clicked into place smartly.

"I'll tell you who is formidable," the old man nodded wisely. "The police."

"Yes." Costain grinned, thinking about the corporal who had nearly urinated on him.

"That's the trouble, you know. Too much formidableness everywhere. That's a very large word for an old man like me."

"I still don't know why you've helped me."

"Maybe because I am not formidable." The old man wiped his mouth with his hand and grinned.

Costain thought the wine must be getting to him.

"No, I am not formidable," he wagged his bushy head, "and I don't like police."

"You'd like them a lot less if they put you in jail, and they'd put you in jail if they found me here."

"I know, I know." The old man gestured impatiently with the empty cup. "At first light I am moving my sheep down to the lower pastures, almost at the foot of the mountain. You can stay here or, if you are able, you may descend with me."

"They'll have you under surveillance, won't they?"

"What of that? They know who I am. They know where I go. Why should they trouble me again?"

"It's still a big risk for you."

"In what way?" The old man poured two cups of wine now. "If you are behind me in the timber—it is very thick, mostly black pine—or off to one side, how do I know you are there?" He offered one of the cups to Costain and watched speculatively as the injured man sat up slowly and then took the libation. "They won't be looking for you with me. They'll be looking someplace else."

Costain didn't reply, sipping his drink thoughtfully, feeling the heavy, slightly sour-tasting wine taking warm charge of his insides.

"Better?"

In the near darkness, Costain couldn't see the full expression on the old man's face, but he knew he was grinning widely. "Better. But what's funny?"

"Much is funny to an old one like me. Very funny." He rocked forward, chuckling rustily.

"You think it's funny to risk your neck for someone like me, someone you don't even know?"

"Ahh, you are like a song that repeats itself over and over. Tell me, are you running from them to some place, or are you just running ... like a rabbit?"

Costain took another swallow before he answered. He owed this crazy old fool his life. However, to tell him too much would be dangerous. He could be taken in for questioning, or he might drink too much of that wine and talk. "I have a place to go," he said quietly.

"Good. Far?"

"Yes, far."

"South? To the border perhaps?"

"Perhaps. For your own sake it's better for you not to know."

"You mean for your sake." The old man put his finger on it bluntly.

"All right, but either way it's better. I don't want to be impolite after all you've done."

There was a silence between them for a few moments. Costain finished his wine and lay down, knowing that reaction was starting to set in fast. The old man busied himself filling his cup. "They will catch you no matter where you go." It was said matter-of-factly, but with overtones of sad finality.

"Possibly."

"Surely."

"Not now, not for tonight."

"Listen, if you go down the mountain with me, you'll be near Budisov. It's not a large place and everyone is noticed. I don't think it would be a good place for you."

"No, it wouldn't."

"If you go west and south, you will strike the river where it cuts between this mountain and another. Do you know this?"

Costain said, "Go on."

"That is all, really. The river is there. It runs south. There are towns on both sides, but if a man like you could lay hands on a boat and did his traveling only by night, with luck he would come to Olomouc ... if that city is a good place to go."

"You've been there?"

"Twice. I didn't like it either time, even the time when I was young and like a bull. Too big, too many buildings, too many people, too much of everything. It might be a good place for you, and if it is where you—are going, the river could take you there best."

Costain forced himself to keep his eyes open. Sleep was an avalanche he was trying to hold back with one hand. The old man's advice was most important. "Suppose I went the other way, southeast?"

"The mountains make their curve that way." He demonstrated with his free hand. "They would not be apt to hunt you in the mountains, but the weather will soon be bad, very bad." He shook his head. "You are not prepared for it."

"No ... I—I wish I could repay you for all this."

The old man made a scoffing sound in his throat and drained the cup. In the morning, his yellow-brown eyes would be filmed in red. "It's good wine ... good wine. You want to repay me, hey?" His voice had taken on heavier, thicker timber. "All right, still my curiosity. Tell me about the killing. Did you kill more than one?"

"One was enough." It was all becoming vague.

"But you have killed others?"

"No ... in the war, maybe ... not like this." He couldn't keep his eyes open.

"He was your enemy. He wronged you."

"I knew him." Costain could hear his own replies, but he was like a man hypnotized. He answered by rote, not caring.

"He must have been someone of great importance to bring so intent a search."

"He was ... He was a security police officer ..." It came out in a whispered sigh.

The old man seemed oblivious to the fact that Costain was nearly asleep. He smacked his crossed leg with his hand and laughed in a high, gnomish cackle. "A police officer! Think of it! ... Hehehehe! Think of it! Hehehehe! You couldn't have made it worse! No wonder you are running! No wonder they are so determined. Hey!" He leaned forward and shook Costain's arm.

"Hummm?" It was more a groan than an answer.

"Why did you kill him? Why did you do a foolish thing like that? You don't appear foolish."

Costain heard the words from a distance. The fog of sleep had all but engulfed him. He replied, but most of it was unintelligible. Only the three words "caught me stealing" were clearly understood.

They straightened the slouched old man like a fist under the chin. He sat immobile under their impact. Then he reached out hesitantly and shook Costain. "Hey!" he said. "Hey!" The wine had made him slightly drunk. He rocked back on his haunches and sat very still again. The meaning of the fugitive's last words had brought a sudden sickness to his stomach. He wanted no more to drink.

"So," he said softly. "So," and shook his head at the enormity of it. "Not only a murderer but a thief as well ... A man who kills for a reason, I can understand. I know it is not for me to judge, but this! This!" He threw his arms wide, his voice rising in anger. "A man who steals! A thief! Pahh! You were caught stealing!" He spat, trying to rid himself of the taste his new-found knowledge had brought.

"A man who is starving and steals," he argued, "that is to be understood ... to be forgiven, but you have not that look! No! No, you are not that kind! You were caught in your filthy work and you killed! Police I do not like, but a thief I spit on!" He shook his clenched fists and spat at the sleeping man.

"One who takes from another is no better than dirt!" He thumped his fists against the hard-packed ground. He was shouting, the effects of the wine lacing his rage. He leaned forward and shook Costain roughly. "You! You!" he cried bitterly.

There was no response, and he got to his feet clumsily and went out of the shelter, walking away with stiff, unsteady steps. The dog moved out of the dark to his side, leaving the bunched and quiet sheep. The wind had blown away the clouds and polished the small, hard brilliance of the stars.

The old man stood looking up at them, feeling the coldness of the wind, a strange old man, who would not judge one who killed but could not tolerate one who stole. He felt tricked and cheated. "I don't understand!" he wailed. "To do all I have done! And this! And this! Let the Devil take him! ... Do you hear! Let the Devil take him and all his kind!"

CHAPTER FOUR

When Costain awoke, it took a little time to orient himself. It was daylight. Clear. Cold. He was stiff with cold. He was lying in the shelter, looking out the open side. He could see that most of the snow was already melted off the grass. Above the trees that bordered it was the white-capped summit line of the mountain.

He saw all this and knew that it was the cold that had awakened him. The blanket and poncho were gone. Everything was gone! The shelter was empty of all sign of habitation. He rolled over and got up quickly and would have fallen without the support of the shelter wall to hold on to. He waited with his head bent, eyes closed, for the dizziness to ebb away.

When he opened his eyes again, it was with the knowledge that the old man, his dog and the sheep were gone, too. He went to the remains of the still smoldering fire, rubbing his arms to restore circulation, noting the rubbery weakness of his legs. He crouched, holding out his hands to the little warmth left in the charred logs, puzzling over the old man's surprising departure.

Of course, it was better not to have gone with him, but why had the old man gone without waking him? Without saying goodbye ... Probably dawn had brought realization of the risk he was taking, and he wanted to clear out fast. Who could blame the old fellow? But he would like to have thanked him properly. Given him something. What did he have to give? The gun in his pocket? No, he couldn't part with that. His watch? It was broken.

He sighed, looking at it. The day before yesterday, he had been the highly thought of Assistant Engineering Director of Research and Development at Aero-Morava ... All the years gone in a thunderous instant ... Could Jan Radek help him now? ... Not for a minute. Not ever.

Maybe the old man had left him something to eat. Investigation proved otherwise, and he was further puzzled and beginning to feel somewhat uneasy about it when he heard the helicopter approaching.

He was standing at the entrance of the shelter, and he ducked instinctively back into the protection of its cover. For a paralyzed moment, he thought of trying to gain the safety of trees, but he knew from the closeness of the sound and his own physical condition that he would never make them in time. Instead, he pressed himself against the overlapping upright that indented the entrance at the shelter corner. There was a dry, sulphuric taste in his mouth, as though he'd run too far. The old man had betrayed him! He waited, gun clenched in his raised hand, the metal tight against his shoulder, eyes pressed to a thin separation between timbers. The helicopter came in sight. It dipped like a dragonfly below the level of the trees and lazily hovered over the pasture. He could see the two men in it clearly. The co-pilot carried a sub-machine gun at the ready. Both men seemed to be looking right in the shelter at him.

If he could hit one of the rotors, they'd crash! Even a fall of ten feet would give him an advantage!

Before he could bring himself to act, the helicopter skittered in closer and dropped to a level where its occupants could look directly into the shelter. The machine's horizontal blades swept the area beneath it, driving a cloud of ashes and burnt bits of wood into the lean-to. Dirt and pebbles and globs of snow joined the hail of flying objects. They pelted Costain where he stood fused to the rough wood. The ash dust clouded his vision and made him cough. The slit through which he peered was not wide enough for the barrel of the automatic. It would make for bad shooting. The only thing he could do was jump clear and start firing.

This sudden attack had caught him completely unaware, and now he was driven close to the edge of panic. He knew what he must do, but he simply couldn't do it. He was shaking all over, dizzy and half-blinded, his legs full of jelly.

"Wait! They don't see you!"

"Do! Can't wait!"

"Can't see! Can't breathe!"

"Got to try! Got to!"

"Give up! Give up! Throw down the gun and give up!"

"No!"

"Wait!"

"Only chance!"

Before Costain could settle the desperate argument that wracked him, the helicopter settled it for him. With the same abruptness of its arrival, the helicopter departed. It rose straight up out of his sight line and, dumb with the reprieve of its going, he listened to its receding sputter, then sank down on his knees, head bowed.

After a while, Costain arose and walked quickly away from the shelter, entering the timber at the pasture's edge. He set a southeasterly course through the trees, pacing himself with care. He left the area, knowing deep gratitude for an old man who had hidden him, fed him, and had not betrayed him. He only regretted he could never repay the incredible kindness.

For nearly two hours, Costain angled down through the heavy timber. He went slowly and with great care, stopping to rest frequently. There was no telling how far ahead of him the line of search extended. He found ample footprints to prove that it had passed, and he had no intention of overtaking it.

As the old man had said, the forest was largely black pine, the trees standing majestically tall with quiet dignity, the woodland floor beneath them thickly carpeted in a soft needle mold. The sun's rays arrowed amidst the pines, creating magical fans of translucent light, dim and rather ghostly. The morning was still and October-spiced, the air strongly scented. An occasional breeze stirred a brief whispering in the pine tops. Half a dozen times, he heard the distant sputter of a helicopter. It was the only indication of danger. Without it and the footprints in the snow-patched ground, he might have been a man out for an early morning hike through the Moravian countryside, nothing more serious on his mind than where he was going. The quietness, the solitude, the grandeur of his surroundings, coupled with what he had endured and the unknowing of what he must endure, had a growing effect on Costain. Each time he sat down to rest, it became more difficult to rise, and only a small part of it was physical. He was gripped by a totally unfamiliar lassitude. He wanted to lie down on his back and look up through the green-black boughs at the rich blue of sky. He was submerged in a sea of trees. He was lying on the ocean floor and up there, way up there, was the surface. If he lay motionless and looked up at that blue long enough, it would put him to sleep. To sleep ... and never to wake again. To stop this running about on a mountain side. To stop everything here and now.

He was not the kind of man to dwell on such thoughts, yet as he walked amongst the close set trees, moving through the filtering light shafts, sirenlike they came to tempt and woo him.

His musing was chopped off by the sight of the cabin. Suddenly it was there ahead, and he was lying on his belly, gun in hand, peering cautiously around a tree trunk at it.

It nestled in a tiny clearing, a small, rough-hewn structure with a stone chimney centering its back wall. From where he lay he could see one side and most of the rear. There were no windows in sight, but what brought fright and apprehension back hard was the thin tendril of smoke that rose from the chimney. He lay unmoving a long time, first to make sure he had not been seen, and then in debating his next move. His immediate thought was to backtrack and skirt the cabin, giving it a wide berth, but the longer he studied the place, the less the idea appealed to him.

"It's either a hunter's lodge ... or a ranger's overnight cabin."

"Never mind whose it is. Somebody's home."

"There's not a sign of anyone but for the smoke."

"Sign enough. You can't see through logs."

"There may be a window at the front."

"Look, what of it? Your only intelligent move is to clear out of here."

"No! ... Not till I have a closer look. There could be food there. God knows, that's getting awfully important."

"Sure, and there's somebody there who'll serve it to you, too."

"One way to find out."

"Fool!"

Costain got up and walked tensely through the trees, knowing that the cabin's inhabitant, or inhabitants, might be away from the building and close by. When he could see the front, he got another surprise. The crude slab door stood half open. There were no windows in the front, either. He snaked forward on his stomach and saw the area around the door had been churned into mud by footprints.

"Now will you clear out!"

"No, wait a minute."

"For what!"

"Wait a minute, wait a minute! Those prints could have been made by the police. Some of them may have been here last night just like they were at the shepherd's."

"All right, that's probable."

"There may not be anyone there now."

"Sure, the fire built itself."

"The fire could be from last night. Look, you can't even see the smoke now."

"Look, my friend, if there's someone in that place, and you go in there, what's going to happen to him?"

"Tie him up."

"Tie him up, my foot! He'd get loose and they'd be down on you like thunder."

"All right, they can't hang you any higher for two."

"But two is twice as many as one."

"I don't have time to moralize. The cabin's there. There may be food and other things. I need them. I've got to take the chance. When your luck's good, ride it."

"It looks like bad luck to me, if you don't get out of here."

"I tell you what," Costain shut his doubting self off. "You get out of here." He stood up and waited a moment, listening. He heard only the sound of his own breathing. Then, jaws locked, he sprinted straight for the door, ready to shoot at the first alien sound. He made a flying entrance, shoulder knocking the door wide, landing crouched and ready in the center of the empty room. He straightened up, nerves unwinding, knowing relief and also that this small effort had badly tired him. The dizziness and trembling were back.

Cigarette butts littered the floor. The furniture amounted to a table, some chairs, and a double-decker bunk. He sat down on this last to get himself back together. There was no denying he was in rotten shape. He'd be no match for anyone or anything. The remains of the fire in the fireplace, the broken latch on the door, and the cigarette butts told him his appraisal had been correct. The searchers had been here. There was no one here now. If he were smart, though, he wouldn't hang around, either, just long enough to see if he could find anything to take away.

Costain found a great deal to take away and was heartened by the luck of it. Now it seemed almost as though he'd been guided here. His reward was eight cans of food, two blankets, a heavy wool sweater which the moths had been at, and a fairly serviceable knife. There were other odds and ends, but he rejected them. He made a makeshift pack of his loot and left the cabin clearing at a trot, eager.

A short while later, he came upon a wildly primitive glen backed by low cliffs where, amidst a tumble of immense boulders, a vigorous, white-tongued stream drove between tree and rock. Here he had another piece of luck that completely changed his plans.

Where the stream leveled out and formed a deep pool, he knelt to drink. When he raised his head, he saw the cave entrance on the far side. He made a torch out of the papers in his jacket and a stick of dead pine. Gun in one hand, torch in the other, he crawled in the entrance to investigate. He found it to be a true cave, the ceiling sloping up from front to back. At its rear, Costain could stand fully upright, and when he did, he felt the draft on his head. He held the flame up to it and saw it drawn. That about settled it. If he were careful, he could have a fire at night, and someone would have to be right on top of him before they'd know it.

Outside once more, he examined the general area more closely. It would be simple to conceal the cave entrance. The only drawback was that the sound of the stream might cover the sound of approach, but he knew, all things considered, he'd take that risk. He'd go to earth like the well-known animal. He'd take up residence here and lie doggo until he had his strength back and the furor of the hunt died down. Fire would help dry out the damp cave interior. Come rain or snow he'd stay snug until his food was gone, and in that time he could plan his next move.

Until now there had been no time to consider the suddenness with which his identity of respectability—that of the dedicated scientist working for the Party—had been destroyed. The dangerous double game which he had played for so long was ended. It had been replaced by a situation deadly and uncontrollable. Everything had been reduced to one basic fact: only his escape mattered and it mattered for a lot more than just his own neck.

CHAPTER FIVE

It was exactly two weeks from the day of his escape that Costain left his mountain hiding place. Though the golden maples had been tempered into bronze, the weather held miraculously mild and fair, and he threaded his way down through the remainder of the timber in a careful but leisurely manner.

Evening brought him to the pastures of the upland farms. Through most of that night, he traversed the foothills, keeping the timber on his left and within easy running distance. Near dawn, he came to the river, and found it an unfordable, fast-surging race, powerfully separating two mountains.

During the day, he lay in a thicket of alders close to the river and let its rushing lull him to sleep. He awoke in the afternoon empty-bellied and chilled. Using the last of his food, he partially stilled the former feeling, but he saw there was nothing he could do about the latter. The weather that had been so kind to him was going to fall in. Dirty gray had murdered blue, a gray that lowered in proportion to the increasing strength of a finely-honed wind from the north. At early dusk, it brought the rain, and by the time he left the alders, his body felt icily waterlogged.

The darkness was complete. Without the river to guide him, he would have gone blundering blindly through the underbrush. But in following the relatively flat, gently curving bank, he was able to pursue a direct course, and he saw the rain-filtered lights of the traffic on the highway quite some time before he reached the bridge.

It was not a long span, for here the river narrowed. If it had been a bridge where duty was collected he would have given it a wide berth, but as he remembered it, it was not, and he also remembered it was necessary for traffic to slow almost to a halt at either entrance.

He had a long, miserable wait, lying in the tall grass close to the approach. A blinking caution light enabled him to study each car and truck as it passed. What he hoped for was a truck with a low tailgate to vault and a body only partially loaded so that he could find a place to sit.

Of course, he had no sure way of knowing where such a truck would be headed. This highway did lead to the city of Olomouc, and a ride of any sort would get him out of the general area.

He was beginning to believe the vehicle he wanted would never come, that dawn would find him caught in the open, frozen tightly to the ground. Then, all at once, it was there. A battered, hard-used machine, it wheezed up the slight incline to the bridge entrance, where it nearly came to a dead halt under a discordant threshing of gears. The caution light blinked owlishly down at the truck, winking at its worn bulk. Costain saw the tailgate, saw the short, billowing tarpaulin like a curtain partly raised, and knew there must be empty space behind it.

No other cars were approaching, and he was up and running stiffly almost as soon as he'd caught sight of the opportunity. He jumped, caught the tailgate rim firmly, got his feet planted at its base and was over the barrier and sitting on a packing crate before the truck was on the bridge proper. He held his breath, listening, waiting to see if the driver was aware of the newly-arrived passenger. He was not. Costain relaxed and tried to make himself comfortable. Heavily bearded, gaunt-eyed and filthy, he sat with his back pressed against a row of boxes and knew how close he was to the point of exhaustion again.

Little more than an hour later, they came to the suburbs of Olomouc. The truck bounced and hoarsely stuttered its way past block-long rows of stone-faced structures, bitterly wedded in their ugly, depressing sameness. It flanked a low-slung factory building, then an open-hearth steel mill going full blast. An occasional car overtook them and went pitching by on the rough cobblestone pavement. Once Costain caught a glimpse of a policeman standing under the weak spotlight of a street lamp.

In trying to make a plan, Costain had reasoned that the truck would stop at one of three places: its terminal, a factory warehouse, or the railroad yards. Since he knew the city to be the rail center for the region, he hoped it would be this last, for he felt the best and quickest method to continue south would be by train, hiding in a freight car. But wherever the truck stopped, he planned to be over the tailgate and away before the driver knew of his presence.

It happened he was wrong on all three suppositions, and the sudden end of the journey took him by surprise.

They had turned off the wider thoroughfare onto an angling side street when, without any warning, the driver pulled in to the curb, braking hard, bringing his machine to a shuddering halt. The engine backfired loudly and subsided with a gusty sigh.

If Costain had remained where he was, the driver would never have seen him. But the swiftness of the halt jerked him sideways, his legs flying high, and by the time he recovered his balance, the truck had stopped. His one thought then was to get out! Somehow he'd been discovered! It never dawned on him that this was where the driver lived.

Going over the side, he caught his foot on a rope across the tailgate. Had he jumped, he would have broken his leg. Frantically, he pulled the caught member free and dropped down to the street. He landed just as the driver came around the rear of the vehicle.

Even in the bad light, Costain could see the driver was a square, heavy-set man with a round, beefy face and a nose that had been badly broken at some time. He wore a black leather jacket and a short peaked cap with a cheap pin in it. He stood staring at Costain, his mouth half open.

"I borrowed a ride." Costain forced a smile. "I hope you don't mind."

The driver's momentary look of astonishment froze up hard and solid. "Who the hell are you!" It was a rasping bark.

Costain saw the thick shoulders hunch and knew that the man had doubled his fists. "It's a wet night. I needed a lift." He tried to keep his voice quiet and friendly.

It had no effect. "You've got one helluva nerve, that's what you've got!"

"I'm sorry." Costain felt helpless and out of depth, his stomach starting to churn. He wanted to ask the driver to lower his voice. If there were a policeman close by, he was finished.

"Not half as sorry as you're going to be, Mister!" The driver took a menacing step closer.

"Wait a minute!" Costain thrust out his arm in protest, anxiety in his plea.

Backed against the tailgate, his movements were restricted. He could retreat no farther. He saw the roundhouse swing coming and tried to jump away, crouching behind his upraised arm. The driver's bludgeoning fist caught him on the shoulder, and the force of the punch knocked him sideways. His feet tripped on the curb, and he fell sprawling. Instinctively, he did nothing to check the roll of his body, knowing the attack would be followed up.

He was on one knee when the booted foot swung in a vicious drop kick for his face. He'd sensed it was coming, saw it in a blur, and ducked away from it. It missed him narrowly, but its momentum caught the driver with his right leg raised high, fighting to keep his balance.

Costain flung himself up under the upraised leg, taking it on the shoulder, straightening powerfully. His hands locked momentarily on ankle and calf, and then released as the driver flipped back in a half somersault. His cry of anguished surprise was cut off as he landed on the back of his head in the gutter. The noise of the connection was a nasty punctuation mark.

The truck driver rolled over limply, and Costain heard the air going out of him like a tired balloon. He came to rest on his stomach, his hands scrabbling weakly at the cobbles, his legs jerking spasmodically. Even though stunned and semiconscious, he seemed to be trying to regain his feet.

Costain hesitated only long enough to see that no one was in sight. The buildings were black and silent, the street lamps few, supplying weak puddles of light. The rain had tapered off to a vapory drizzle, decimated in the wind's drive. He went down the street, staying in close to the building fronts, not running, but striding as fast as he could.

He'd been in Olomouc a number of times. However, he didn't know it well enough to set a course for the railroad yards. It wasn't a large city, only about sixty thousand. There were a good many historical landmarks. In fact, if he could only see the cathedral with its three towers, he could use that for a mark. Right now, he had nothing to guide him, only this street whose name was meaningless and whose direction might be taking him the wrong way. He had to get off this street. He had to get under cover fast!

There was no telling what the truck driver would do when he got his wits back. If he reported the incident, the police would figure it out, or at least be suspicious enough to center their attention on the city. Maybe the driver wouldn't want to get involved. Maybe he'd rather keep his mouth shut. No, he couldn't assume that. He couldn't assume it for a minute. It was just damn bad luck, and he hoped it wasn't a sign there was more to follow. One thing was for sure. He must have a change of clothes, get clean, stop looking like what he was. How did he do it, though? How could he do any of it!

He saw there was an intersection of sorts ahead and approached it cautiously. This new street was even narrower and more twisted than the one he was on. It looked equally desolate and empty. He was debating whether to take it when he thought he heard footsteps approaching rapidly from behind. He didn't glance back but went around the corner and began to run, keeping on his toes to deaden the sound. He passed several faceless edifices before he saw the thin border of light framing a pulled curtain. It was a window on the top story of a building on the far side of the street.

At the time, Costain had no clear thought on why he saw it as a place to try and reach. It meant someone was still awake. It meant a chance to enter a lighted room. Mostly, it was a chance to get off the street. Of course, if the front door of the building were locked, it was no chance at all. Whether it was or not would depend on how much custom had given way to newer regulations.

He moved quickly to inspect the building. He paid no attention to its dingy features. He saw that the low iron railing fronting it was divided in the center by a single stone step. The door beyond was a worn, wooden affair with rough metal bracings. It possessed a small judas window, a badly tarnished name-plate, and a massive iron knob. Twenty-five years ago, it might have been the front entrance to a fashionable home in a quiet, fashionable street. At this hour, only the quiet remained.

Costain took a breath, his hand fastening on the cold knob. He twisted slowly and firmly. The handle turned, squeaking in unoiled protest. He stiffened tensely, waited a moment. In the slight pause, he thought he heard again the sound of hurried footsteps. He put his shoulder against the panel, but the door held firm and unyielding. He twisted the knob the last notch and heard a rusty click. The wood gave a little, sticking stubbornly. He thrust his weight forward, and the door came open with a shivering, vibrating snap of wood and metal.

He silenced it with his hand clasping the rim. The judas window had told him there was no light in the foyer or hall. He entered and closed the door quietly. Then he stood in darkness, ears straining, waiting for his eyes to become accustomed to the blackness as best they could.

The building was full of muted sounds, creakings and whisperings. Someone was snoring. A child whimpered. Of equal proportions was the smell. The cold, clammy air was stagnant and thickly pigmented with conglomerate odors of cooking, bodies, and inadequate plumbing.

Shortly, Costain could distinguish indistinct boundaries of the foyer and hallway entrance. With hands outstretched, moving a single step at a time, he made his way into the hall and there found the ascending flight of stairs.

The tenement's unceasing cacophony aided him in his climb, for the squeaking of stairs underfoot was more than matched by other noises. One was a quick, furtive patter flowing ahead, behind, and to either side. The rat population was extensive and busy.

Despite its industries, he'd always thought of the city as a rather clean, picturesque place. Undoubtedly, he was in the poorest section, and this must be one of the most run-down structures in it.

He went up four flights before he reached the top. The light he'd seen from the street inched out from under the first door at the head of the landing. He paused again, listening, examining his surroundings as best he could. He was out of breath. What heat there was in the building had risen to this level, but still he felt chilled and wretched in his wet clothes. His fatigue was no less. He was tense and shivering, unsure of his next move.

"If the door's locked, you can't break it down."

"I know. I know! I can knock on it."

"Sure, and who would open it?"

"I'll say I'm the police."

"And if they're stupid enough to believe it, then what?"

"I'll show them this." He glanced down at the gun as he took it from his jacket pocket.

"You can't shoot them."

"Don't be an ass! I warn them all to be quiet. I—I put them all in a closet. I get out of these clothes, find some dry clothes."

"And then what do you do with them?"

"If there's a sink, I can get rid of this beard."

"Sure, get a shave and a haircut while you're about it ... maybe a manicure."

"If there's food, I'll eat."

"And then what do you do with them, whoever's in there? I mean, honestly, what can you do with them?"

"I don't know how many there will be."

"You sure don't! What do you do with the children?"

"Would there be this light if there were children?"

"Why not? Illness, maybe. Maybe a million things."

"I'll have to find that out. I'll have to see."

"Suppose they won't obey you? Suppose they yell bloody murder?"

"They'll obey me! I wish you'd shut up. I've gotten this far. What have I got to lose?"

"But if it goes all right in there, what do you do when you leave? What do you do with them?"

Costain knew this was a question that could not be avoided. Everything he did now was extremely risky, built on intangible "ifs." His only alternative was to return to the street, and that he must not do now. He really had no choice, regardless of what lay on the other side of the door. He could look at it as an opportunity or an act of desperation.

The insistent questioning of his more cautious and doubtful self merely laid stress on the one point that was not intangible: What did he do with them? Or her? Or him? Or variations of the same? Tie them up, gag them, wait till first light and then make tracks, hoping they wouldn't be found until he was out of the neighborhood—out of the city. That was all very well, providing no one tried to oppose him. But if they did—what did he do with them?

There was no margin for error because there was no visible margin. He was operating in a void as thick as the void in which he now crouched, trying to get a look through the keyhole of the door. The hole was sealed tightly with something more filling than a key.

Costain straightened, jaws locked, hand clenching the barrel of the gun. His free hand fastened on the knob. It twisted easily and the door gave without hesitation. He went across the threshold in one swift step, checked the impetus of his advance, and reshut the door very fast.

He stood in a crouch, eyes blinking feverishly in the sudden glare of light. The room's sole illumination came from a large, old-fashioned kerosene lamp. Its flame genuflected fearfully.

The lamp was on a small, paper-littered table. Behind it sat a man, pencil in hand, momentarily transfixed, staring at the unexpected intruder.

Costain's first half-blinded glance indicated to him that there was only this one large, high-ceilinged room. Part of the cot along the wall was against a boarded-up door. Beyond the bed's foot, there was a washstand. In the corner to his left, he glimpsed a small stove with a pipe going up into the ceiling. There were several shelves with cans and utensils to either side. The room was sparsely furnished, in sore need of paint and plaster. The two windows facing on the street were covered with pull-down shades.

Even in that first second, he was aware that, poorly as the room was decorated and furnished, it was neat and clean. The only disorder was the papers on the table.

Costain judged his unexpected arrival, gun in hand, would be a shocking surprise for any man. Add to that his thoroughly unsavory appearance, and there would be good grounds for terror-stricken speechlessness. And so when that first hushed instant had passed, he was about to speak reassuringly. Instead, he was thrown off guard himself, for the man behind the table arose and said, "Well! … Well! Come in!" The voice was light and clear, musically modulated. There was surprise in it, but no sign of fear. In fact, it struck Costain that in back of it lay a touch of sardonic humor.

"I don't mean to harm you." He said it with an obvious "unless" in his inflection.

"No, no, of course not." The man started to come from behind the table.

"Stay right there!" Costain halted him. "You're alone!"

"Oh yes, quite." The answer was calm, patient. He stood leaning forward, his head slightly cocked. "There's Euripides, of course, but I don't think he'll hurt you." The smile was faintly amused.

Costain's eyes swept the room in search of Euripides. He saw nothing that was animate. He knew the man was waiting for him to ask the obvious.

"He's under the bed. You frightened him. He's a cat. If you'd been a rat, he might have eaten you by now … I don't think he'll hunt you." It was all said lightly in the soothing, musical tone, and translated, Costain sensed it meant, "You haven't frightened me. I'm way ahead of you." It was almost as though the man were waiting for something to radically change the situation.

Costain backed against the door. At least that way he'd know if anyone were out there. "You have no key for this, no lock?"

"No," the faint grin remained. "No, my door is open to anyone … It's a way of getting back at them, you know. A man whose door is unlocked has nothing to hide."

"Keep your voice down!"

"Yes, to be sure." The reply dropped to a conspiratorial level. "We are invested on both sides by wicked Philistines."

"What do you mean?"

The man gestured gracefully with either hand. "To the left of me there are six, to the right, five. They'd complain bitterly should their slumbers be disturbed."

In the lamplight, the close-cropped, sandy hair carpeted the beautifully formed head like a pelt. It ended in a sharp peak on the brink of a broad forehead. Costain found the large, rather fawnlike, pale gray eyes startling in their quality and depth. "How is it you have this place to yourself?" He said it almost angrily, his suspicions pouncing on the incongruity.

The other showed a set of even white teeth, and Costain didn't know whether he was smiling at the question or the tone in which it was asked, or both. "I have friends in high places.

The landlord owes me a certain debt of gratitude." He gestured, "This is all the payment I require."

There was no guessing the man's age. He was far past youth, but youthfulness was in his every move, his voice, his hands, his rather pointed, classical features. Yes, there was youthfulness, and intelligence, and something else. It was the something else that bothered Costain most, partly because he was too tired to put his finger on what it was and partly because he wanted to believe that the man wasn't planning to trick him, wasn't just playing with him. That was it! Playing with him!

He could feel the muscles in legs and shoulders twitching in dull protest. He had to have rest! He had to get out of these clothes!

"I warn you," he said with quiet harshness, "if you're lying to me, if anyone comes here, I'll kill you."

The smile vanished. The cheek bones were flat and high, and the eyes above turned smokily remote in their gaze. Costain gathered a decision was being made and threats of violence had little to do with the reaching of it.

The reply came seriously. "I can't promise no one will come here. However, I've never known anyone to come at this hour ... uninvited ... except yourself. There's no key for the door, but if you'll feel better, you can place that chair against it. That will give you some warning."

It was all helpful and to the point. Costain took in the straight-back chair indicated. It suddenly hit him that this was some kind of wild dream and that he was playing a part out of character and not playing it very well. "You sit down there where you were," he signaled with the gun.

The man sat down and, as he did so, Costain was disappointedly aware of his slight build. His clothes would never fit. With the gun in his belt, he picked up the chair and set it on an angle with its back wedged in under the door knob.

"Excellent! It would take an Alexander to break it down now." The grin was back, the same relaxed inspection. "Tell me, if you don't mind, what brought you here?"

"The light in your window."

"Ahh!" The man swung about to take in the offending blind. "Do you mind if I adjust it? If it brought you, it might bring someone else, and I don't think either of us wants that, do we?" He got up, not waiting for Costain's approval, and went to the shade, tugging it lower.

"You can see it on either side, too." Costain's attention went from the window to the one comfortable looking chair in the room. It was a battered, brown leather monstrosity, its covering cracked and peeling. He crossed to it, shoved it to the wall and sat down. He was unable to contain a sigh of exhaustion.

"I'll put on some coffee. I usually have a cup about now. There's food, too, if you like." The man went on fixing the shade in the second window, his back to Costain, the invitation an obvious reply to the visitor's sigh, all very polite, all very normal.

"Who are you!" Costain growled, not meaning "What's your name?" so much as "What the devil manner of man are you to so calmly accept a dangerous and armed fugitive in the middle of the night!"

"I?" He swung around. It was clear the question was welcome, that the subject was a stimulating one. "I'm one of the few survivors of a time that is gone … a breed forgotten, ignored. I'm not quite extinct, but like a worn tombstone, I'm neither noticed nor recognized."

He might have been an actor performing before a packed audience. The pitch remained little more than a whisper, but it was full of melody and vibrance. Every gesture, whether small or expansive, flowed with the words.

"You have learned a secret." He wagged his finger and winked. "You have found me at my work. There is not one other person on this earth who knows how I spend the watches of the night. You share my secret. It gives us something in common, because I share yours. We have other things in common." He nodded with a crafty look and stood silent a moment, his shadow blackly climbing the wall behind him. Then he spun about. "Excuse me, I'll put on the coffee."

Costain leaned his head back and closed his eyes. Now he knew what the "something else" was. He was in the company of a friendly madman. "What are you writing, a book?" he asked.

"No. I'm a poet." The poet busied himself with pot and coffee jar. "When I am finally dead, if my poems have not been used to light fires and stuff windy cracks, and there is anyone left on this planet who can read, perhaps they'll discover me … The beauty of my words will awake them from a long, long sleep." He placed the pot on the stove and lit the gas burner with exaggerated finesse. Then he faced Costain again, grinning broadly. "They'll wonder how such a giant could have walked amongst them as an obscure, unnoticed office clerk in a steel mill."

There was laughter in it and joking, but Costain saw that, though this might be a friendly madman, he was certainly not a modest poet. He made no reply, and the poet laughed softly, returning to his tiny scullery.

"Yes, I'm a poet, by night at any rate. I don't suppose there are any real full-time poets left, but then I'll bet you've never met a poet of any sort before." He chuckled, wagging his head, as he sliced several thick slices of bread from a loaf. "I'll make you suffer for it. You came unannounced. I'll treat you to some of my poetry as a penalty. If you don't like it, I'll ask you to leave."

He shot a glance at Costain over his shoulder. "I think you'd better get out of those wet clothes. We can string a line across the room to help them dry. You can put a blanket around you."

Costain might have been an expected and welcome guest. He was losing control of the situation but then, he reflected wryly, he'd lost control of it the minute he entered the room. "I'd like to get rid of this beard," he scratched at the heavy growth of hair.

"There's a razor at the sink."

"This is all very generous of you ... completely, not understandably generous of you, so just let me mention for the last time that if there's a trick in it, you won't live to enjoy it." It sounded blatantly melodramatic.

"I imagine someone in your position is bound to be suspicious," the poet replied matter-of-factly, licking his finger.

"It seems to be necessary."

"Yes. Well, as I also mentioned, if someone catches you here, it won't be my fault. I won't be considered an accessory to whatever crime you're fleeing. I can say you forced me to do your bidding. But since I have an inquisitive and adventuresome spirit, whether you be devil or beast, I make you welcome and offer you what small hospitality I possess." It was all said with mercurial good nature. It bubbled with tolerance and open franknesss. "More than that, we can talk and you can hear my poetry, because if I'm your captive, you're mine."

Costain's instinctive liking for the man overcame his worn but wary defenses. Silently, he accepted the invitation in the manner that it was offered. He got up and started to undress.

CHAPTER SIX

He was dry. He was reasonably warm. His hunger had been nicely spiked. The poet made good coffee. Sausages, bread and Olomouc cheese was a repast fit for a king. The beard was gone, clipped close with the aid of scissors and then bravely eradicated by a rather dull razor. The portion of his face that it had matted was cold in its new nakedness, but it was clean and, psychologically, he felt as though he'd regained a part of his lost identity. He sat in the big leather chair, a heavy wool blanket swathing him cloak-fashion. With his lean, hawky features, he had the appearance of a brooding Indian. His clothing was hanging from a cord stretched across the far end of the room. Somehow it made the room seem smaller, more cluttered and crowded. The clothing would dry slowly, and Costain knew when he put it on again, it would still be damp.

It was a minor consideration in a number of possibilities that he now must weigh. Sleep. Did he dare? Or if he did not, could he possibly remain awake? And when it became light, what then? ... He could tie this incredible man up and leave, but the more he thought about venturing out by day in a relatively unfamiliar city, the less it appealed to him. Then, too, a day's rest would restore him greatly. The poet, who had been silent for the last few minutes, leafing through pages on the table, broke in on Costain's deliberations as though he'd been taking part in them.

"I have to leave here at six-thirty, you know. If I don't report for work, the chances are that someone will check on my absence." He peered around the lamp, smiling apologetically. "It's not that they know how important I really am, but they like to have everyone in his place at the proper time."

Euripides rubbed against Costain's leg, purring strongly.

"Ahh! He likes you. He's very particular, very discerning, very wise. Listen to what he says."

The effect was uncanny, chilling. It left Costain gaping in amazement, for it seemed that the cat was actually speaking to him. "Look to the things of God," it purred, arching its back and eyeing him. "Know you are bound to help all who are wronged." The voice faded away in a bubbling laugh, and Costain jerked to his senses, looked across the table at the laughing poet and knew he had other talents besides making rhymes in the night.

"Forgive me," the poet said. "Ventriloquism is a gift I have. I shouldn't use it unkindly."

"You're very good." He smiled. He couldn't be angry with the man. It was good ... even if the words didn't mean anything ... or did they?

"I'll tell you something." The poet shook his pencil gently at Costain. "As I see it, either you leave before I do, or you stay."

"That's right." The cat jumped up into Costain's lap, and he began to pet it absently, not taking his eyes from the poet. "That's exactly right."

"Is daylight a good time for you to travel? I expect you're traveling." There was no levity in his manner now. He spoke seriously, a man concerned, trying to be of help.

"We'll discuss procedures, if you like, not causes, or results ... or aims."

"Very good. What I don't know can't hurt either of us. I'll make an offer. If you want to stay here tomorrow, I think you'll be quite safe ... providing I go to work."

"You mean I'm to trust you, to put my life in your hands."

"Yes, it comes down to that, doesn't it? You know I've never had anyone's life in my hands before." He studied his half-cupped hands, put them together and then looked down at the small entrance between his thumbs. "Life ... so delicate, yet so tough and enduring." He closed the entrance tightly. "You can imprison it so easily ... chain it to a rock like Prometheus." He opened his hands and let them drop. "We have found so many different ways to be Prometheus. The modern version is to deaden the mind and senses, to spit on the soul. We have been so long at proving we are descended from apes that we have become their brothers." There was no bitterness in it, only a sad weariness, and for an instant, the man looking at Costain was very tired.

In the next instant, the effect was gone, melancholy and age extinguished with an impish smile. "I told you you'd pay for coming to my door! Now you're going to. Now you are going to find that we are both fugitives. You, physically, and I, because I choose to think. Listen!" He stood up and began to recite.

"In Greece and Rome monsters were idolized;
The Nile was thronged with victims dazed by fear
From images of ideas beasts have symbolized.
And already by such votaries on this hemisphere
An ideology of like proportions would appear
To be taken for a god, though in the form of a beast."

The words jarred Costain. It took him a moment to understand their meaning, and then he wasn't quite sure. "Wait a minute!" he interrupted. "Say it again." He leaned forward to hear more clearly.

"Ahh, you understand it!"

"I—I don't know." He caught himself. "I'm not much on verses. You'll have to go slower."

The enigmatic smile on the poet's mouth faded slowly. It remained in his eyes until he began to speak again.

Now Costain did not interrupt. To show complete indifference would be rude. To reveal that he knew exactly what the man was talking about would be out of character, and so he chose a middle ground that might mean anything … head back, eyes closed, hand stroking the cat's back.

Even though he was not particularly familiar with the art of poetry, he felt the words being driven home with hammerlike accuracy. Nothing could deny them. There was in their quality a timelessness; the warm, stimulated voice could be echoing down a corridor two thousand years long, or from the darkness of two decades … or today, this very night … and tomorrow.

> "We need not forfeit the firmament for the stye.
>> Or else in our festivals and feasts
>> On doleful husks we dine,
> Against the gloom unable to hold the line.
> Either we fall back
> Upon our songs, our women and our wine—
> Or once and for all we attack;
> Our wits we clarify, our ideology define."

The poet went on, and Costain listened and saw the man had not lied, had not exaggerated. He was one of the last of a lost breed … here, at any rate. It was true they were both fugitives.

If this man were caught speaking the lines he now recited, he'd be treated in the same fashion they'd treat Costain for having killed a police officer.

"Nothing in Nature on an orbit of its own
    Has ever been complete;
And there must be a miracle somewhere in a human
    That moves on common feet;
Or the idea of a Deity we would have to treat
As a ruthless ogre torturing the small.

    We are—we must be—great;
Love itself within Nature's very arsenal
    Destined to indoctrinate—
Or we are being preyed upon by powers we do not rate.
    To no purpose at all."

It was the poem that decided Costain, the final words so quiet and clear they might have been a distant clarion call, whispering back from a time where men still fought and held.

    "We will be seen and heard.
    Ours is the coming consciousness of man!"

He did not suspect that the poet had reasoned on the effect of his writings. He simply knew beyond the effect that such a man was in no position to betray him. The poet might be mad, or fey, but he was not a fool ... far from it. Of course, he gave the impression of knowing all about his unexpected visitor, which couldn't possibly be. Whatever he assumed, Costain would do nothing to change his assumptions ... Let it go the way it would.

"You're going to leave here at six-thirty?"

"Yes ... I'll also return at six-thirty in the evening. Are you going to accept my invitation to stay?"

"No one will come here?"

"It would be surprising."

"It would be more than surprising for me."

"There's that chance." He nodded thoughtfully, kneeling on the floor and lifting a board that appeared to be just as well nailed as the rest. Costain watched him put the sheaf of papers into the recess in the floor and then replace the board carefully. "You'd rather leave by dark, wouldn't you?" he asked, straightening, looking down at his handiwork.

"Yes ... It will be light shortly."

"You'll have the whole day to rest."

"I know."

The poet grinned his youthful grin. "It will give you a better chance to hear my poetry ... when you're not so tired."

"I'm afraid I'm not much of an audience."

"I know what you are."

Costain was startled by the quiet, flat statement. Some of the tenseness he'd managed to shuck off rearmored him stiffly. There was nothing hidden in his questioning stare. It was cold, hostile, dangerous.

The poet ignored it and went toward his bed, supplying a sufficient answer. "You're very tired ... There's only the one cot, and it's too narrow for both of us." He stopped, turning slowly and looked at something not in the room but inside himself. "You're my first overnight guest in many years ... My last one's name was

Eva, and it didn't really matter how wide the bed was. She—" His voice faded, and he was gone with the private memory of Eva. When he spoke again, Costain could barely catch the words.

"In some walled ancient town this home must be,
And near—as always—must be heard the sea.
Where nights our foreheads cool, where drowsily
The vested robins choir upon the lawn;
Where we can feel, half dreaming—"

His voice was blown out in a sigh.

Costain could hear the sibilant pattering of the rain tapping mockingly at the windows. He got up, clearing his throat and pulling the blanket snugly about his shoulders. "I'll sleep on the floor or in this chair."

"What! What!" the poet returned reluctantly. He squinted across the room at Costain, cocking his head, annoyed at being pulled away from his memories.

"Oh yes! Yes!" He moved to the closet built out from the wall. "I have a coat that will soften the floor for you. You can keep the blanket. When I leave for work, you may have the bed. We'll talk later." He spoke no other word that night, and Costain might just as well not have been there.

At first, Costain fried to resist sleep, to fight it off. His mind warred furiously over the decision to take this chance, to stay here, to trust anyone. Finally, it fell into the pit of its own exhaustion, and he went away to a limbo of disconnected and incoherent dreams. It was cold in the room, and the coat did little to soften the hardness of the floor, but in spite of coldness, discomfort, and fear-seduced dreams, Costain slept.

He awoke, stale and shivering, to the soft, still light of early morning. Though the shades remained down, he could tell the rain was gone and the day was clear.

The poet was already dressed, busy at his stove, fixing his breakfast. Costain could hear the rise and fall of voices in. nearby rooms. He hadn't realized the thinness of the walls. He raised himself on one elbow and cleared his throat, not wanting to speak out.

The poet turned and smiled, raising his finger to his lips and nodding his head in understanding. He picked up a steaming mug of coffee in each hand and crossed to where Costain lay.

He was dressed in a threadbare, dark blue suit, and he wore horn-rimmed glasses. With the smile gone from his face, he looked completely nondescript. There was a dull cast to both eye and feature. Youthfulness was gone. This was a tired, dispirited man, confused, defeated … a face in the crowd lacking identity. Then the smile flashed again. He handed one cup to Costain, pulled the big chair closer and sat down.

Costain sat up, tugging the blanket around his shoulders. He held the mug in both hands and silently toasted his benefactor, sipping the hot liquid, feeling its heat warm him.

The poet pocketed his glasses. "Good morning," he said softly. "I hope you slept."

Costain nodded again. "I didn't realize the walls were so thin."

"No one heard us, I'm sure … They're sound sleepers, too. How do you like the coffee?"

"Life-giving."

"Good." The smile again. "I'm talented … in lots of ways." The look of confusion and defeat winked on, then off.

"You're very good. I didn't recognize you for a minute."

"That's the way I fool them. I'm harmless ... nothing."

"What about today?"

"I've got to leave in a moment. Stay here, if you like. I think you'll be safe. If you keep the chair against the door, be sure to take it away about six-thirty tonight. It wouldn't do to be seen knocking on my own door."

"No ... If I stay, I'll do that."

"Is there anything I can get you?"

"I need a map of the city."

"I can tell you how to get most anywhere."

"No." Costain shook his head. "There's no need for you to know where I'm going."

The poet grinned and put his hand on Costain's shoulder. "Wherever you're going, I'm glad you came here. So is Euripides." He glanced at the cat where it lay at the foot of the cot, yawning complacently.

"Why! Why do you say that?" He couldn't conceal his wonderment.

The poet drained the last of his coffee and stood up. "I've got to go." He appeared not to have heard Costain's question. "I'll try to get a map. We'll talk tonight." He winked slyly. "You'll have to hear more of my poetry before you leave."

CHAPTER SEVEN

When the poet left his room, he was once again an elderly man without purpose or hope. His was an empty face with squinting eyes, blinking in foggy defeat at an uncaring world.

He went down the stairs slowly, as was his habit, pausing now and again to sigh an innocuous "good day" to his faster-descending fellow tenants. Within him, his heart was singing. A line from Herodotus chanted its proud paean: "Freedom you have never tried—never known how sweet it is. If you had, you would urge us to fight for it not with our spears only, but even with hatchets."

Some higher power had brought his visitor … Oh, he was tough, that one … A Ulysses on the run. All right, they were hunting him. Out of the darkness he had come, showing his teeth like a wolf, the gun in his hand a dangerous thing. Into the darkness he would go again, and perhaps the next time they would bring him down, but in the interim between now and the time he went forth again, he would have help … whatever small help there was to give.

It was one thing, the poet told himself, to play this part, to revel in fooling them, to write his clandestine and unpublishable poetry, but in the long run, it was nothing but a form of self-indulgence. It did no good. It helped nothing … no one. Now, at last, had come this amazing chance to help. Now the words he wrote could take on some real meaning, and the part he played would be for a good cause.

He'd known in that first fused moment of meeting, almost before the man had spoken. Oh, he was good, that one! There was no doubt about that. Only someone who had spent a great many years in the study of speech, who had specialized in languages, would detect the flaws. But they were there. Absolutely! Of course, added proof was in the poem itself. The visitor had understood it clearly because it was written about the things he was obviously fighting. It might be well, this evening, to caution him about certain inflections. The man was definitely not a native of the country. In fact, the poet was willing to stake his professional background that his visitor was not even a native of the same hemisphere.

The poet reached the street and began his plodding advance along it, amidst a growing throng of workers. The rain had washed the sky a pale autumnal blue. The chill remained, and in it was the foretaste of colder weather to come.

Head slightly bent, hands in shabby pants pockets, the poet moved with the swarm which he suddenly realized was slowing in its flow toward the intersection. He looked up and then stopped stock-still. An inadvertent gasp made a ghostly puff of steam before his face. What he saw atomized the proud, assured thoughts of an instant past. The narrow end of the street was blocked by a police van. A pair of policemen stood on each corner, scrutinizing everyone who passed. A few they stopped and signaled aside into the street, where three of their comrades ushered the unfortunates into the rear entrance of the van.

The poet's first startled reaction was to run. He squashed the impulse but, nevertheless, glanced over his shoulder. Although the street end curved out of sight, he knew from the slow movement of those who traveled in that direction that the same situation existed there. His fear was only a momentary thing, reaching its pinnacle when he saw policemen issuing out of one building and quickly moving into the one next to it.

The street closed off and a house-to-house search! The visitor was trapped!

It struck him that to stand still too long might attract attention. He began patting his pockets in bewilderment, and then, with a shake of his head and a disgusted mutter, he turned and started walking unhurriedly back the way he had come. He must warn the man! Must find a way out! He beat down the desire to walk faster.

"Hey, you!" the voice snapped from the opposite side of the street. His hesitation was more a pause in thought than in action. He continued on, unheeding, hopeful that the challenge had not been directed at him. Even when he heard the fast-approaching footsteps, he held his gait, seemingly oblivious.

The hand fell heavily on his shoulder. He cried out, flinching away, pulling his head in turtlelike. He was spun about roughly and would have fallen but for the bruising fingers that gripped him. He stared up open-mouthed and palsied at his inquisitor.

The inquisitor was dressed in plain clothes. He towered stiffly, his hatchet face a mask of sharply chiseled lines. "Where are you going?" The voice matched, devoid of inflection, devoid of humanity, unalterable.

"I—I—I—" the poet stuttered, "to—to—to my job!" He was cringing, a victim, abject, terrified, eyes blinking, his breath coming fast.

"Is this the way to your work!"

"No! No! That way!" He pointed. "But I forgot my lunch. I—I thought I had time to get it."

The inquisitor made no reply. He stared down at the trembling poet. The trembling was not all play-acting. This was the appearance of death. "Where do you live?"

"Right—right there."

"What's your name!"

The poet told him.

"Where do you work!"

The poet not only explained but began to describe his duties.

"All right! All right!" The inquisitor cut him off, punctuating his command with an impatient slice of his hand. "Go along!"

The poet babbled his thanks and went. He didn't look back until he was at the foot of the first flight of stairs. The front door was open, and through it he could see the inquisitor standing in the same spot, immobile, waiting.

He didn't dare run up the stairs, but he knew he must hurry. The searchers were already in the next building. He'd realized in his encounter that they were operating in teams.

Three of his fellow tenants passed him going down, down in a hurry. None spoke. All threw him curious glances.

He gained the top landing just as the door next to his room opened and his bellicose neighbor stepped out. He slammed the door angrily, making the walls shake. "That woman! That woman!" He shook a fat fist at the door. "Come! We'll walk down together."

The poet evaded the outstretched hand, and it flexed into an admonishing pointer. "You know you talk in your sleep! I heard you talking. You woke me up. I wish you'd try not to. Come along."

Again the poet side-stepped. "I have to get something."

"All right, get it, but hurry. I don't want to be late."

"You go along. It'll take a minute." The poet spoke in an unnaturally loud voice. "The police are stopping everyone, you know, going through all the buildings in the block."

"No!" The face took on an even more lumpy form. "Why! How do you know!"

"I saw them from the window."

"The window! I've done nothing! I'm a good worker."

"Yes, of course. You'd better go along. I don't want to make you late."

"I wonder what it is. I mean—"

"Why don't you ask them?" The poet took the last two steps to his door. If the chair had not been removed!

"Hey, you'd better come along."

"In a minute." His hand rested on the knob.

"Ahh, the devil—!" There was more fear than impatience in the brusque remark.

The poet turned the knob, and the door opened. He went in, his legs feeling like those of a bedridden patient who's gotten up for his first walk. He closed the door and stood leaning with his back against it, listening to the heavy footsteps fade. He was conscious of his heart's accelerated beat, of the perspiration on his neck and forehead, and for the barest instant, he dared to believe that his visitor had already departed. Despite the seeming emptiness of the room, he knew, even as he had the thought, this could not be, and Costain stepping into view from behind the far end of the built-out closet grimly verified it. The poet saw that Costain was fully dressed. In his eyes was the same taut glaze that had been there when he'd first burst in.

"They're coming!" It came out of the poet's mouth in a hoarse, whispering cry of warning.

"I know! How do I get on the roof!"

"No!" He shook his head. He was terribly out of breath. "The door is padlocked! … Get under the bed! I can bluff them!"

"Don't be a goddam fool!" Costain grabbed the poet by the arm and forcibly swung him out of the way. "Is there a cellar!"

"You'll never reach it." The poet struggled to hold on to Costain. "No! … Wait! They know I came back! I can fool them! I fool them all the time!"

"Go on fooling them!" Costain shoved the poet away angrily. The smaller man tripped and fell, sitting down hard.

There was a flicker of shame in Costain's eyes. Above all, he didn't want to hurt this man. "Thanks! Good luck!" He tried to express it all in three hurried words and knew that no words could ever express it.

He was out the door and at the landing when he heard them surge into the building, heard their dog-voices, the swift, naked staccato of their boots! He was trapped! Trapped fast with no trees to climb arid mountains to scale and sheep to hide amongst! Trapped by his own stupidity and a poor, dumb lout of a truck driver!

There was nowhere to go now … but down.

Before he could move, the poet had hold of his arm with a strength that surprised Costain. If, a moment ago, he had succeeded in pushing the smaller man away, now the smaller man literally flung him back into the room. "Get under that bed!" he ordered, pointing. His eyes blazed with a flame that seared.

Wordlessly, Costain found himself obeying. They could kill him under a bed as easily as on a staircase. But this madman was going to get himself killed, too. In Christ's name why!

Because he was mad.

All right, because he was mad and maybe just mad enough to bring it off and save them both.

The door to the poet's room stood open, and three of them came through the entrance, the inquisitor and two uniformed men carrying lightweight submachine guns. They found the poet waiting, clasping a paper bag to his chest as though it held the crown jewels. He blinked at them in fearful stupefaction.

"What are you doing here!" the first to enter the room barked. "Don't you have a place to work!"

"I—I—I—" the poet gathered enough strength to jerk his head at the inquisitor, "I—I—told the gentleman I forgot my lunch." He displayed the bag with a trembling hand.

Costain was beyond trembling. He lay on his left side, right arm flexed against his chest, finger on the trigger of the pistol, one eye squinting through a small hole in the blanket which had been dropped to the floor of the unmade bed.

He would start shooting when the two uniformed men finished their examination of the closet and turned their attention to the bed. In the chair, he could see the cat, Euripides, curled in a black muff, unconcernedly asleep. God, to be able to change places!

The poet was a shivering wreck of a man. "Please!" he squeaked. "May I go to my work! I—I'll be fined for lateness."

"Who lives here with you?" The inquisitor's gaze imprisoned the two coffee mugs.

Costain saw the reason for the question, but the poet didn't. "I—I live alone."

Costain groaned silently.

"And you drink your coffee out of two cups, hey?"

The closet examiners, through with their investigation in that area, turned their attention to their superior where he stood by the stove holding the two accusing cups.

The poet gulped out his answer without hesitation, a perfect answer of frightened sincerity. "M—my neighbor, he—he had a fight with his wife. He came for coffee. I—it—was how I forgot my lunch." He held the bag up for them to see and shook it in a pitiful desire to please.

No one had anything to say to this explanation, and the sounds of similar rapid search could be heard going on in the adjacent apartments.

"He—he often fights with her," the poet added weakly. "M—may I go?"

"How is it you have this all to yourself?" The inquisitor stonily contemplated the room's size. "It's big enough for a family of six."

"I—I don't know. I—I never asked. I—"

"I'll just bet you didn't! We'll see if we can change that for you. Take it down," the inquisitor snapped at his nearest subordinate. "Don't dawdle."

In his eagerness to assist, the poet was like a man reprieved from death, babbling about the glories of life to his executioners. He gave his name, his age, his occupation, his weekly wage, and had started in on his infirmities when the cataloguer of it all cut him off rudely.

Dust had gotten into Costain's nose. To suppress the sneeze that would surely be his death rattle, he had managed to move his right hand so that the fingers pressed against the flesh between upper lip and nose. The hard barrel of the automatic lay on his cheek, the barrel's edge cold on his forehead. Tears blurred his eyes and, helplessly, he knew that deeply as he pushed his fingers into nerves below his nose, the sneeze would not be choked off.

Dead by a sneeze! By his own sneeze! Why didn't he just go on holding his breath until he suffocated or the blood in his veins broke loose and drowned him!

The inquisitor started toward the door. The taker-of-information followed, and the chief-examiner-of-possible-hiding places halted them with a question. "What about the bed, sir?"

The pause after it draped the question in a shroud. Although Costain still fought to strangle the sneeze, he knew it was unimportant now. For a brief moment, he had dared to believe fool luck and that a fool poet might bring off the impossible.

"You're sleepy?" The inquisitor's sarcasm didn't require a change of inflection.

"No, sir, but—"

Three pair of eyes focused on the bed. The fourth pair, the poet's, fastened on the submachine gun held loosely in the black-gloved hand beside him.

"May—may I please go to work?" The voice chirped with frantic worry. The inquisitor shrugged his shoulders and walked out of the room. "Hurry up," he said.

The eager one started across the room quickly. Costain aimed to kill.

The heel of the eager one's boot hooked into a loose floor board. He tripped forward and nearly fell, catching himself against the big chair. Without seeming to have awakened, the cat jumped off the chair and ran under the bed.

The combined curse of annoyance and snort of derision died stillborn as both men saw that the offending board had been knocked loose, exposing a paper-filled recess beneath it. Simultaneously, the two pounced on the unexpected discovery, pulling the papers out, calling to their superior.

The poet straightened with a sigh, shucking off the role of the groveling man. He became himself. He'd been careful replacing the board last night. When he'd fallen, he must have knocked it loose.

For a short space, the only sound in the room was the turning of pages, a breeze through withered corn stalks.

"Coming back for your lunch, were you." The inquisitor handed the pages he'd been reading to his cataloguing subordinate.

"Exactly!" The poet smiled and the three men stared at him, aware of the sudden metamorphosis, aware that they had been tricked, but not minding it because of their chance find.

"Do you like it?"

"I like it," the inquisitor monotoned, "but you won't." "We should have more investigations like this," the holder of the poetry snorted emphatically.

"Well, I'll tell you something," the poet grinned, speaking conversationally, as though they were all friends. "I'm glad it happened like this ... for all of us."

"I'll tell you something," the inquisitor said. "I think you'll live long enough to change that opinion." He nodded an order to his subordinates, who took the poet by either arm and marched him roughly out of the room.

Costain's sneeze had died, shocked to death by the poet's unlucky apprehension. Dumbly he heard the inquisitor say, "Have them send some people to make a thorough search. There may be more of that filthy stuff." And then there was only the sound of receding footsteps.

Those last words of farewell from the poet left Costain lying torn and sick with remorse. The hideous irony of the whole thing screamed at him. The cat rubbed against his cramped legs, purring contentedly.

Costain left the building a scant fifteen minutes later. He waited only long enough to be sure that the rapid, concentrated search had swept the street from end to end and moved on. It was like the aftermath of a sudden, violent storm, it left the street silent and empty. No one quite dared to venture out yet, quite dared to open their door to see how their neighbors had fared.

He saw no one in his descent and, on reaching the ground floor, he proceeded quickly down the hall to the rear of the building. He found a back door that exited onto a dank, refuse-cluttered alley. It was little more than a narrow division between the backs of twin rows of tenements. He went along the alley at a fast walk. The night's rain had softened the carpeting of assorted filth on which he stepped, helping to deaden the sound of his passage, but he took no comfort in it.

Far overhead lay a long sliver of blue sky. Like hope, he saw its beauty remote and unattainable. He was a wanderer in the lower depths, stumbling amongst a graveyard of tin cans, breathing a thousand noxious stinks, imprisoned by bleak walls of cold, dark stone. He walked with the gun exposed in his hand, overpowered by a dizzying sense of despair. He'd shoot anyone who got in his way. He almost wished someone would.

The more balanced side of his nature knew that his mood was unrealistic, careless, and very dangerous. It tried to reason that either he must be dedicated to the extremely difficult and hazardous goal of escape, or he should stop right now and give himself up. Anything in between could only result in disaster, making it all a wasted effort.

The poet was not his fault! It was all luck! All luck ... good luck, bad luck ... And madmen, who wrote their silly verses and sacrificed their lives for strangers in the night, had to look after their own luck! They didn't really exist ... as Radek didn't exist.

What existed was a man named Costain, alive, feeling, thinking, walking down a narrow, stinking purgatory. Toward what?

Toward his own death.

Why walk then, why not run? If there is no hope, why not run?

Because as long as a man named Costain is alive and feeling and thinking—as long as he can look up and see that ribbon of blue, no matter how far distant, there is hope. Never mind its smallness, its dimensions, or its color. Never mind the odds against it ... it is there. While you live ... it is there. Now if anyone should, or could, look out of these dirt-filmed windows, they'd see you, and that would put an end to living. So find cover, find a place to hide ... until noon ... until the streets are crowded and, even in these clothes, you won't be noticeable.

"And then?"

"And then to Saint Wenceslaus ... and from there to the railroad yards."

"And then?"

"South to Breclav."

"And then!"

He found the place he sought where the cramped alley widened in some inexplicable manner to form what might be generously termed a small courtyard. Taking advantage of it, some small boys had gathered wood from somewhere and built a hut. It was hardly bigger than a good-sized dog house, but Costain managed to squeeze into it on hands and knees. By drawing up his legs, he was able to remain hidden from view, his back resting against the far wall. He placed the gun in his lap, and there he sat and rested, and thought his dark thoughts, waiting for the morning to pass.

CHAPTER EIGHT

Costain made his entrance onto the street by way of the corner tenement. He emerged through its front door, having passed down the hall from the rear. He met two women in the hallway, the first leaving her room and the other coming in the front door. He gave them both a cheerful "Good day," as though they were familiar to him, and they returned his greeting in kind.

On his head he wore a flat, peaked cap, found in the poet's closet. Under his arm, pressed to his side, he held the paper bag that contained the unlucky man's futilely prepared lunch.

Hands in pockets, body stiffened against the chill that had lessened but was kept alive by a gusty breeze, he walked like a man who knows where he's bound. The rain had washed much of the mud and dirt from his clothes and, despite their worn condition, they did not make him appear overly conspicuous. He might have been a worker in any kind of factory job on his way to anywhere.

His destination was the cathedral. In the now hazy autumn sky, its triple towers stood out as a guide amidst lesser building tops. He crossed a small park in which noontime strollers lazed, and at its end struck a main artery. He followed it on foot, rejecting the idea of taking a tram car. Better to move in the flow of the thickly thronged street. This kind of weather not only brought workers out for their midday break, but it invigorated them and made them walk briskly, which suited his own urgency.

Once he reached the church, he'd know how to get a bearing on the railroad yards. There would be a bridge to cross over, if he remembered right. Yes, there was the river to consider. When he had the railroad yards in sight, he'd find some place to hole up until it grew dark. Finding such a place might not be so easy. He might have to keep walking until the day was over. So far, no one had paid him the slightest heed, not even the police he passed. After all, what better place to remain unnoticed? Ahead he saw a larger park which he thought he recognized. If he crossed it, instead of following the street, he'd save time.

In the park, he paused by a fountain a moment to drink and then looked up through the black filigree of tree branches at the cathedral towers rising in gothic majesty … for man to create, but not to reach. Old. Old! … Silently, everlastingly, unalterably old, and the wickedness of mankind lapping, lapping far below.

A voice spoke out of nowhere to Costain. "You are being watched," it said distinctly. Part of the shock was in knowing that no person had spoken to him, and he did not think he had spoken to himself. He hesitated, fighting down the desire to turn around. He started walking, shouting at himself to keep the pace normal. Moderate!

Each step was a step! … was a step! … was a step! … A step to the street! In crossing through the tide of traffic, you can pick up the step. You can even run!

He went across the avenue at a fast lope and, upon reaching the curb, let the paper bag under his arm slip and fall. In stooping to pick it up, he managed a frantic look behind. It was enough. The follower in plain clothes stood out like a weed in a flower patch.

To run now would be fatal. To suddenly change his tactics and amble along leisurely window-shopping would be equally bad, for it would give the follower time to catch up and confirm the suspicions that had drawn him in the first place. Should he continue his present course and gait, he would also be overtaken.

There wasn't time to curse his own stupidity! Walking about in broad daylight, carefree as a bird! They knew he was in the city. They were alert and watching, and now—!

He saw that the store on the corner was a new market. It appeared quite crowded, and he was moving toward its entrance even as he straightened up with the paper bag in hand.

With its white counters and indirect lighting, the interior was polished and glossy. Even the shelves of food seemed to shine. He realized the store must have just opened and that most of those present were there to examine the newness of the place and not as customers. The prices would be much too high for the average.

Costain still moved as though he had a purpose and a place to go. He knew he had to give the impression that his surroundings were completely familiar. If he were to be stopped and asked where he was going, he must have a ready answer.

There were three doors at the rear of the store. The aisle he was in would take him to the center one. That was his choice. No one paid any attention to him until he was clear of the counter and a few feet from the door. Out of the corner of his eye, he saw a man moving hastily toward him. "Hey, you, where are you going?" It was the voice of querulous authority apprehending a culprit.

Costain had the door open when the hand fell on his shoulder. "You!" It was a shrill command.

Costain turned, to all outward appearances bland and unruffled. He held the heavy fire door open, having seen that it led into a large storage room which terminated at a loading ramp, where several produce trucks were parked.

"What? What's the matter?" Costain asked. He saw that the man was obviously a floor manager of some sort.

"Where are you going? This isn't the way out. What have you got in that bag!" He was fussy, a nervous hen of a man, peering up sharply through his pince-nez, his bald dome glistening in the bright lights. Fortunately, the thick hubbub of the slowly milling crowd put a damper on the range of his trumpeting falsetto.

"I'm going to my truck," Costain said with gruff belligerence, "and in this bag," he shook it at the little man, "is my lunch, which I didn't buy here because I'm not a rich man."

"You have no right to reach your truck through here. This store is for customers," the pudgy man scolded, eyes snapping with annoyance.

"Paaah!" Costain said it as though he were trying to literally blow the man off his feet. He turned away and entered the storage room. The fire door's swift closing chopped off the floor manager's insulting retort. Costain nodded to the half dozen men, truckers and loaders, who sat scattered about with their backs against packing boxes, eating their noonday meal. He could feel their eyes examining him with mild curiosity.

There was that empty weakness in his legs, and he was starting to sweat. They'd remember him. That little turnip would remember him. He had to move fast now.

He reached the edge of the loading ramp and dropped down into the building-surrounded courtyard. There was one entrance in from the street, and he didn't run until he turned the corner into it. It was empty and only about one-hundred-and-fifty feet long, but he sprinted down it, not slowing before he reached its end. He mustn't attract the attention of those passing by. His re-entry onto the street had to be casual, very casual.

It didn't work that way, for he stepped out on the sidewalk just as the package-ladened woman crossed his path. Her arms were full, her bundles stacked on them. She only had time to gasp before Costain collided with her, and the four packages were knocked from her arms and fell to the pavement. She would have fallen with them if Costain had not instinctively thrust out his hands and grabbed her, steadying her and regaining his own balance.

In that first instant of shock, he was aware that she was a small, smartly dressed woman. "I'm terribly sorry!" he apologized, stooping to pick up the bundles, dismayed by the accident and not wanting her to get a good look at him.

"Clumsy!" she hissed furiously. "Oh, if you've broken my perfume!"

He picked up the small square package which he thought held the perfume and shook it gingerly. Grimly, he knew pedestrians in the vicinity were watching with sardonic amusement. "I don't think it's broken," he said, straightening before her tensely, anxious to be gone.

Her brown, almond-shaped eyes were cold and hostile, the yellow flecks in them iced. "You stupid lout!" she said, in the same hissing breathlessness. "Can't you see where you're going!"

He was holding two packages in each hand, looking down at her. The chic white hat perched on her dark, fluffed up hair somehow leant an added touch of imperiousness. There was no doubt she was a striking looking woman, but he did not like her. He knew that if he left her abruptly or rudely, she was just the kind who would attract more attention. "If you please, Madam," he said with the proper amount of deference, "I'd be glad to carry your packages to your car … if you're driving."

He saw disdainful rejection rise to her full lips and die, saw it die first in her eyes which widened in a new expression. She was staring at him.

"My car is right there." She gestured toward a small, black vehicle parked a few yards up the street. She didn't glance in its direction. She kept looking at him.

"Allow me," he said, turning his back on her, walking toward the car. What the devil did that look mean! What was it? Surprise? Speculation? Both … Could she have recognized him? Impossible! … Well, if not impossible, improbable.

God, he had to get out of here! He realized he'd left the paper bag containing his lunch where it had fallen. He had to get it, too.

Costain was standing by the car waiting for the woman to come and open the door when the idea hit him. He flung it away. It wouldn't work! Madness! Too risky! The idea refused to be flung off. It came back stronger and tried to take possession of him. There was no time to debate it down. He compromised. If the possibility arose—.

The woman unlocked the car door wordlessly. He stood back and watched her get in, the skirt of her expensively tailored suit pulling tightly against her well-shaped, smoothly hosed legs. He could either hand her the packages where she sat or bring them around to the opposite door. It had to be the latter if he were going to attempt this thing. He saw that she was staring at him again. "I'll bring the packages around to the other side," he said.

She didn't reply, busying herself starting the engine.

Did he dare go through with it? This woman was totally unpredictable, volatile, to say the least. He didn't want to harm her, and she didn't seem to be the type that frightened easily. If she called his bluff, he was done for. The streets were crowded. They were right in the center of everything.

Then he didn't have any choice. He ducked, yanking open the car door. The follower and the floor manager had just come into view at the entrance of the truck driveway. They looked left and right. He saw them spot the paper bag.

Costain leaned across the seat into the small back compartment of the car. He set the packages on the floor and swung around into the seat, slamming the door shut, swiveling his body down as low as he could. "If you want to live," he said in a snarl, "drive!"

Her eyes flared at the sight of the gun, her breath sucking in, the color draining out of her face.

"Drive!" he repeated, the urgency of his command explosive.

She swallowed and put the car in gear, eyes straight ahead, white-gloved hands gripping the wheel. She backed out into traffic, nearly colliding with another car and finishing it all right there.

As they moved forward, Costain raised his head high enough to see the follower striding up the sidewalk in the opposite direction and the floor manager watching him go. He sat up, switching his attention back to the woman.

In profile, her cheek bones were more pronounced, her short, straight nose arrogant. Tension gave her olive-hued skin a taut, sickly quality.

"Listen," he said, not wanting to frighten her into doing something rash and, at the same time, not wanting her to recover fully from this first shock, "I don't mean you any harm. I don't want to hurt you. Just keep driving carefully and slowly. Don't try to disobey me. I have nothing to lose."

Her tongue flicked out and licked her lips. He saw her throat work as she swallowed again. The faint, slightly musky smell of her scent came to him. "What do you want with me?"

He was surprised at the almost normal tone of her question. The trouble was this had happened so fast and unexpectedly he wasn't sure what he wanted of her. She was certainly a liability. If she got the idea he was bluffing, he was done for. If she didn't, as soon as he let her go, she'd yell bloody murder. The first thing was to get out of this city. The method of transportation had been miraculously supplied and that was a stroke of good luck. Come to think of it, why couldn't she drive him to Breclav, or better still, Mikulov! This could be the luckiest break of all! "I want you to cross the bridge and take the highway south toward Prostjov."

"You won't get two miles out of the city in any direction you go."

Both the statement and the mocking way in which it was delivered startled him. "What are you talking about!" he snapped.

"You!" she replied, and the word was a scoffing sound.

"What about me!"

"I know who you are." The husky timbre of her voice was assured.

"How do you know that!" He couldn't hide the note of dumbfounded surprise.

She laughed sarcastically, giving him a quick look. Her lips went up in a smile, but her eyes were like glass. "Fantastic, isn't it? Utterly fantastic! ... God, you must be a fool!" Her nostrils arched as though she smelt something offensive. "A complete idiot, walking about in broad daylight ... Bumping into people!" She snorted with derision. "Drive south! I don't know how you've managed to keep out of their clutches for so long. I don't suppose you're aware that they're practically turning the city inside out trying to find you," she scolded contemptuously.

"How do you know about me?" he repeated angrily, confused. "How did you recognize me? The newspapers?" He was completely bewildered, off balance, and as with the poet, he knew he'd lost control of the situation almost the moment he stepped into it. Her scorn-sharp laughter infuriated him.

He was on the verge of ordering her to shut up and thus put himself even more on the defensive when he looked down at the gun he still held tightly in his hand.

In it he saw a clear fact. If this wretched female knew so much about him—never mind in what way for the moment—she knew that, having killed, he would be desperate enough to kill again. She'd been frightened in those first seconds back there. If he put that fear back into her, he could restore the proper balance of power.

He said nothing, continuing to stare at her, watching her every move. She was aware of the intentness of his gaze and, after a protracted silence, favored him with another quick look. He saw her face starting to turn in his direction and did everything he could to make his features ugly and dangerous.

It had the reverse effect. She began to laugh again, and this time she had more difficulty stopping. There was a wild bitterness in it, as though some hidden fury had hold of her and was going to push her over the border of hysteria. It began to get in the way of her driving.

"Watch where the hell you're going!" He yanked the wheel to the left before she rammed into the rear of a parked truck.

The near miss sobered her. She wiped the tears from her eyes with the back of her hand, and Costain saw they'd come to the river, and the bridge was close ahead. "Go across the bridge and head south," he ordered.

Again he heard the sucking sound her indrawn breath made and knew the mannerism was one of habit. "Listen, do you think I'm making jokes with you? We'll be stopped!"

"You'll do as I say," he said stubbornly, hoping his unyielding attitude would bring some clarification.

"Look, let me park the car, and I'll explain."

"All right. Instead of going over the bridge, take the street to the left there."

She let out a sigh of relief, and he said nothing more until the turn was completed and they were moving along a tree-lined drive bordering the placid river. "Why this great concern for my safety?" he asked.

"Not yours," she said bluntly, "mine. I happen to be with you. I happen to know what will happen if you're recognized." She glanced down meaningfully at the gun and then looked forward.

"How do you know so much?" He disliked asking her questions of any sort, but it was clear she had knowledge that might be helpful.

She made no immediate reply, seeming to have all her attention on driving. In a second he was going to lose his temper! He'd wring her blasted neck.

"It's really fantastic." She nodded, as though talking to herself. "Incredible!" And then shaking her head in disbelief, "Do you know, of all the people in this country, you couldn't have picked a better one to get hold of than me?" She paused and then continued flatly, "I happen to be the mistress of the man in charge of tracking you down. Yes, in charge of it all!" She laughed shrilly. "Krupina, Director of Security Police for the entire Hana region. You murder one of his idiotic subordinates in Ostrava, and you pick me to help you escape! It—it's really too much!" She went off into another fit of laughter, and Costain sat watching the road, making sure she didn't drive into the muddy ditch or run into another car. "You listen to me," she broke off her laughter, getting her breath. "You listen to me, Mr. Murderer-of-Policemen, I knew who you were the second you stood up with my packages. Yes, I did!" She said this last with a proud toss of her head.

"What do you suggest I do, pat you on the back?" If she were telling the truth, there was a certain inescapable irony in the whole thing.

"You miss the point," she said impatiently and then repeated heavily, "I recognized you … I should despise you, really. Four o'clock this morning, he got word you were here. That didn't do anything for my sleep. But just now, I recognized you." She hammered at it again, and then added, "I thought you might even try this."

"No doubt," he intoned with heavy sarcasm, "and when I did try it, you not only weren't frightened, you were overjoyed."

"I was terrified," she said with simple candor. "You see, I wasn't really considering what you might be like, what you might do to me, until I saw the look in your face and that awful gun. I do wish you'd put it away."

"What were you considering, your perfume?"

"I knew who you were," she ignored his gibe, "and although I didn't have it thought out at the time, I told myself if you tried to get in the car with me, I might think of something."

"I'm not sure that makes any sense to me."

"I said you couldn't have been luckier to bump into me. All right, maybe I couldn't have been luckier either. It's what struck me as being so—so droll." She gave a short laugh to illustrate.

"So we're both lucky," he said, knowing he wasn't going to let this go on much longer. "I know why I'm lucky. I find it a bit difficult to understand why you consider our meeting a sudden good fortune. Why?"

The animated expression her confusing admission had produced faded. She gave him a cold, withdrawn stare. He sensed something tortured beneath the surface of her disturbing eyes. "Watch the road!" he ordered sharply.

She obeyed, and then asked quietly, "Did you hate the man you killed?"

"Never mind that! I want you—!"

"No, it's important," she interrupted. "I'm trying to explain."

"Then answer my question!" It was difficult to keep his voice down.

"If you'd hated him," she went on, "you know what hate is … know what it can do to you, and if you know that, you'll find it easier to understand me."

"I'm damned if I can do that," he snorted ruefully. "What's hating someone got to do with you?"

"Krupina!" It was an obscenity spat from her mouth. "Krupina! I loathe the brute!"

The sudden violence of her outburst took Costain by surprise. The naked depths of her feelings were starkly chiseled in both face and word. She paused, as though having to swallow down the bile of her own bitterness.

"If I knew how to get away with killing him, I would kill him." She reflected with chilling calmness, discussing something clinical. "But I don't know how … and up to now I haven't had the courage to try … Besides, my mother, my sister and her children would all suffer. My position gives them certain advantages … So you see, my dear murderer," she did not favor him with a glance, "I am a woman with a purpose in life who has never found the method to carry it out." Her voice dropped to its hissing whisper, venom-filled. "And more than simply killing him, I would like to destroy him while he lives!"

The intenseness of her desire left her emotionally unable to continue, to find words, or in finding them, speak them.

So she bore the man who was her master no abiding love. That might well be. She'd be mistress to a man like Krupina through his choice, not her own. And she'd like to get even.

"And because of the way you feel toward him, you'd risk helping me." He said it thoughtfully, a man having solved a riddle.

"If he fails to find you … if you should escape … or even remain free for another week or two, it will ruin him. He will come crashing down!" This was a sight she would revel in. "I know that. He's had his warning."

"Maybe you're a good actress ... a fine actress," he said with a faint derisive smile.

"No!" she shot back bitingly. "No, I'm a fool for trying to talk to a fool! For the past weeks, I've heard little but what a clever fellow you are. I even began to admire you ... to hope that you would do the impossible. I was foolish enough to think you would be clever enough to grasp what I'm saying to you, but I see you're not. It's a matter of stupidity. They're just more stupid than you. However, I'm sure if they simply stopped looking for you, you'd walk into their arms."

He hardly heard her scathing tirade, his mind jumping straight to the point. "How can you help me?" he asked when she ran out of breath. "How can you do anything without getting yourself in trouble?"

"I don't plan to get in trouble," she said firmly.

"To help me is to certainly risk that."

"I don't mind a small risk to get what I want." She said it as though she'd taken other small risks.

"According to your information, you can't drive me to the border."

"Nor would I think of it," she said loftily, "but I can take you to a good hiding place." She laughed nastily at the thought. "A simply lovely hiding place."

"Where? Your home?"

"No, not my home. His!"

Costain felt his temper rising. He'd had just about enough.

She checked him before he could express himself in a manner that might convince her it wasn't all fun and games. "You know, I thought of it almost at once," she complimented herself. "He's got a chalet in the foothills not far from Jevicho. He uses it for hunting and parties, and that sort of thing. It's not over ten kilometers from here."

Jevicho! He jumped on it, trying to place it on a map. Beyond the plain. Northwest … mountainous. The highway didn't run through it, but—"I thought you said the roads are blocked."

"This is a private government road."

"All the way to Jevicho!"

"No, it's not that far, just in that general direction. It's really on the edge of the farmlands. Who would ever think of looking for you in his chalet!" It appeared she could have clapped her hands with joy at the thought, a stroke of pure genius.

"How do we get there without being stopped? They'll be watching all roads, private or otherwise."

"You have to have a special pass to travel that road." She nodded at the official-looking sticker on the window … "They'll know who I am," she added somberly, pointedly.

"They'll know who I am, too," he countered.

"If you make yourself small, you can lie on the floor back there. There's a robe to cover you."

He looked back. "I don't know whether I can make myself that small."

"Something will inspire you to shrink, I'm sure," she said, swinging left onto a broad, gently curving avenue, and in so doing, reversed their direction, heading back toward the heart of the city.

"Is this road Krupina's special preserve?"

"Not his alone. There's a sort of colony. This time of year, there's no one there except on week ends, and your nearest neighbor is half a kilometer away."

"So I take up residence in Krupina's chalet. How can you be sure he won't decide to do the same thing?"

She made a snorting sound of disgust. "He hasn't time for relaxing in the hills, or haven't you heard he's hunting bigger game? And as each day passes and you're not found, he'll grow that much more desperate!"

He saw she was about to go off into another flight of revengeful anticipation. "What about food? How do I eat?"

"You'll find it well-stocked. The pig is not given to dieting."

He didn't know whether this last statement was supposed to be a proverb or simply a description of the chalet's owner.

"There's no caretaker?"

"On a farm below, but he never comes around unless there's someone there."

"You know that, of course," he said sarcastically, "having watched him when you weren't there."

"You don't want much, do you? So you'll have to be careful and not lie in bed all day, eating caviar and drinking champagne."

Deeply suspicious as he was, Costain couldn't deny that the offer, on the face of it, was better than anything for which he could have hoped. If he had the time or the inclination, he might pause to wallow in the beautiful irony of taking up residence in the country abode of the man in charge of his capture. He'd leave that to the amazing creature sitting next to him.

She was amazing, no doubt about it, and if he rejected her invitation, he'd have to do something physical to her to keep her under control ... Tie her up, leave her somewhere, or keep her with him ... Then try to travel by back roads, cattle tracks. Anything, but get out of here. It wasn't a very bright prospect. If he did anything to bring discomfort to this handsome witch, she'd turn on him and probably be more dangerous than Krupina and all his bully boys. All right, to accept her offer was to trust her and, aside from the fact that he'd only known her for a few minutes, he had no trust for her whatever. Over the years, his perception, his ability to accept or reject, with little but instinct to go on, had by circumstance and nature become extremely acute. He was alive now because of it. But even if he'd been the dullest of clods, he'd have known that this unpredictable woman operated largely on impulse. Likes and dislikes and nothing in between, the heights and the depths, with an imbalance in perspective that made it impossible for her to see any situation except as a means of gain or of personal loss. He'd met a few women of this calibre before, and there was the look and feel about them that meant trouble. It was in the small, darting movements of their gestures, eyes that struck at the heart and fogged the brain, their cruel, sensuous lips, and the shrill yelps of almost hysterical laughter. Oh, she had it all and no mistake. Because she hated the man who kept her with an insatiate passion, she was willing to get at him by harboring the fugitive. But let something happen to jeopardize her position and the fugitive would be thrown to the wolves in an instant.

Of course, she could be leading him into a trap and, of course, a lot of other possibilities, but he didn't think so ... not at this moment. And in the end, it was a matter of matching his own cunning against hers. Hiding out wasn't getting him any closer to the border, yet going to earth again for a week or ten days would be better than risking movement.

"Well?" she said quietly with a knowing smile, "Have you decided that you need a rest for your health?"

"Understand one thing," he replied, choosing his words carefully. "You're doing this for your reasons, and I'm accepting for mine ... We have no secrets, and if you attempt to betray me, you'll run a very great risk whether you succeed or fail." He let it sit there for her to chew on.

"You're not very grateful, are you?" she said, and some of the surety had gone out of her voice.

"A man in my position has no time for being grateful … If there is ever time, I'll be grateful. Now, as soon as we're out of the traffic and I'm sure I won't be seen, I'm going to climb in the back and find out if you're right about my ability to shrink. Then it's in your hands. Better to remember what I'm holding in mine." He shook the gun gently.

He saw that he had finally convinced her he meant business, and she was wondering whether getting at Krupina in this way was worth the personal risk. "I don't want to harm you," he said with oblique reassurance, "you know that. All you have to do is take me to the chalet, as you offered."

CHAPTER NINE

There were two ceiling-to-floor wall maps, one a detailed street plan of the city and its environs, and next to it a topographical chart of the entire region from the Polish to the Austrian border. The shadow of the man who stood before them climbed darkly on both.

A shadow is a distortion, but in this case it symbolized the man who cast it. It was the combination of height and breadth that, in part, created the effect, for if Krupina stood six feet tall, he was nearly half as wide, not just in shoulders and chest, but also in belly and thighs, and in the way he planted his black-booted legs. His body was on the order of a rectangular flask and the head it supported above the almost nonexistent neck was the cork. He weighed over two hundred and fifty pounds, and there was no excess fat on any part of him.

The subordinate, who stood several paces behind Krupina, focused his eyes on the roll of neck-muscle bulging above the tight uniform collar. He saw how the light struck the back of the large, square-shaped head with its close-cropped pelt of pepper-and-salt. He mused that if it were possible for a bull and a bear to mate, this is what they would produce. Proportion was all that saved the man from being completely grotesque, but because there was proportion, the overall effect was impressive.

It was a pity, he thought without pity, that the mental powers didn't measure up to the physical. Oh, it wasn't that Krupina was a bungling fool. His innate shrewdness, his utter ruthlessness made him extremely dangerous. But he'd spent most of his life being a soldier, and soldiers, even if they rose to general, seldom made good policemen. Theirs was the direct approach. They lacked a sense of subtlety necessary to secure their position internally and the ability to attack anything smaller than an opposing regiment. This was a good case in point. The organization was all right, efficient. It was in its execution that it became clumsy and inept. No, Krupina, for all his gargantuan size, was out of his element, in over his head. Now, were he in charge instead of this mountain—

The mountain turned to face him. The small, granite eyes, deeply entrenched in bulging pads of flesh, raked the subordinate with a touch of sardonic amusement. "You, of course, would have a better plan." The voice was soft, a little raspy. The contrast in modulation and the man's size was always startling to those who first met him.

Now it was startling to the subordinate for other reasons. It manifested itself in several agitated blinks of his eyes. Inwardly, his balloon of ridicule exploded at the first prick of his superior's words. For a horrified instant, he wondered if Krupina could read his mind. "No—no, sir!" he cried in instinctive protest. "It's an excellent plan, sir. I—I'm sure it will work."

Krupina returned his cigarette to his mouth. The way he pursed his meaty lips, it just seemed to fit. He gave a noncommittal grunt and strode to his desk. He walked with a stiff, military bearing, his tightly tailored uniform accentuating the powerful grace of his body.

"Get out," he said to the subordinate. There was no inflection to signify approval or displeasure. It simply said "go," and the subordinate went gladly, daring to think, as he closed the door, that it was actually a stupid, unimaginative plan, and that if he were only patient and bided his time, one day the office he'd just left would be his own.

The man he'd left was also being patient and biding his time, for that was the essence of his plan. And if there was a single characteristic more important to Krupina's rise than another, one half of it was the ability to wait, and the other half was knowing when not to wait any longer. That the man from Ostrava was still at large might well have driven a lesser person into frenzied action, particularly since the security of his own position depended on quick success. Not Krupina.

Before the maps again, fresh cigarette in his mouth, he reviewed his plan of battle. He couldn't think of it in any other terms. It began with a known fact. The man was somewhere in the city. Even though that incompetent had let him slip away, the fact had been clearly established. And so it ended with what must become a fact: There was no possible escape.

Between that which was known and that which must be, he'd deployed his forces. He saw no need or reason to disrupt the entire city in their deployment. Aside from the inconvenience and resentment, it wasn't politically smart. A house-to-house search, such as that idiot had suggested, was out of the question.

The whole affair had become a delicate matter for more than the obvious reason that the fugitive had been able to avoid capture for so long. The public, alerted at the time of the crime, was fully aware that the man still remained at large. And these days the fools in Prague—even Moscow—were extremely touchy over the fact. But what really upset them—and he had to admit troubled him also—was the still unanswered question, why had this brilliant engineer, one of the top people in a highly sensitive area of research, killed Hans Goltz? If Goltz hadn't been such a secretive ghoul, never taking the rest of his organization into account until he was sure of his victim, there'd be no doubt as to the answer. Undoubtedly, Goltz had caught the fugitive in some serious crime. The one that came most readily to mind in this case was espionage. If the research engineer from Ostrava were indeed a foreign agent, his apprehension was more than imperative ... Radek and his Prague crew took the view that this was the case, and yet what had anyone been able to uncover at Aero-Morava? ... So far, nothing was definitely incriminating. The fact that the man seemed to have no close friends, had kept largely to himself, could be suspicious, or, as the fugitive's colleagues pointed out, he was dedicated to his work and had little time for else. But between the time he had disappeared over that mountain and had been definitely identified in Olomouc, where had he been? Someone must have hidden him. And if someone did, willingly, it meant clandestine friends. It could mean a spy ring, and if the engineer was handing over to the enemy what was going on at Aero-Morava, then it was serious ... Well, no matter, conjecture could be a waste of time unless it definitely tied in with laying hands on the man.

All indications showed that the fugitive did not know the city well, that he had no friends here, no reserves he could call on. Right now he'd be shivering in some dark alleyway, half starved, for if he was indeed the member of a filthy spy ring, would his cohorts have dumped him here? After all, his only chance would be to get out of the city. He might just as well try to get out of a locked cage with his keeper watching. Every method of travel, every route of travel, from highway to cattle track, was under close surveillance. There wasn't a car that could leave the city without being stopped and inspected, not a train, not a bus, not a truck, not a cart, not a boat, not a single thing that moved larger than a rabbit! So one waited, waited for—

The phone on the desk purred metallically. He plucked the cigarette from his lips, chuckling to himself. Yes, one waited until the phone rang.

His hand holding the receiver gave the instrument a puny, delicate look. The diamond nippling the solid gold band around the fourth finger twinkled its cold brilliance. "Yes ... Where? ... Was she alone?" There was no change in tone. The pauses seemed evenly spaced. "And she returned at what time? ... All right ... No." He replaced the receiver with one hand and stubbed out his cigarette with the other, holding this latest information at a distance where he could examine it objectively.

Why would she go there? ...

It was a pleasant day and, for all her sophistication, she exposed her origins in her love for the country. That was reasonable enough.

Would she dare to have an affair with anyone else? He weighed the point reluctantly. It gave him an unpleasant twinge. Would she be unfaithful to him? He was not fool enough to think he held her through affection or respect. He held her by force, mentally by what he could do to her and, physically, because once sexually aroused, she needed a Krupina to give her satisfaction. She might not like herself before or after, but she couldn't resist the desire to want more. He enjoyed her antagonism. It was stimulating, made their encounters battles, battles in which he briefly conquered and subdued her.

He was tremendously jealous of anyone to whom she gave a second glance. He had never shown it, and he never would. In his own narrow, brutal way he loved her, a strange, animal kind of love that whispered, "Let no man touch her! Let her touch no man!"

And now, could it be? Did he not have enough on his mind without this added concern? She could be completely unpredictable in her actions, impulsively do the most unexpected things, but impulse was swift, and unfaithfulness took more time. She had brains. She knew when she had a good thing. She wouldn't endanger it. There'd be an explanation.

He was going to her apartment from here at six-thirty. He looked at the expensive Swiss watch, girding his thick, darkly-matted wrist. It was nearly six.

She sat before Krupina, silently watching him as he ate. One would expect him to shovel his food down, to tear at it like an animal. But no, he ate delicately, fastidiously, swallowing one mouthful before taking another, using his napkin frequently. Consequently, he ate with infuriating slowness.

Look at his hands. They were more like paws, the hair running right up the fingers. One would expect them to be hard and rough, the fingernails uncut and not too clean. Instead, they were soft, scrupulously manicured. They could be gentle ... or brutal. She knew.

She knew. If anyone knew Krupina, she did ... Knew what time he would arrive, what he liked to eat and drink. The power he held ... what he could do to her if she made him angry. Outwardly, he was nerveless, unruffled, but she knew what lay under that awesome calm, knew that when aroused, he'd shed his placidity like a robe and reveal his true nature. And, she told herself, the only reason she was able to tolerate and accept his furious virility was that in their joinings, she became the master. His need made him subservient to her, and in this way, she humbled him and gained her only satisfaction in their relationship.

Above all, she knew that she hated him. She had not exaggerated her feelings to Costain. That she did not question the reason for her feelings was of no moment.

She was not the kind to examine her emotions. What she felt was enough; enough to know that she sat here while he slowly and politely gorged himself, not by free choice but because she had to. Given the choice, who could say whether she would be here or not? She let her thoughts tumble on, knowing that she did it to keep herself from dwelling on the realization of what she had done.

But the enormity of her act slowly made itself clear. She hadn't really thought of the possible consequences until after she'd left the man at the chalet and started back. Since then, she'd been fighting against the thought that she'd made a hideous blunder. It wasn't hate that held her now. It was fear—a terrible fear. How could she expect to outwit Krupina! He'd find out, and then—!

Dear God! What had possessed her to think—! If she got through this night safely, she'd go out there tomorrow and tell him he had to leave. Right now she must show no signs of nervousness. She must remain calm. Calm! Calm!

He put down his knife and fork on the plate, finished the last of his wine, and belched politely behind the cover of his napkin. He lit a cigarette and then sat back, smiling faintly at her as though he'd noticed her presence for the first time. "Well, what did you do today?"

She'd known the question was coming. "Nothing very exciting. I did some shopping … And oh yes, I drove out to Eagle's Nest this afternoon."

"So I heard." He put his head back and exhaled a cloud of smoke.

"I wish you'd hurry up and catch your man. It's getting to be a nuisance, being stopped wherever you go. Haven't you found him yet?"

"What's of interest out there this time of year?"

"What? Oh, I don't know. I like it out there any time of year. If it's a nice day tomorrow, I may go back and do some painting. Do you want more coffee?" She realized she was talking too fast, that her voice sounded strained.

"No, thank you." He looked at her. "It might be better if you didn't travel about until this thing is over."

"Why? What have I got to do with it?" She stood up and began to clear away the dishes. It gave her something to do. She wasn't going to sit still and let him look into her with his eyes of stone.

He shrugged and didn't reply.

"At the rate you're going," she said snidely, "it'll be another six months before you find him."

"Really?" He yawned. "I didn't get enough sleep last night. I think we should retire early."

It was like a slap in the face, and it was ever the same. He didn't say, "Well, I've satisfied my hunger, now I'm going to satisfy my lust. Go take your clothes off." No, he yawned and pretended he needed sleep, when they both knew he could go for two days without sleep! They both knew she would obey him, too. It was a part of the ritual and she couldn't deny that, by the time she had undressed, the heavy river of her desire would have begun to flow.

The telephone rang and she nearly dropped the tray and cried out. Before she could set it down and answer the ring, he'd risen and crossed to the instrument.

"Yes ... Yes ... Where?"

She couldn't move. She stood staring at his ramrod back.

"Won't move in until I get there. I want him taken alive ... Right away." He set the receiver down and moved toward his coat and hat on the nearby chair.

"I shouldn't be too long." He didn't turn.

"You—you found him!" It came out in a stricken whisper.

"Yes." He put on his coat, facing her. "Didn't you think I would ... for another six months?"

His face told her nothing. "Where!"

He stood motionless, his head cocked slightly, taking in her obvious agitation. "Does it matter?"

"N—no! No, of course not! I—I just wondered where."

He picked up his hat and put it on. "Yes," he said. "Yes, you might at that." And then he was gone, the door clicking quietly shut behind him, and she was standing alone in the room, the tray of dishes in her hands. She set it down with a choked cry, and pressed her hands to her mouth. God in heaven, what had she done!

"Stupid! Stupid! Stupid!" she cried aloud. "Oh, you stupid! ... Now look what you've done!"

Could she get out of it! Could he prove anything! Oh Lord, the criminal would think she'd betrayed him. He'd tell! He'd threatened that he would! Oh why in God's name had she ever—! Why hadn't she called a policeman right then and there!

Could it be a mistake! Could they have the wrong man some-place else!

"No! No! No!" she moaned, and threw herself down on the couch, her whole body trembling. He knew! He knew! He was just torturing her. He'd come back here, and—and—! She had to get out!

"How!" she cried aloud, as though by voicing it she'd get an answer. There was no answer. She was caught in a web of her own making.

CHAPTER TEN

Costain lay on a ridge several hundred yards above the chalet. He'd positioned himself there amongst the pines shortly after the woman had left, and now in the still, clear night, he observed the stars flickering frostily and felt the cold's bite on head and neck.

The excellent sleeping bag he'd selected from amongst a half dozen in the chalet housed his body warmly. The Mannlicher .308 he'd confiscated from the well-stocked gun cabinet might be of little use against submachine guns and the like, but anyone who tried to take him now wouldn't find it quite so easy. This last he knew was largely morale-building braggadocio. However, the precision-made weapon did offer comfort, whether false or foolish. Just to heft it, to sight it, gave a lift to his spirits. Now it rested close to his head, fully loaded, safety off. Beside it were the high-powered binoculars, also supplied courtesy of the chalet. Through the long afternoon, he'd put them to good use.

As the woman had said, the chalet was perched in the rolling foothills overlooking the broad, gently undulating plain. The valley spread out in a vast carpet of narrow, rectangular fields, divided irregularly by the river and met by a similar countryside at its far edge.

Behind him, the land tapered down into a sparsely wooded valley, splotched with undergrowth. Through it a stream coursed. Beyond the stream, the ground shot up steeply to form a portion of a jagged, rock-faced escarpment.

Costain knew the valley must be ideal for bird hunting, but anyone trying to come down the cliffs and cross the valley to attack him from the rear would find it tough going. He'd have plenty of warning, possibly more than he would have from a frontal attack. If the latter happened, they'd have to approach along the road to reach the chalet, and even in this darkness, he was sure he would hear them, should he fail to see them.

Against various eventualities, he'd worked out a series of counter moves. Of course, everything swung on the woman herself. Having gone so far to help, would she turn around and expose him?

She'd been the instigator of an almost macabre piece of good fortune. His stomach was filled, his body warm, his ability to fight back increased tenfold, all through the good offices of an impulsive bundle of female nitro, whose name he didn't even know.

When they'd had to stop at the guardhouse check-point where the private road began, she'd been arrogantly cool. He'd lain huddled on the floor, twisted and cramped against the back of the seat, covered by the robe, her packages and pocketbook. He was completely helpless. She could have handed him over to them with impunity.

She could have arranged for it again when she halted at the farm half a kilometer or so down the road where it was gated. She'd left the car, gotten the woman of the house to open the gate, and so brought him to the chalet, and barely a word out of her.

She hadn't remained long, at first pacing up and down the lengthy, high-beamed room, watching him with furtive glances as he examined the premises. Then, after he'd built a fire in the wood stove, she'd shown him the well-stocked larder next to the small kitchen and even helped prepare a meal.

Their conversation was largely monosyllabic, and when he'd finished eating, he saw that she was in a hurry to go.

"What happens now?" He stood up.

She began to pull on her gloves. "You'd better clean up this mess."

"I plan to. I mean, when will you come back?"

"I don't know. I don't want to attract attention."

"Neither do I, and 1 have to eat. There's only the wood stove to cook over, isn't there? If I light a fire, the smoke will be seen."

"Well, what do you expect me to do?" she snorted. "Come up here every day so you can eat? You'll have to figure that out your-self. There's plenty of canned food you can eat cold." She picked up her bag from the long, red leather couch.

"Suppose I stay here two weeks? What then?"

"Then I'll have kept my part of the bargain. He'll be through. Finished!"

"You won't help me after that?"

"Of course not!" Her head shot up with annoyance. "I'd say I'd risked a great deal already. If it weren't for me, where would you be now?"

"I'll have a medal made up for you." He stared at her coldly, not really feeling cold toward her, almost wanting to smile. "If, after you get what you want, you decide maybe you'd like to talk to your boy friend's replacement, you just remember what I said earlier."

He thought for a moment she was going to slap him. "If, after I get what I want," she said, as though measuring each word, "you're still here, I won't be responsible."

"No one's asking you to be responsible," and now he did smile. "But for the good of your own neck, you'd better let me know when Krupina gets the axe."

She considered this and then nodded thoughtfully. "If I can ... safely. If you don't hear from me in two weeks, you'd better clear out." She turned and started for the door.

His hand fell on her shoulder, stopping her. "Wait a minute."

She swung around, shrugging herself free. "Keep your hands off me!"

"I just wanted to thank you ... for everything."

She didn't enjoy the irony. If she had a sense of humor, she kept it well-hidden, he thought. "If you're caught through your own stupidity, don't blame me."

Then she was gone, and he watched her from the window, speeding down the dirt road in her black car, leaving a trail of brown dust to briefly stain the air.

A short time later, he'd left the chalet and found this dominating ridge. It was a fine place to take cover, giving him a good, sweeping view on all sides.

Now he lay comfortably dozing in the sleeping bag, thinking. The woman, the look and the sound of her, drifted in and out of focus, delicately intruding over his main stream of conjecture about the plane.

The plane was a possibility to be approached warily, to be approached slowly and from a distance, with caution—great caution. When he'd first seen it, he'd thought it was hunting him. It was flying very low over the plain directly toward where he lay. Even as he was sure the woman had double-crossed him, the aircraft turned in a steep bank and reversed its direction. Grabbing the binoculars, he quickly learned its purpose, and his fears died stillborn. It was a crop-dusting machine and, because the fields had already been harvested, he thought the faint, descending cloud that it laid must be winter wheat or possibly a restorative chemical for the land. He'd heard of such projects taking place on an experimental basis.

The plane was not large, a small, single-engine craft with a high wing. Stamped on its bright yellow fuselage, there was a government insignia. He first thought it must have come from Olomouc.

From where he lay, he could see the city straddling the river in the near distance, could see the trains moving north and south from it, could see the automotive traffic on the main highway west of the river, but could see no aircraft rising from the city or its surrounding territory.

Through the shag end of the afternoon, the busy little machine had plied its monotonous, repetitive course. Back and forth, back and forth, from field to field. Whatever its job, the tillers of the land must have found its operation new and welcome. It was saving somebody a lot of manual work.

It wasn't until daylight was breaking into the soft amethyst of dusk that he got his answer as to its home base. Because it was flying so consistently low and a haze curtain was gathering over the plain, he nearly missed its landing. He hadn't been watching it constantly, and when its faint buzzing stopped suddenly, it took several seconds of looking to spot it.

It had landed in a field close to a low barn-like structure, which he realized must have been built to house it and its equipment. Close by, there was a small farm dwelling. Costain saw the plane taxi up to the barn and swing around its tail to it. The engine was cut, and through the binoculars he watched the pilot climb out of the cockpit and stretch wearily, flexing his arms and shoulders. Even with the aid of the powerful glasses, the pilot was a tiny miniature of a man. He was joined by another man who came from the house. Together they lifted the tail of the plane and pulled the craft out of Costain's line of vision into the hangar. He saw them reappear, the pilot going to his car parked beside the barn. The other man waved his farewell, and the flyer drove off down the dirt track toward the intersecting highway.

The plane was something to be considered, to be considered at judicious length; to be considered while the darkness gently sucked substance and color from the sky and hid the place where the plane lay; to be considered as tiny flecks of light dotted the plain, quietly reaffirming the pattern of life, and the massed, glittering lights of the city proclaimed its supremacy; to be considered now, here, at this moment.

"How far distant? ... Say, three kilometers."

"What airspeed? ... Say, one hundred. Wind negligible."

"How far to the border? ... Say, 100 kilometers by air. Say, forty minutes flying time."

"How swift. How sure!"

"Swift, my friend, swift, but not sure, not at all sure."

"Aye, there's the rub."

"Take it in steps, one step at a time ... A hunted man walking across a treeless, open plain by night, skirting farm houses, moving through the starlit darkness."

"Are there others out there on that plain, waiting, watching? ... On the roads at various points? Yes, of course."

"Is it possible to stay off the roads? Not altogether. Necessary to cross several, but not too difficult."

"All right, if sense of direction does not fail, if dogs do not bark, and watchers do not hark, our man reaches destination well before break of day."

"And then?"

"Then he must take care of occupant in house."

"Not knowing whether the occupant has family of seven."

"No, not knowing."

"First bad obstacle."

"Agreed, but leaving it for now, hunted man gets plane out of hangar and takes off for points south."

"All very well, but—"

"Never mind 'BUTS.' Important question is, can they shoot him down at the border?"

"It's a very serious consideration."

"A second bad obstacle."

"Yes."

"But if he takes off, say at three in the morning. He is making a run for it of approximately forty minutes. If he hugs the mountain tops, flies east of Brno and West of Kroměříž, avoids towns of any size, his chances are not too bad. They are better than the chances of a man lying on a ridge, dependent for the next two weeks on the whims of a very dangerous woman, better than the chances of a man lucky enough to survive those two weeks and then having to figure a new move."

"Agreed, but for two counts."

"I know them."

"Can the hunted man fly the course required or, to raise the greatest obstacle of all, can the hunted man simply fly the plane, when he has not flown any sort of aircraft in over sixteen years?"

September 24, 1943 ... that was the exact date. He'd often considered it from the point of view of fate, of a man's destiny, for it had been a flight he had not been scheduled to make and would not have made, if some lieutenant, whose name he'd long forgotten, had not gotten drunk and fallen through a plate glass window.

Knowledge that he'd been chosen to replace the lieutenant came in the middle of the night. It was a bitter awakening. He'd protested to no avail, not much caring whether his anger covered the gut-sick fear which had come to live in him ... Yes, fate, particularly now, because one could say if the pilot who was supposed to fly had flown the mission, a man named Costain would not be lying here in the darkness on an alien ridge some sixteen years later.

All right, but the question remains the same: Having not piloted a plane of any type since that day of long ago, could he expect to step into the cockpit and take off and fly in the dark, and land somewhere in the dark without killing himself?

Costain knew if he decided it was worth the attempt, once committed, there could be no drawing back.

In sixteen years or fifty, one did not forget the mechanical operation of controls. What one forgot and lost was the feel of flight, the touch and the sensitivity of mind and body in its realm. Granted, but if he could just get it off the ground, get it up in the air, it shouldn't be too difficult to keep it there. It was a fine, clear night. He'd be able to see all right. By God, was there any better way to get out!

"Now wait a minute, wait a minute!" he cautioned himself. "You won't even know how to start it up."

"Ahh, master switch, if it has one, magneto switches ... mixture. That's right, mixture ... prime ... and start."

"Suppose there is no starter? A light plane like that, you might have to spin the prop by hand."

"I doubt it, but if so, chock the wheels, crack the throttle, switch on, and pull her through."

He found himself becoming excited, pleased to find out how much he could recall. The more he concentrated on it, the more should come back.

Of course, it wasn't really so amazing. Although he hadn't been a pilot in years, aviation had been his career, no matter how advanced his work. Before the war, he'd started taking flight training in college. He'd flown small planes similar to the one down there. He must think only of that time, not of B-25s, or of jet design, or of missile design, or the new design that went even farther.

"You'll need carburetor heat in case of icing."

"What about gas?"

"There should be enough in the tank or a supply in the barn."

"If one could stay relaxed, not tighten up, let the plane fly itself. I can do it! I know I can do it! I can't afford not to try. How long can I stay here like this?"

"God, it certainly looks like a golden opportunity."

"I've had good luck. You have to keep moving with your luck, like getting here in the first place."

"There's no good in moving foolishly. You don't know how many people are in that farmhouse."

"True, but—"

"Wouldn't it be better to give it another day, watch the farm all tomorrow? Watch the plane, too, study it, learn more about it?"

"It's dangerous to delay. Who knows what that woman will do? And the plane may go someplace else."

"There's more danger in going down there now, not knowing how many you'll be up against. The woman's not going to try anything funny. You won't ever see her again."

"Perhaps."

"It's really better like this, much better. You've got time to plan, time to work it all out, so you'll know the odds better, know what you've got to overcome."

"What about the weather? Suppose it turns bad?"

He examined the sky against the possibility. There was a small night wind quartering out of the northwest. This was a season of sudden change, but now he saw nothing that indicated it.

In the end, he heeded the more cautious approach. If the weather turned, the plane would not fly. It would not go someplace else. In delay, it was true, there was danger, but he could not put it on a comparative basis with the danger of going down there now, not knowing who was in the farmhouse, and not being sure what it would take to start the plane. It was worth waiting another day to find out.

Costain wormed his way deeper into the sleeping bag and prepared to sleep. He'd come a long, strange way since this time last night.

CHAPTER ELEVEN

An hour before midday, Costain saw the car approaching. With the binoculars, he was able to recognize both the vehicle and the driver before they passed out of sight beneath the bluff where the caretaker's farm lay. From all he could observe, she was alone, nor was there any indication of a second car following. Still, he did not like it. He did not think she would return so soon, or even at all, unless something was wrong.

He hadn't reconnoitered the general area since the first light, but from his position on the ridge, he'd been able to keep all of it under watch. He had seen nothing disturbing, other than the thick quilt of fog that had closely blanketed the valley until the sun had gotten high enough to burn it off.

The fog worried him. He'd want to make his take-off before it formed, but he did not know at what time of the night that would be. He supposed it all depended on the temperature during the day and how fast the ground cooled off after dark.

This worry had been somewhat tempered by the definite answer to one important question and a possible answer to a second. The pilot had not taken off until the fog was fully dissipated, and Costain learned that even though it had been necessary for the helper from the farmhouse to pull the propeller through its arc a half a dozen times by hand, the engine was started from the cockpit.

After the plane was air-borne, the helper had disappeared into the barn and, as far as Costain could tell, he was still there.

There was no sign of anyone else living in the house and, after careful watch and deliberation, Costain thought he had the answer. The place was deserted as a farm, the house in a very bad state of repair. The spot was being utilized for the express purpose of servicing the plane and housing the two men assigned to its operation. If the pilot did not leave as he had the evening previous, it would mean there would be the two of them to handle. It might also mean he could force the pilot to fly him across the border.

Now, suddenly, these speculations had been scattered by the woman who was unexpectedly returning. Suppose he remained here on the ridge ... She'd come to think he'd already left. What then?

No, it would be better to find out what she was up to. Even if she were up to no good, she might have information that would be helpful. Before the car came into sight again, he'd slipped down through the trees, using the chalet's bulk as further cover against anyone watching from below. He sat crouched in a tangle of underbrush close to the corner of the building. He carried the rifle and the binoculars with him.

He admired her tight-fitting beige slacks. There was a handsome suede jacket to match, and a red silk scarf at her neck to add just the right flare of color. It also highlighted her pale olive complexion. It was obvious that she was frightened.

She left the car for the chalet, and when she reappeared again, it was full of purpose, as though she'd long planned exactly what she must do, an actress playing a scene. She went back to the car, parked at the chalet's entrance, and began unloading it. It took him a moment to realize she was setting up easel and canvas. She was doing it out in the open. The valley was to be her subject.

She didn't speak until the easel was in position, sketch pencil in hand. "If you're here, you'd better let me know." Her voice, despite its throatiness, carried on the quiet, autumnal air.

He made no reply, and the sound of the distant plane was a small, insistent buzz, scratching the gray-blue haze.

"You've got to leave!" He heard the crack of desperation in her statement. It was there in the quick, jerking strokes of her pencil. "He suspects!"

"Don't turn around," he cautioned. "How do you know he suspects?" He could see her in profile. He saw her body start and tense at the sound of his voice. The curve of her neck traced a lovely line.

"I'm sure this place is being watched right now. If you've showed yourself—"

"I haven't. Why does he suspect? What did you tell him?"

"Nothing! Last night, they caught someone they thought at first was you. I—I've never seen him so upset." Her pencil made a slashing stroke at the remembrance. "I want you to go!"

"You're not making much sense. Why does he suspect this place?"

"Because of you! Because! Because!"

"Calm down!"

"He—he's jealous. I told you that. He knew I came here yesterday. He knows I'm here now."

Costain thought he saw what she was trying to say. "You mean he suspects you have a lover and this is where you're meeting him?"

"Yes!" It came out in a low, hissing wail.

"I'm flattered," he couldn't keep the humor out of it. "But why come back here to tell me and make him even more suspicious?"

"Because I know him! Because I know he'll send some of his people here to uncover what they can."

"He hasn't so far." Was this all a bluff, a method of holding his attention while something was going on? Her nervousness and fear were genuine enough ... Maybe it was from having to play the sacrificial goat.

"I'm sure he would have sent someone last night, but he thought he'd found you, and that took his mind off me!"

"Whom did he find?"

"I don't know! Some poor wretch. He was in a frightful rage! ... Horrible! I couldn't sleep all night. Get out of here! He's bound to send people tonight!"

"Now wait a minute! If you did have a lover, would he be foolish enough to stay here and wait through the night for you to come visit him during the day?"

"If I had a lover," and she emphasized the word 'had,' as though spitting, "he would leave some trace of having been here—a—a cigarette end, footprints in the dirt—a—a hair on a pillow. Evidence. That is what would be gathered, and when there was enough, Krupina would start to torture me with it. That is his way!"

"I'm going to crawl up in the brush behind you. You just go on with your work."

The underbrush and uncut grass was such that he was able to reach his new resting place without fear of being seen by anyone watching from the valley. From where he lay some twenty feet above and behind her, he could see she was actually making an effort to sketch the scene. He didn't think it was going to be very successful.

"Don't you think you're exaggerating his suspicions about you a bit? If he—"

"No!"

"Now, just take it easy. He's got me on his mind, not some theoretical boy friend of yours. If he's got this place under watch, he'll know that you arrived alone, that you're here alone … painting the view."

"I tell you he'll send someone!"

"And if he does, and they're any good, they'll find plenty of traces of my having been here, so where does that leave you?"

"We can remove them!"

"Look, he hasn't got time to be worrying about you now."

She stamped her foot. "Will you stop telling me what he has time to do and not to do! Do you know him! Do you live with him! If I were not worried for my own safety, do you think I'd take a chance of coming here! You've got to help me get out of this!"

"I've got a rifle and a pair of binoculars I'm going to keep. I've eaten more food than you could ever eat yourself. I'll probably carry some with me when I leave. These are traces nobody can remove. But even if they were, once a person has spent some time—even a short time—in a house, he leaves additional evidence that can be found, so I'm afraid there's not much I can do to help you."

She didn't reply right away, as though totally occupied in mixing paint on her palette.

He saw the plane was still air-borne. He knew from his earlier observations it should be landing soon. Nothing had changed at its landing place.

"I told him I thought I might come up here and paint today." She spoke carefully, slowly, her tone less edged with emotion. "From the gate entrance, they can see I'm doing just that. At noon, I'll stop and go inside. You can join me there."

"For lunch, of course."

She ignored his sarcasm. "Since it seems to be impossible to hide evidence of your having been here, I have another idea."

"I'll just bet you have," he said silently.

"I've helped you. The least you can do is return the favor." "In what way?"

"Suppose I were to be found here all tied up ... maybe a little the worse for wear. I could say I didn't know what had happened ... that when I went inside, I'd been struck down."

"And naturally, that would satisfy his oversuspicious nature." He chuckled nastily to make sure she knew what he thought of the idea.

"Why shouldn't it!" she flared. "What else would he think!"

"Maybe that you were suspicious of his suspicions and staged the whole thing," he said blandly.

"Oh really now!" She flung down the paint rag in her hand.

"You'll have to do better than that, Lady Bountiful."

"Listen, if I'm willing to chance it, what do you care? It's my worry!"

"Is that so! Well, if everything you've said is correct, and you don't leave here by dark, he'll have his lads up here fast, and that doesn't leave me where I want to be."

"No," she argued. "I told them at the gate I was planning to spend the night."

Curiouser and curiouser, he thought and then replied with the same open disbelief, "You really wanted to make him suspicious, hey?"

"I often spend the night here."

"Sure, and does he often check up on you to see that you're alone?"

"God, you're a stupid bastard!" Her unexpected profanity sharpened the point of her anger. He had a feeling this painting was going to look like someone's nightmare.

"And you're no doubt an excellent liar, but in this case, you haven't got much room to move, and I'm not buying any of it."

"Please, I—!"

"Don't turn around!" The command caught her face in profile. It checked her, and again he was looking at the back of her head. There was a long silence between them, and in its space, he watched the plane make its landing and saw the pilot and the helper servicing it. They had just finished the job and were walking toward the house when she spoke again.

"Please," she said, choking on the word, and it was the plea of the helpless female. "Can't we talk inside? This is very difficult. All I'm asking is your help. I helped you. Please!"

Was that it? If she got him inside, Krupina's boys could move in fast. There was no sign of that, but for all he knew, they were waiting on the far side of the ridge. But why wait? To protect this female Rembrandt? No, hardly. She could be telling the truth. Her capacity for reacting implausibly made it plausible. She'd gone way out on a limb and, now having considered the consequences, she was trying to get off it by going even farther out in another direction.

He could thank himself for having convinced her that any attempt to betray him would only result in an act of selfbetrayal for herself.

"What's the matter!" Her head moved from side to side tensely.

"Nothing. I'm thinking. You go on with your painting." And then after several moments, "I don't think I can afford to tie you up and leave you." He said it pleasantly, regretfully.

"I was a fool to expect anything from one such as you," she said bitterly. "I saved your life yesterday. I'm warning you to leave here now, and you're not intelligent enough to take the warning."

"You know, I don't even know your name to thank you."

"What!" She gave a short burst of angry laughter. "God!"

"Now look, you tell me something. If you stay the night, is he apt to send someone up here during it, or will he wait until you've left?"

"I—I don't know."

He was going to tell her what he thought of her reply and then decided against it. "I'm going to do some looking around. You stay put."

He went away on his stomach to a point where the chalet shielded him from the valley and, then crouching, ran in amongst the trees. When he was sure they screened him, he strode quickly to his former vantage point on the ridge line. There, on his stomach, he painstakingly looked over every foot of ground within his range of vision. The binoculars ferreted out nothing suspicious. Even so, he remained where he was until the sun was directly overhead.

He rested with his chin on the flat pillow of his crossed hands. Looking down across the russet fields, it suddenly seemed that the season was out of joint. Where the sun's rays glazed the thick strands of tassel-topped weeds, they shimmered and swayed as though coated in stems of ice. It gave a strange, fairyland effect to the fields, a zillion silver lances saluting the sky. Pity she hadn't picked this for her subject. He went over her every word. He weighed every possibility that came to mind and saw it swung on two things: One affected the woman, and the other, his intended time of take-off. He didn't like either, and now he told himself he should have made his move the night before.

When he got back, she was sitting on the ground beside her easel and paints, smoking a cigarette. He got up quite close to her before he made his presence known. "You can go inside now. Fix us something to eat."

She started with surprise, and then sat very still. "I heard you leave," she said, as though making a point.

"Didn't you think I'd come back?"

"No, I was thinking something else. I recall your profession is engineering ... I didn't know you were a woodsman as well." She got up and strode gracefully toward the chalet's main entrance.

He waited another half-hour before he made to join her. By then, the plane was back at work but, though it could not be long past noon, he felt a new chill in the air. The sky remained cloudless, but its blue had taken on an unhealthy tinge of white that, close to the horizon, gave it a colorless complexion. There was going to be a change, and no mistake. He only hoped it would be gradual in its coming.

It was his preoccupation with the weather that nearly cost him his life. He had planned, before entering the chalet, to have a look through the window to see how his benefactress was faring. Now he neglected the precaution, slipping directly into the main room through the small side door.

He saw instantly that she had been waiting for him. She was standing braced and tensed by the gun cabinet, the double-barreled shotgun clenched in her hands pointed at his midriff. From the whitely pinched, glassy-eyed expression congealed on her face, he had no doubt that she meant to use the weapon.

In the fractional pause of realization, he damned himself for not having seen that she was desperate and determined enough to try this.

His reaction was so fast that he had actually dropped the rifle and was catapulting through the air, as the self-castigating thoughts seared his mind. He launched himself not toward her, but to his right and the protection of the big red couch, hoping that his speed would take her by surprise and throw her timing off balance.

He hit the floor as the room shook to the stupefying blast of the closely confined double charge. The sound was still reverberating as he gained his knees and, like a football lineman, drove forward with shoulder and hands against the back of the couch, charging across the room toward her.

Though his ears were ringing, he heard her sob of despair. There'd be no chance for a reload. With a heave, he sent the couch on alone and rose behind it. He saw she was running to escape its entrapment. She got clear of the arm as the center part slammed into the gun cabinet, shattering the glass doors, splintering the framing, and knocking most of the firearms from their individual racks.

He caught her easily and she twisted around, fighting to pull free and hit him with the gun. He got hold of her wrists, and she kicked at his shins and tried to bring her knee up into his groin. She was extremely agile. Fear and rage gave her added strength. She fought, sobbing wild, unintelligible curses. He moved in close, daring her flailing legs, and tripped her up, purposely falling on top of her, hearing the gun go clattering across the floor. She screamed in pain at the impact and then began to writhe convulsively beneath him, moaning, her mouth wide and tortured, trying to drag air into emptied lungs.

He raised the upper part of his body off hers, keeping her arms spread wide, his hands tightly pinioning her wrists. So she couldn't use her legs, he forced them apart with his knee and lay between them.

He'd never treated a woman like this, never thought to, but she'd tried to kill him and, by God, he was going to teach her not to try it again! He didn't say a word, holding his position, letting her get back her breath. He watched her head twisting from side to side, her mouth working spasmodically. Weakly, she struggled to dislodge him, thrusting her hips upward in futile jabs.

Angry and shaken as he was, he found himself becoming increasingly aware that she was a woman, a woman whose physical qualities had already brushed the wellspring of his desire. Both his location and her bodily reaction began to make themselves felt.

As she began to breathe more normally and some of the color came back in her face, she ceased trying to move her body free of his. She lay quietly, not looking at him, her head turned to one side. There was a faint sheen of perspiration on her forehead and above her upper lip. The scent of her body was excitingly provocative. He could feel the contour of her thighs and belly molded to him. It struck him that sometimes the act of love was little removed from the emotions that gripped them now. Certainly, the position was correct.

"That wasn't very nice," he said, knowing that his voice sounded thin from more than the after-effect of her attempt. "You shouldn't have tried that." He drove his hips down against hers in a hard punctuation mark.

She gasped and looked up at him. Some of the newly returned color left her face as she stared at his.

"I should, you know," he said icily, and repeated the punctuation. "You want to get even with him," he grated. "What nicer way? I should think you'd like this better than killing the man he's after. I know I'd enjoy it more. Pity you didn't wear a skirt."

He didn't know whether it was the expression on her face or some inner barrier of conscience, but suddenly the words and the hot thoughts behind them were repugnant to him. There was also the terribly important question of whether the sound of the gun's report had attracted any attention.

He released her and rose so swiftly, it wasn't until he'd recovered the shotgun and the rifle that she moved. Then, it was to roll wordlessly on her side and start rubbing the circulation back into her wrists. He wondered if her crying indicated relief or anger. She looked small and helpless, like a discarded doll.

He surveyed. the results of their brief encounter. "I'm afraid traces of my having visited here are going to be rather permanent," he said, his voice still troubled by an unnatural thinness. He held out his hand and saw that it was trembling. Now, having left her, he knew a strong urgency to return, to strip the clothes from her and pay her back in kind.

He stood back from the central window, fists doubled, taking in the valley. "Get out of here," he said thickly. "Get on back to your painting until I tell you otherwise."

Krupina drove his private car amidst the flow of homeward traffic. He willed himself to drive with care and patience, holding at bay the double spear of his displeasure, one sharp tine for the enemy still at large, and the other for her. Self-controlled as he was, he could not completely dispel the turmoil still squalling within him.

The fiasco of the past night must not be dwelt on until the campaign was successfully terminated. But the enormity of the blunder and its possible results could not be laid to rest simply by concentrating on driving his car.

He strongly suspected it had been more than an inefficient case of mistaken identity. Somehow, it had been planned for the express purpose of embarrassing him, of hurrying his downfall. He had no illusions about the invulnerability of his position. Why should he? Upon occasion, he'd used similar tactics to gain it.

When he finished this ridiculous mission, the heads were going to roll. The call from above had made it clear he had little time in which to act and restore his own prestige.

It wasn't like the old days. Now the administration was concerned about public opinion on certain levels and, although nothing had been reported in the newspapers about last night's action, the story was all over the city and, no doubt, would spread far and wide. An innocent man had died ... Well, lots of innocent men had died and, as for himself, he'd survived far more serious ambushes than this piddling attempt.

Not by one twitch of an eyebrow did those back-stabbers realize that it affected him as anything more than a stupid attack against the wrong salient ... for which they would all be held responsible. Let them try their tricks on him, and they'd learn his touch to their regret.

Krupina sighed. In another hour, these streets would be empty of traffic, only authorized vehicles allowed on them. By 2000 hours, the population would be curfewed to their homes or places of work. The attack in depth would begin.

He didn't like it, and the citizenry wasn't going to like it either. The sensitive, bureaucratic boobies who were compelling him to take this course weren't going to win any friends by it. To try and counteract a relatively small error, they succeed in making a far larger one.

They were wildly criticizing him for not having made this move sooner, too frantic and dull to know that, although his own plan might take a little longer to bring victory, it would not create general havoc. Now, the entire city was to be turned upside down.

All right, he'd attack. Every man he could lay hands on would be thrown into it. He'd tear this city apart street by street, house by house, room by room, alley by alley, and he'd let those whey-faced administrators try and put it back together again ... like humpty-dumpty. Well, all right, tonight would settle it and as for the temper of the people, it was none of his concern.

Krupina looked at his watch and then switched on the radio receiver to listen to the interchange of reports. He shouldn't be here now. He wouldn't be here now but for her! ... He'd break her silly neck! More and more, of late, she'd been acting up, going against his wishes. He had no time to be interrupted and plagued by her activities, but now her activities had put him in a bad spot.

If she tried to come back to the city while the curfew was on, she'd be picked up, embarrassing him on several counts. Right now, he could not afford it. It would be another piece of ammunition for the opposition. They'd say Krupina's curfew applies to everyone but his mistress, or he's not very efficient if he forgets to tell his woman her place. They could say things like that and plenty more.

To send someone else to bring her back or have them tell her to stay put would be equally embarrassing. God knew what she might say or do to the someone, and besides, he wasn't going to have anyone reporting that he'd used a single man for other than the offensive now being mounted. So, like some kind of dog in heat, he, Krupina, the General, had to go sneaking off to make sure his paramour didn't endanger his position! It was enough to—! Oh, she was going to pay for this! She was going to do as she was told from now on, or he'd get rid of her! He-could find someone else more appreciative and, if by any chance he found *her* there with someone else—!

Krupina touched on the hidden source of angry flame and then fiercely stamped on it, forcing himself to concentrate on the monotoned voices reporting ... reporting. He was hoping to hear words of success, hoping against the zero hour in which he must order an attack whose victory might never measure up to the disruption and enmity it would create.

At times like this, Krupina sourly wished he'd been content to stay in the military, that his ambition had not pushed him into the deadly arena of politics, where no man was to be trusted and the enemy became an illusive, fleeing shadow.

The traffic began to thin as he approached the turn off to the private road. Before he'd set out on this degrading trip, he'd given orders to have the guards posted at the road juncture withdrawn. Everyone would be required to join in the attack. Only at key points would road blocks be manned. Not only was the move above suspicion and logical, but it also meant his own actions, for the next twenty minutes or so, would not be easily traceable. He'd left without a word to anyone. After last night, none of them at Headquarters were foolish enough to speak to him without first being addressed. Fortunately, he could be anywhere, and no one would dare question his brief absence. And, of course, with the radio, he'd be aware of any important developments as soon as they happened.

He noticed how quickly it was growing dark. It was going to storm ... all to the good. He switched on his headlights and speeded up. He had to get that fool back to the city before the curfew. Perhaps he'd make her stay there. If it snowed, she'd work hard enough to keep warm. Keep warm. God help her if she weren't there alone! God help her for putting him in the monstrous position of having to fetch her, simply to guard against a weak point in his defenses.

"You wilful bitch!" he said aloud. "You wilful bitch, I'll teach you!"

Krupina swung the car into the private road and saw that his orders had been obeyed. The guards were gone. He switched off the headlights. He knew the road well enough. It was straight to the farm, and then the hill would hide him.

At the farmhouse, he shouted for the woman to leave the gate open. He didn't know whether she recognized him in the dark, but she knew enough to keep her mouth shut whether she did or not.

He traveled the final distance lights on, accelerator to the floor, a man in a furious hurry, who told himself that his hurry was due to a shortness of time, knowing it was overridden by the explosive desire to surprise.

He braked the car to a skidding halt beside her own and was out and loping the few feet to the door almost before the vehicle stopped. The soft lamplight, shining from the windows, was glaringly indicative of a clandestine meeting. He went up the half dozen steps in a single bound and without checking his stride, flung wide the door and crossed the threshold.

The couch had been swung around to face the door, and he saw her lying on it bound and gagged, her eyes enormous in their imploring stare of warning. The completely unexpected sight of her stopped him in his tracks. In that instant of unmoving surprise, he read her silent cry and heard it matched by a cry from within himself. He had started to turn, when he was struck viciously from behind. The instant of warning gave way to one of blinding flame. Then there was nothing.

It wasn't until Costain had Krupina securely tied that he recognized him. For a long minute, he could do no more than look down at his unconscious adversary in awe and wonder.

After what had happened earlier, he was sure the woman had been lying about anyone coming to investigate. Nevertheless, he'd spent most of the afternoon on the ridge keeping a sharp lookout. He'd seen the weather slowly deteriorating, had watched the plane complete its day's work early and been further disheartened by the sight of the pilot and his helper adjourning to the farm-house together. It meant two men to handle instead of one. His lowering spirits had been tensely sharpened, first by seeing the two guards depart at dusk, and then by the unexpected appear-ance of the car turning into the private road and switching off its lights. If he had not been looking through the binoculars at that particular moment, he might have missed the car altogether, not been aware of it until it shot into sight around the bluff. Instead, he was ready and waiting, ready to take whatever measures were necessary, no matter how drastic.

Yes, he'd been badly surprised by the car's approach. Now he was dumbfounded to learn the identity of its occupant. He straightened from a closer examination, and said, "It's him!" It was as much a question as a statement. Her glare was confirma-tion and fear together.

He began to laugh. He couldn't help it. He'd caught the man who was leading the hunt for him! "Lo, look how the mighty are fallen," he intoned through his laughter. "Lo, Lo, Lo! High, low, jack and the game!"

"What can you do with him?" he asked himself.

"Nothing … Just leave him lay where Jesus flung him. Just get the hell out of here."

He crossed to the couch and undid the handkerchief he'd used to halter her jaws. Freed, she lowered her head, shaking it painfully, drawing air heavily into her lungs. "I owe you an apol-ogy," he said dryly. "He really is jealous, isn't he?"

"You'll find out," she panted, not raising her head.

"I should think you'd thank me. You asked me to make it look like you'd been set upon by brigands. Well, now you've got him to back it up … You've really got him now, you know!"

"What do you mean?" She raised her head and stared at him with sullen distrust.

"Suppose you were to mention that the great General Krupina had been captured, made a fool out of ... by me!" He barked with laughter, seeing the thought penetrate and receive tentative acceptance.

"Who would believe me?"

"I owe you something," he smiled. "I'll leave my old jacket in place of this more serviceable mackinaw. Is it his?" He'd found the short coat in a closet and, although it was large for him, its warmth and quality made it a valuable possession.

"That jacket," he pointed to the badly used garment, "will prove who I am ... your attacker and his captor. You let it be known he was here with you when I broke in and overpowered him. Oh, I'm sure you'll be able to think up something convincing."

"You didn't kill him?"

"No. His skull is pretty thick. Would you like me to?"

"It would be better for you."

"Your consideration for my welfare is overwhelming. I tell you, if you get free before he recovers, why don't you do it?"

"Let me free now."

He saw she was serious. "You know, if I believed in witches—" He turned away. The urge to get moving was becoming overpowering. Previously, he'd planned not to leave until much later. Now, with the weather and this latest development, he'd be smart to go right now.

She did not speak again until he'd dragged Krupina to the far end of the room and rechecked the trussing job he'd done on the man's wrists and legs. Neither of them were going to get free very easily.

"You're going to leave?" He was surprised at the concern in her tone.

"Yes. I won't put the gag back. I don't think anyone is going to hear you if you shout."

"They might not find us!"

"Oh, I'm sure they will!"

"Goddam you!" Her face was suffused with a ruddy tinge, her features etched in satanic fury.

"I don't know your name," he said, "but I have a name for you … Medusa. It'll be uncomfortable, Medusa, but actually, if you lie there and think about it, you've pretty well accomplished what you hoped to do. When they come looking and find that jacket, well—pleasant dreams."

He blew out the lamp on the table and walked to the door.

"You filthy, murdering whore's pig! You goddamned—! You goddamned—!" Her foul, keening cries of rage followed him out to the car. Even with the front door closed, he could hear her cursing him. "They'll get you! They'll get you!"

He put the rifle, binoculars, and small knapsack full of food into the back of Krupina's car. He'd wanted to take the sleeping bag but, with luck, he wasn't going to need anything like that. With luck, he'd be out of this bind by midnight. But oh God, it was going to have to be good luck … impossibly good!

CHAPTER TWELVE

Costain had not thought to relieve Krupina of his watch, and so it became necessary for him to measure the passage of time by events. The open gate at the farm was the start. It struck him, as he drove slowly through it, using only the dimmer lights to guide him, that the quality and size of his luck had gone on too long. It gnawed at him, punching holes in his ebullient hopes, whispering dark warnings, making him feel tense and edgy. He had no idea that the car contained a police radio, and when it blared forth as though someone were sitting next to him, he nearly drove off the road.

He'd already decided that to attempt to drive to the border would be foolhardy, but he had considered driving to the plane. Now, as he fumblingly cut back the volume on the receiver and forced his nerves to calm down, he realized that the radio, too, was good luck. It was the second event, and it told him of the curfew already in effect.

He brought the car to a halt and switched off the lights. He wanted to let his eyes become fully adjusted to the dark, and he wanted to decide what he would do next. From his meticulous observations on the ridge, he knew there were no wooded areas bordering the road. But for an occasional tree or two, there was no cover on the plain. There were the scattered farms, which he wished to avoid, but there was no place to hide the car. The only thing to do was to drive along the road to a point which he judged would be opposite where he wanted to go, then turn the car off the road and guide it across the fields as far as it was feasibly safe. The farms were positioned in his mind. He didn't want anyone to hear the car out in the fields, and he had the feeling the fields were going to be too soft to drive across. However, he must get far enough away from the road so that if anyone should come looking before daylight, they wouldn't spot the car and know the direction he'd taken.

For a few moments, he sat listening to the cryptic police reports. They quickly made clear what was happening, what was going to happen. When the first query came over as to the whereabouts of General Krupina, Costain put the car in gear and drove slowly down the road, looking for a good place to turn off.

Finding it had been the third event, and from there it had gone: Car mired in soft ground no more than fifty yards from the road ... Extensive commune skirted, but dogs voicing his passage ... Rain, dreaded rain, falling coldly, intermit-tenly, sky and earth blackly merged, and time passing, passing ... Precious minutes falling with the rain, and he plodding on over the gently undulating limbo ... Plodding on through the close, baffling darkness, no longer sure of his own or the plane's location. He'd thought to use the lights on the highway as a marker, but now he saw no lights. He'd judged the distance from the private road to the farm no more than five kilometers. He felt that he had already walked twice that.

The belief that he'd overshot the farm grew stronger with each step. It finally halted him. There was nothing to see. The rain had a different feel. He raised his head to it, and knew from its touch that it had become mixed with snow. "It couldn't last," he said in a whisper. "I told you it couldn't last. You can't have that kind of luck and expect it to last."

Even if he found the plane now, what good would it do? What was the point of going on in this manner, using up the rest of the night, if he had no direct place to go? … What place?

Why not return to the chalet? He'd fixed her car so it wouldn't run, but he could repair it. So he could repair it, What good would that do?

Every thought he had, he brutally clubbed down. He'd overplayed the whole thing. If he'd moved last night, he might have made it. Well, there wasn't any point in standing here in the middle of this god-forsaken nowhere and debating the badness of it.

If he could only get some kind of bearing on his position, he could at least make tracks westward into the dubious protection of more rugged country. He wouldn't be caught out here in this naked, colorless land, like some species of wind-blasted tree.

Using the binoculars, he began to turn in a slow circle. From past experience, he knew that even in darkness as thick as this, binoculars did have the power of some clarification.

He'd managed about 45 degrees of nothing, when the glasses picked up a squarish, black object. He held on it but couldn't be sure of anything other than it was there. He moved the glasses away from it and completed the circle without further success. He came back to the object and, lowering the binoculars, began a cautious advance. The rifle slung on his right shoulder, the knapsack on his left, had grown increasingly heavy, their straps furrowing into his flesh. Now, as much for preparedness as for relief, he unslung the rifle and carried it at the ready in his hands stiff with cold.

Every few steps, he halted and had another look with the binoculars. He was quite sure that he was approaching a farm building. When he'd verified his suspicions, he stopped, wondering what he might gain by going still closer. Why shouldn't he? He was armed. What could he lose by it now?

It wasn't until he was actually standing next to the barn that he realized it housed the plane. Even then, he would not allow himself to believe until he had laid his hand on the aircraft itself. Moving around the tail of the plane, he brushed against a big metal drum. He sat himself up on it and rested. He'd been slogging around out there for a helluva while. His legs—his whole body—were weary, but now everything had become dizzily softened and colored by this miraculous find.

Some higher power had a hand in this. "This sort of thing can't happen without direction. It can't ... the whole thing ... It's nothing I've done. It's things done for me ... It—it's coming here like this ... More than luck, Costain ... More than luck. A man's life has got to have some meaning ... If it does—if it does ..."

"How do you know yours does? Why are you so important?"

"It's not a matter of that kind of importance; it's a matter of being alive. That's the importance. It is given, and for a purpose ... not just a biological joining. I'm here, and there's a purpose to it beyond my knowing."

"Sure, you're blessed. You'll get in this plane and fly up into that muck, and soar on wings of song to a better land, I know. You'll bust your arse all over the landscape! There's a lot of purpose in that."

"Look, I'm not going to argue. I didn't get this far alone. I couldn't have done it all alone."

"Well, you sure as hell can't fly this thing out of here alone."

"I know, but since I've come this far, I'm going to try."

"You've got a pilot in that farmhouse. Make use of him."

"Maybe."

"Just don't get the idea you're immortal."

"Whatever I am, I am ... and for a reason ... not by mistake. You know where you can shove your putrid dialec-tics."

Costain stood up. He moved to the cockpit entrance. The door was open, hooked on the strut. He could see that the plane had originally been a tandem two-seater. Now, where the back seat had been, there was a large metal drum, whose length extended beyond the cockpit wall. There wasn't going to be room for two in this crate.

Extending out from the fuselage and anchored to the wing struts, there was a thin pipe with faucetlike outlets. It was from these faucets that the dust or seed was sprayed. It all added up to one bad element. Weight.

At the chalet, he'd found a map of the area, and study of it had caused him to change his original plan of flight, providing the weather remained clear. He would stay very low, right beside the river, and follow it to Breclav. Now, the weather meant that he probably could not follow the river and that he must fly high, not less than 3500 feet. With all this added weight, how could he expect to get anywhere near that?

Was the drum removable? From what he could see and feel, it was firmly connected to the plane by bolts. There was a forked pipe running from the face of the drum along the floor out each side of the fuselage to feed the dusting pipes. It would have to be disconnected. The whole unit was going to have to come out of the plane before he thought about taking off. He couldn't do the job himself, but he knew two people who were going to do it for him.

He had not fully made up his mind that he was going to try this crazy thing. Nevertheless, he went about making prepara-tions as though he were. He explored the barn-hangar. On a wall bench, he found a heavy, well-stocked tool box and lugged it to the front of the plane. In the back of his mind, he began toying with the idea of delaying the take-off until first light. In this rain and snow, visibility would not be good, but it wouldn't be good for the hunters either. They might pick him up on their radar at Gottwal-dov, or they might not, if he could stay low enough. Even if they did, they'd have a dandy time scrambling jets to locate a slow-flying bird like this, particularly in such weather. But that was just what was bad about the idea. Weather. He didn't know what it was going to do. It could turn to freezing rain, or heavy snow, or a multitude of impossible combinations, and if it did, they'd have him. So for now, he'd go on the assumption that he was going to take off as soon as he could get things ready and see what happened.

When he'd put the knapsack and binoculars in the cockpit, he was ready to take the next step. It would be both decisive and dangerous. There were no lights in the house, which was little more than a cottage. The pilot's car was parked at the end of the barn. Costain could count on there being two men in the house. From his observations, he didn't believe there was anyone else, but he must be prepared for any eventuality. He wasn't going to enter the house. He wanted to get them outside, and the best way to do it was to frighten them out. If he could frighten them, he'd have an advantage he could keep. When they saw he was armed and meant business, they'd behave. Either that, or he could wait until day-light when they came out voluntarily. The wind, gusting a handful of wet snow in his face, cried, "No!"

He took a deep breath and ran across the space between the barn and the house. He could feel the reassuring heaviness of the pistol jogging in his mackinaw pocket. It was added strength.

With the rifle butt, he hammered on the weathered, decaying door. "Outside! Outside!" he shouted.

The door latch gave to his blows. It slammed open, adding to the sudden racket.

"Outside, you two!" he thundered. "You men there! Cover the barn! Lieutenant, post a squad at the rear and watch the road!"

He whistled shrilly, trying to imitate a police whistle. "Out! Out!" he roared.

He was beginning to think it hadn't worked or that he'd frightened them so, that they were afraid to come out, when two figures materialized at the door, stumbling over each other in their dumbfounded hurry to obey the strident voice of authority.

They were badly startled, still foggy with sleep and only partially dressed. He saw that, in their haste, neither had put on shoes.

"This way!" Costain barked, motioning toward the barn with the rifle barrel. "Hurry it up!"

"What is it!" the one who was the pilot gasped. "What's happened!" He'd recovered enough to feel the cold snow under his bare feet, and he obeyed Costain's command in a kind of high-stepping jig.

"We—we haven't done anything!" his round companion chirped nervously.

"Jesus, let us get some clothes!" The pilot began flapping his long arms around his back.

"Shut up and move!" Costain knew in another moment they were going to realize it was a hoax. He herded them toward the plane, halting them at its front. "All right, the sooner you get done what I tell you to do, the sooner you'll get warm again. I don't have any time to waste, and you don't either. If you try to disobey me, I'll kill you both. Now pick up that tool box and go around to the cockpit."

It took a menacing thrust of the rifle to jar the mechanic into action. Dumbly, he picked up the box. As the pilot followed him, his head swiveled about in little jerks, sizing up the situation.

He stopped by the cockpit and looked over his shoulder. "Jesus," he said hoarsely, "are you the one they're looking for in the city?"

"I'm the one. Now, I want that thing in the rear removed and I want it done fast."

The mechanic put down his tool box and stood hugging himself dazedly. He didn't seem to know what was going on yet.

"Take the drum out!" the pilot said, a hard note in his voice. "It can't be done without taking the plane apart."

"You'll get it out without taking the plane apart, if you want to go on living."

"His tools won't do it," the pilot argued. He half faced Costain, and Costain knew he'd recovered his balance and was becoming dangerous.

"Shut up and turn around, or he'll do the job without your help!" The pilot turned slowly.

"Go on," Costain said to the mechanic. "Get at it! Fast!"

"I'm freezing," the mechanic protested.

"Working will warm you. If you don't do as I say right now—!" He left it there.

"It's foolish to remove the drum," the mechanic sighed, shaking his head, squatting down to find the necessary tools. He handed a large wrench up to the pilot. "Disconnect the rear bolts, I'll—"

"Disconnect them yourself, pig!" the pilot snarled, savagely thrusting the wrench back at the shivering butterball.

Costain heard the breath pop out of the man as he caught the force of the tool in his stomach. "Ohhhh!" It was a painful gasp.

It angered Costain. He jabbed the barrel of the rifle hard into the small of the pilot's back. The pilot cried out, his body arching upward.

"Help him, you bastard!" Costain said. "You think maybe I'm kidding!"

Where the baggage compartment once had been, the fuselage opened up so that the rear fastenings of the drum could be gotten at. The pilot reluctantly worked on their disconnecting, while the mechanic fumbled around in the cockpit. "Please, sir," he wheezed, "I need some light."

"No light. You do it by feel. Hurry!"

"You think you're going to fly this plane in this stuff, you're crazy." The pilot saw the plan. He sneezed loudly. "How about letting us get some clothes on."

"You get that drum out of there, and you can get all the clothes on you want."

The pilot sneezed again. "Christ, at least let me put on some shoes!"

"When you're done," Costain said. For the moment, at least, the weather was working in his favor.

When they unfastened and raised up a portion of the fuselage blocking the rear of the drum, Costain knew its unloading was not going to be impossible, or even too difficult. He was not ready, however, for the unexpected suddenness of its removal, nor the pilot's use of it.

The mechanic had just climbed out of the cockpit, wheezing mournfully. The pilot half turned, saw that his companion was clear, and with a mighty heave freed the drum from its rack. The drum hit the ground rolling, making a hollow "bong!" coming straight for Costain. Had he been standing any closer, or had the drum had more momentum in its advance, he'd never have gotten clear.

Instinctively, he threw himself out of its path in a sprawling dive, going under the wing, landing on the muddy ground just clear of the barn entrance. He was on his back, making a final roll to regain his feet, when he saw the extended blur of the pilot's body in mid-air.

Costain had kept his hold on the rifle, but there was no time to bring it into line. All he could do was steel himself for the impact. The lower half of the pilot's body smashed into his chest and face, but the impetus of the dive, plus Costain's twisting action, made it impossible for the man to hold his advantage. Only his legs made firm contact, and Costain slithered away from their piston-like blows, fighting to regain his feet. He was up on one knee when the pilot rushed him again in a flying leap. Somewhat off balance, rifle barrel raised skyward, he managed to swing the rifle butt up in a vicious stroke. The metal-bound stock caught the attacking man above the chin in a wicked uppercut, smashing into mouth and nose, his own momentum adding to the devastating effect of the blow.

Costain was knocked sprawling, the rifle wrenched from his hands. Largely unhurt, he fought to get free of the pilot's thrashing body. The pilot unknowingly aided him, rolling over and over in the mud, hands clasped to his broken face, howling in pain.

Costain tugged at the automatic in his pocket, swinging around to face what he was sure would be the mechanic's attack. He saw the little round man standing in front of the plane, looking on stupidly.

By the time Costain had recovered the rifle, the pilot was lying on his stomach, moaning. He moved to stand behind him. "You!" he panted at the mechanic, the word a hot sob in his throat. "Get some rope, quick!"

The mechanic hesitated only an instant, then disappeared into the deeper darkness of the hangar. Costain knew the man was too frightened to try anything. He knew that if the mechanic had been the same sort as this one, he'd be all finished now. His difficulty in breathing and the trembling in his legs were partly in reaction to such knowledge. Carelessness! All carelessness! ... Damn fool!

The pilot got his elbows into the ground and started to lever himself up. Costain pushed the rifle barrel into his back. "Stay right there!"

The pilot collapsed, choking a curse through his hands. He took them from his face, coughing, spitting out blood, his breath coming in a series of stunned hiccups.

"Hurry up, you!" Costain shouted angrily.

The shivering mechanic came trotting out of the barn carrying a long length of rope. He'd found and put on a ragged, grease-covered jacket. He came up to Costain, head hanging like a dog with its spirit gone.

"Tie his hands and feet," Costain said. "Tie them securely. I'll check what you do. You'd better do a good job." The mechanic gave a great, shuddering sigh. Costain handed him his knife. "Cut the rope into four equal lengths," he said.

The mechanic took the knife gingerly and did as he was told, handing back the weapon haft first.

"Tie his feet ... tight!"

The pilot made no move and said nothing, intermittently coughing and spitting, until Costain said, "Put your hands behind your back."

"You broke my nose!" It was a blurred snarl of censure.

"You broke your own nose. Do as I say, or you'll get something else broken."

The pilot cursed him bitterly, finally turning his head to rest his cheek carefully in the mud. He put his hands behind his back. The mechanic knelt to tie them.

"You son-of-a-bitch," the pilot swore at the mechanic. "When I get loose, I'm going to break your goddam face in!"

"Shut up!" Costain snapped. "Come on, make it fast." He prodded the mechanic with the rifle barrel, galvanizing him back into action. Together they dragged the battered flyer into the house. There were two bunks in the farm's main room. They laid the pilot on one. Costain checked the mechanic's tying job by feel and was impressed.

The darkness was very thick, but he was not going to light a lamp.

Using the mechanic as a shield and a guide, he found there were two small rooms off the main one, and the remains of a cow byre. Naturally, the longer he could keep the pilot from getting free, the better. Separating the two of them would help.

Before Costain tied the mechanic up in the cow's stable, he allowed the frightened man to get fully dressed, and bring his bedding. The mechanic nearly fell over himself in his desire to be accommodating. After Costain had tied his hands and feet, he covered him over with the blankets, and nearly laughed aloud when the little man thanked him.

Costain felt his way back into the main room. His nerves had settled down, but the urgency of time was on him. He quickly rechecked the pilot, relieving him of a pocketknife.

The pilot raised his head as Costain turned to leave. "I hope you break your neck," he said hoarsely.

"I trust you're comfortable," Costain replied and went out of the house, closing the door behind him.

He strode hurriedly toward the hangar, rubbing his chest where the pilot's feet had struck him. "Boy, you nearly bitched that up … Comes of thinking you're invincible."

"Comes of being careless. Having such good luck can work against you."

"You should know it."

He stopped and raised his head. There was only a slight drizzle now. It could mean the ceiling had lifted. To the south, he could detect a faint, reddish glow, which he thought must be a reflection of the city lights. The wind was gusty, out of the north.

That meant a downwind take-off, unless he taxied the plane to the opposite end of the field. But that would be starting out in the wrong direction. It would require a turn of 180 degrees in the dark. He didn't want to have to make any turns. It was going to be all he could handle to make the take-off, climb straight ahead and keep the wings level. If he had visibility enough to see the river, maybe he'd try to follow it. He wasn't sure. He wasn't sure of anything other than precious time wasted.

Costain sat in the cockpit, trying to familiarize himself with the plane's controls and instruments, trying to call back a knowledge long discarded, rusted in time, feeling himself become shakingly appalled by the incredible act he was considering.

Yes, the control stick still moved, as all control sticks must move in working elevators and ailerons. And yes, the operation of the rudder was no different than he'd ever known ... The throttle, with its round, black knob extending from its slot, was not alien to his left hand, nor was the smaller mixture lever beneath it. The instrument panel offered a bare minimum of information, but information he could recognize and read. Air speed ... Altimeter ... Tachometer Fuel gauge ... Oil temperature and pressure ... Compass in its rack above. What more did a pilot need? Nothing, providing the weather was reasonably clear, but the weather was not clear, and he was no longer a pilot, and this whole idea was utter madness!

"All right, madness. What's the alternative, and don't say wait till daylight?"

"It seems to be improving."

"The way it moved in, it can only get worse."

"All right, then madness. There's half a tank of gas. Switches and starter are right there. Start it up and take off."

He heard the wind hit the barn a rattling blow. Christ, he was cold and sweating at the same time! He looked behind at the empty space where the drum had been. He felt he was looking into the entrance of a cave, that the plane's vitals had been ripped out of it. It made him think of weight. He found the stabilizer over his head and, after studying its position, he set it as best he could to compensate for the drum. Over the chemical smell, he could detect the familiar cockpit aroma of gas and metal. It, too, was a memory.

"Either start it up, or get out of here," he said aloud, and then to himself, "Take the pilot's car, head north, try to find a way around the city."

"Balls to that! Start it up! Start it up, dammit!"

His groping hand found the primer on the right side of the instrument panel. He worked the lever in and out slowly. Before he'd gotten in the cockpit, he'd pulled the prop through half a dozen times. It should be ready to fire.

Godalmighty, if this wasn't suicide, what was! The hunters hadn't trapped him, he'd trapped himself. He dropped his head on his chest with a sigh, wagging it dispiritedly. "God," he whispered, "God, what am I going to do?" He heard the wind's heavy insistence ruffling the barn slats.

Costain lifted his head, looked up through the canopy, and saw the star. He saw it so briefly, he wasn't sure he hadn't imagined it. For a breathless, flickering instant, it had shone through a small rent in the dark sky covering, an infinitesimal fleck of pure gold. It beckoned.

He was surprised how easily the engine started. The mechanic might be a pathetic warrior, but he certainly knew his aircraft, despite its vintage.

"To the good," Costain said, looking for and finding the carburetor heat control. He pulled the lever out all the way.

"Keep talking, Costain. Listen to yourself ... Brakes. Where are the brakes?" His feet found them above the rudder pedals.

The release was a handle extending out from under the instrument panel. He pushed it forward, and the plane moved slowly out of the barn, heading toward the farmhouse.

"Rudder!" His right foot jammed down on the corresponding rudder with entirely too much force, the muscles of his leg locked in tension. The plane turned gently, despite his roughness.

"Relax, goddamit! Relax!"

Some of the rigidity went out of him at the command. He neutralized the rudders and advanced the throttle minutely.

"Take it slow." And as the plane cleared the protective shielding of the barn's length, "Left rudder."

The wind's rude clutch pawed and teased the craft, making it jerk and shiver. He realized his hand was clenching the stick so tightly his knuckles hurt. "You've got to simmer down! You've got to relax everything. Hands! Legs! Body! ... Brains! Keep the stick forward."

He had the plane straightened out now, clear of all obstructions, headed for take-off. He halted it with the brakes and could feel the wind troubling the tail. A tail wind was bad taking off, but if he got off, it was going to help him get where he wanted to go all the quicker.

Through the windshield canopy, he could see the dim form of the engine covering. He could sense, more than see, the blur made by the turning propeller. Beyond that, he could distinguish the difference between the dark of sky and the dark of earth, but it was a viscous difference and something like the propeller, in that it was sensed almost as much as it was seen. Within the cockpit, the faint luminosity of the instrument panel offered no reassurance. Right now, its various readings meant nothing, could not register past the barrier on which he now stood fearfully poised.

He thought of checking out the engine and then decided the sound might be heard, and someone would have that much more time to alert the hunters. Besides, the way the plane had started, he'd trust in the mechanic's ability, that it would not fail him now.

"Costain," he said, "you won't trust in anybody's ability now. You'll trust in God because, if you try it, it isn't in your hands any more."

He took a deep breath and let it out slowly. "Now," he said quietly, dropping his feet to the rudder pedals and advancing the throttle. The plane seemed to leap forward. The sudden, blaring increase of sound hit him a frightening blow. His body convulsed rigidly. His mind battled against the net of panic.

"Relax!" he shouted. "Throttle all the way!"

He had the impression that he was tearing through the dark at a fantastic speed, yawing left and right as he overcorrected the plane's weaving course. Never had the sound of a plane's engine been so magnified. It riddled his sensibilities with its deafening roar. It lent a kind of wild frenzy to his actions.

"Left rudder! ... Right rudder! LEFT RUDDER! STICK FORWARD! NOT YET!"

The plane began to bounce, and he had to fight against the mechanical reaction of bringing the stick back. "Leave it alone!" he fumed wildly. "Leave it alone!"

In spite of his rough handling of the controls, thrust produced lift, and lift overcame gravity. The plane staggered off the ground in a nose-high attitude, struggling to hold and improve its purchase on the air.

The fact that he was actually off the ground and flying left him momentarily helpless to react. It saved him, for the moment, from doing anything to hinder the plane in its upward sweep.

As he felt the climb steepen, he did react, bringing the nose down sharply. Then, it was the glow of the city lights that saved him. They gave him a point of reference, allowing him to orient himself and so keep the plane on a relatively even keel.

The take-off had been very fast, a dark kaleidoscope of sound and movement. To it now was added a greater degree of vision. It registered with him that, even without the city's illumination, he could see better being air-borne. There were other scattered lights and a horizon of sorts, more clearly defined in its variation between earth and sky than when seen from the ground.

His first coherent action was to retard the throttle. He did it to stifle the unbearable racket of the engine and to slow the feeling that he was hurtling through the night at tremendous speed. He was still very close to the ground. The altimeter registered only two hundred feet, and the fast-approaching lights of Olomouc appeared to be on a level with him. In their reflection, he saw the dull sheen of the river. Then, all at once, it and the city were gone! Smudge of horizon and scattered lights were gone! He sat paralyzed. Then they all came back, and he knew he'd flown through a piece of cloud.

My God, if the ceiling was no higher than this! He knew he didn't want to try and follow the river now. It didn't stand out clearly enough, and its twistings would add to his confusion. Could he get above the overcast? He brushed the sweat from his eyes. His whole body was bathed in it.

"Try to go higher," he said. "Shallow climb. Give it more power."

With the nose raised, he checked the plane's attitude by pressing his face to the plexiglass window, trying to keep lights and horizon in view. The city was behind him now, the darkness of the land more intense and so more distinctive.

When he hit the rain, its sudden thrumming on wings and fuselage, its million triphammer blows on the windshield, made him gasp in horror until he identified its sound. The rain cut off all forward vision but did nothing to impede his ability to see out the window. Still, it was one more source of worry. If it continued—if it grew colder—if it froze on the plane—If! If! If!

Oddly enough, the air was not as rough as he'd expected. Only occasional spots of turbulence buffeted the plane, and then he was glad he'd thought to fasten the safety belt.

He had just reached the one-thousand-foot level, when he found the belly of the overcast. It was a monstrous incubus, sucking him up into its maw, blotting out light. The plane trembled and shook in its clutch.

He shoved the stick forward and fled. God, only a thousand feet! If he stayed at this altitude, he'd hit something sure. That reddish glow to the right … must be the lights of Prostějob. Kroměříž would be the next place to watch for. Damn, if only this rain would stop!

He leveled the plane off and pressed his face against the right window, then the left, trying to spot a telltale glow. Nothing! Nothing but the dreadful abyss of night.

"Go lower. Go find the river as you first planned."

"No, I can't see it. I've lost it!"

"Go lower. Find it."

"No!"

"Turn and go back to Olomouc. Pick it up there."

"No! Not going to turn!"

"What then! What then! You can't just sit here. Try to go up through the overcast!"

"Never! Spin in, sure."

"All right, go lower! Follow the contour of the earth!"

"Sure, right into the side of a mountain."

"What then! What then!"

"Jesus, I don't know! I don't know!"

He realized that he was shouting at himself, that his indecision was driving him to the point of helplessness.

"No!" he yelled. "No, stop it! Get hold of yourself! You're flying! You got off the ground! You're flying! That's more than you expected, isn't it!"

"Yes, yes, all right! All right!"

"You're flying! You used to fly. You know how. You're doing all right. You're doing fine. What's your course?"

His eyes went to the compass and then beyond. The rain had stopped beading the windshield. Its mad hammering had ceased. Something was different out there, a diffuse and lighter degree of darkness. Lights! A mountain! What!

And then he saw what it was. He had shoved the throttle against the stop and was climbing the plane through a wide, jagged tear in the overcast. He was climbing a deep valley, rising up and up, brushing away tattered pieces of cloudscud. He was wonderfully pleased at the improvement in his ability to see. There was no moon up there, but there were stars! Stars to light the way! To guide his way! ... Could he get through before the winds molded and sealed up this great tear?

"Come on, climb! You want to get out of this as much as I do! Climb! Climb!"

Turbulence began to toss and jerk the plane. It seemed indetermined whether to help or hinder, dropping the craft one second, flipping it upward the next.

"Don't stall her! Take it easy. Don't watch the cloud wall. Look up, look up! Make a gentle turn right ... Good! Good! Now left ... Easy, easy, not too steep! Up, up, rise up!"

The altimeter read thirty-four-hundred feet when the plane rose clear of the main body of the cloud layer, and Costain's feeling of release was momentarily complete. A drowning man, he'd miraculously risen from the bottom of the air-sea into a transcendent realm in which the spirit, as well as the body, had been set free.

The blue-black vault of the heavens! This far-flung reach of starlight! Never had there been so many stars, and never had they seemed so close. The cloud plateau with its towering black crags, its angry, shifting mass, roiled, writhing, a place of desolation and horror. Stay clear! Stay clear! And this little plane, its engine a small, strident beat against the night. All this, all this, and himself, sitting at the heart of the plane, sitting here now, knowing a sense of relief beyond all words, all description, feeling for the first time, not in just weeks but in years, that a great weight had been removed. He had slipped the bonds of earth and now, at this height and this time, had escaped the prison of his life ... There was only himself, feeling the sweat of fear drying coldly on his body, feeling the cold invading the cockpit, and not minding. Not minding, for now he had but to fly for only a few more minutes on his present course. Then, somewhere in that dirty mess of clouds, he'd find another opening and go back down, believing that whatever had brought him safely to this moment would guide him down to see another dawn, not minding anything in these few scattered minutes in which he drank up the pure beauty of the scene and knew its meaning, not minding anything until the engine coughed ... coughed again in a racking gasp, as he pumped the throttle in a frenzy of instinctive movement ... coughed once again in a sputtering death rattle ... and then died with a gusty sigh.

He had always thought the hissing whisper of the slipstream a pleasant sound, a rather musical sound. Now, it became the viperous hiss of an evil god standing by for the kill. The plane lost speed, became sluggish in its passage, and not until it was trembling on the brink of a stall, did he react, thrusting the stick forward. The plane nosed down steeply, quickly recovering its flying speed. He leveled it to a more gradual descent.

Through his actions and lack of actions, his eyes swept the instrument panel with stupid despair, trying to read the cause and so find the cure. Vainly, he tried to restart the engine a half a dozen times before he had reasoned the cause for failure. Ice clogging the intake manifold, probably because the carburetor heat control was faulty.

The transcendency of a few moments before was gone, and where there had been exhilaration, there was a great yawning emptiness, an emptiness into which he was now falling.

"Quicksand," he said dully. "Drowning in quicksand." And the dirty sea of clouds had reclaimed him.

"Going down," he said. "After having been there … Well, what more did you expect from this?"

"Nothing."

He could see nothing outside the cockpit. The plane began to twist and writhe in the ugly cloud-currents. He felt pressure building up and brought the stick back with care, then neutralized it. Now it seemed he was turning right … Now left! … Going down! Faster! Spinning!

"It's vertigo!" he shouted. "Leave the controls alone!"

Hands and feet off rudder and stick, he could hear the slip-stream's rising warning, and outside nothing, nothing! And inside, a man falling to his death.

"All right, Costain! All right … No man wants to give it up without a fight. Fight the good fight."

God in Heaven, I commend my soul into your care.

"Better this way than the other."

"What altitude!"

It took great concentration to read the instrument's fast-changing indications. "Seventeen hundred! ... Close! Air speed! ... 150! Probably in a spiral. Soon now!"

"Slow it up! Why don't you try to slow it up!" The strident, angry inner voice brought a reaction. Hands and feet went back to position. Stick came back and to the left ... air speed checked and the needle began to run back up the dial. It was just on 100 when the plane fell out of the overcast.

It was all so rapid that Costain never was sure what he saw, or what he did. He sensed the plane was in a tight spiral to the left and yanked the stick over to the right, hauling back on it at the same time. The plane checked its motion violently, and he was jackknifed forward, the seat belt digging painfully into belly and hips. He managed to block his face with upraised arms before both slammed into the instrument panel.

There was a nasty, ripping, shredding noise as the plane's forward motion was checked, its fabric snagged and torn by tree branches. This, followed by an instantaneous moment of pause, in which he and the plane seemed to be suspended motionless in time and space, and then everything fell and exploded in a roar of sound, and he was flung head-long into a bright red tunnel. Then nothing ... Then the red was black ... and cold ... quiet. He was rising upward ... Upward through what? Through the overcast? ... No ... What then?

He opened his mouth to take a breath and swallowed water, choking, drowning! He clawed his way upward, threshing with arms and legs. He had to have air! Had to breathe!

He surfaced, dragging air into his lungs with grateful sobs, choking and spitting out water that got mixed in.

He didn't know what had happened. He only knew his body was terribly tired and heavy, and that if he didn't keep up a constant motion of arms and legs, he couldn't keep his head above the water.

He must get out of this water. Its frigid grip had penetrated through the weight of his clothes, punishing his body. And his coat … He had to get rid of it … It was pulling him down. No, there wasn't time! It would take too much of his failing strength. Swim! Swim, damn you!

He began to swim clumsily toward a dark line that he thought must be the shore. His head went under, and he swallowed more water. He struggled to rise, and his feet touched bottom.

"A little farther," he urged himself … "Just a little farther!"

He made a final effort, kicking his legs, trying to move his arms in a crawl. He was capable of no more than a dozen strokes, and when his feet sank this time, he was able to stand with his head clear. He waited until the coughing and choking subsided before he floundered the rest of the way through the leaden pull of the water to the wooded shore. When he reached it, he fell on the ground and lay panting, unaware of the small, dry flakes sifting down around him.

CHAPTER THIRTEEN

The breeze had died completely at first light, and the snow came down in a thick, gentle fall, a white screen against the gray of early morning.

To Costain, who had been following the wagon track, quiet, falling snow was in keeping with the state of his mind and body. The latter, badly chilled from its frigid immersion, felt as though it were incased in a constricting prison of ice. There had been no way to dry his clothes.

The presence of mind to know that he could die of exposure if he didn't keep moving had started him on his way through the woodland that bordered the water into which the plane had crashed. He hadn't gone far when he struck the wagon track, and though stunned and shivering from his recent experience, he'd realized his luck hadn't deserted him altogether. For a while, he'd even dared to hold on to the hope that he'd come down in safe territory. But as time wore frigidly on, and the cold tightened its grip on him, he began to lose contact with reality.

Now, following the track out of the woods and across an uncut upland meadow, he had crossed a border of the senses into the very dangerous realm of not caring. He knew he was Costain. He knew his safety depended on his location, but he didn't care … didn't care at all. Right now, the only thing that troubled him was a sound he could not properly place. It was not made by his numbed and aching feet, erratically marking the deepening snow. It was not the rusty breaking of withered, waist-high weed growth that tried to impede his passage. It was a faint, crackling sound, a not unpleasant brittle crackling ... a most intriguing crackling.

He discovered its source a moment after he detected the obstruction rising in a bulky, black mass at the crest of the meadow. The sound was made by the ice particles on his mackinaw snapping to the movement of his body. Stopping in his tracks verified this. It was not caution that halted him ... only curiosity.

When he started to walk again, he stumbled and fell. It took a great deal of effort to rise, and he told himself angrily that if he did it again, he wouldn't get up. It was foolish. He knew it was some kind of building, even before he reached the top of the gradually sloping incline, but he did not know it was the ruins of a castle until he was on level ground. The knowledge stirred his failing faculties. He stared up at a wall of crumbling stone. It would be empty ... ghosts. He could build a fire ... a big fire.

"You can like hell!" he snarled with sarcastic cunningness. "What are you going to do for a dry match!"

He mumbled some meaningless reply to himself and made a staggering approach across the remains of what had once been an extensive formal garden. The snow was a friend to it, covering its ragged corpse.

He reached the castle wall and began to follow its decaying expanse, searching for an entrance. "If I had a horn," he said crazily, "I could sound it, and they would bring me into the great hall and let me sit by the fire and drink strong wine from the south."

He broke off his prattling when he turned the corner of the wall and saw the compact stone house. It stood some distance from the castle front, next to a drive that entered through a screen of fir.

He hardly checked his weaving stride, for the light coming through the casement window was a star that drew him like a magnet. Who or what was inside the house made no difference. In the light there was warmth, and warmth was the only consideration which his mind was now capable of accepting.

His impressions of the house went no farther than his eye balls. He had to get in where it was warm! The difficulty he had in raising his arm and grasping the white-frosted iron knocker made him cry, "Get in! Get in! Get in!" He said it over and over, unaware that he was saying anything. He was still saying it when the door was unlocked and partially opened.

Her blond hair was short-cropped, a profusion of yellow-brown curls. Her wide-set blue eyes were very large in their surprised appraisal of him. He saw them from a great distance, saw the gentle line of her lips part in sympathetic recognition of his condition, sought to reassure her, to explain, and could only manage an unintelligible croak.

Innocuously, he wanted to say, "Thou art gentle, thou art fair, Isolde, and I have traveled the length of my life to find thee."

"Oh, you poor man!" And the warmth and timbre of her voice drove a bright shaft through the frozen fog of mind and body. He tried to smile.

When she took his arm and brought him into the house and then led him to the fireplace, he stumbled and fell against her, and vaguely knew she was wearing a heavy, woolen bathrobe. He wanted to apologize for having awakened her and felt a helpless surge of frustration when he was unable to form the words.

She was stripping the frozen mackinaw from him, when he heard a man's voice calling with husky concern from another room. "Lisa? Who is it? ... What do they want?"

"It's all right, Father." In the quiet reassurance of her reply, Costain knew it was all right.

Later, his memory of what followed was all in patches. The painful strength of her hands massaging his hands and feet and then his arms and legs ... She holding the cup, while he burned his tongue and mouth on the bitter coffee ... A gray-bearded man, with a gaunt, harshly seamed face, staring vacantly at him, and from somewhere her words, "I don't care who he is. We can put him in my bed for the day. I'll call Otto from the Conservatory. He's the doctor. He can decide what's to be done."

"No ... No doctor!" He was able to say it.

A long silence and then, "Yes, better wait, Lisa." The man in the wheel chair cleared his throat.

"Wait!" Her voice was full of impatience. "For what? To have him get pneumonia and die! He needs medical attention."

"No," he'd repeated. "No doctor."

And then she was helping him into a big four-poster bed, and he was sinking down and down into its warmth, and in his nostrils a fragrance beyond any fragrance, its possessor's face hovering with its lovely look of concern above him. "Thank you, Lisa," he whispered. "Thank you."

He awoke to a feeling of heat. He'd had two experiences with near freezing now, and he'd thought that ever and always he would welcome heat, but he did not welcome this heat. It was an uncomfortable feeling that seemed to emanate from a painful tightness in the upper region of his chest. His mind was functioning normally but with jagged jumps and starts, and he realized with annoyance that he was running a fever.

The light in the room had not appeared to change in its grayness, and so he thought he could not have slept long. He'd sleep again, and when he awoke next time, he'd get up and find out where he was and make his plans accordingly. There was something about a doctor he didn't like. He didn't want her bringing one until he knew where he was. He just wished she'd bring herself back. He missed her. He smiled to himself. "Costain, you're delirious."

"Maybe … Maybe I dreamt her because of the way I was. I'll find out."

When he opened his eyes next, it was to the cool pressure of her hand on his forehead.

"Hello." He saw that she was dressed in an artfully decorated woolen sweater and ski pants.

"How are you feeling?"

"Fine. Much better."

"I think you've got a fever."

He started to reply, thinking, "No, it wasn't your condition … she is what you saw" … and he coughed, and the coughing hurt his chest. It took a moment to get his breath. "I'll be all right. I'm sorry to impose like this."

"Nonsense." He realized that they were looking into each other's eyes with the same surprised intensity. "I—I wasn't able to reach Doctor Gerlach today, but I left a message."

"I don't need a doctor, really."

"I know." She smiled faintly.

"Where am I? I mean, where is this?" He indicated with his head.

She smiled again, and he liked what it did to her face. "Well, this," she said, with a flowing motion of her arm, "is Hostelec. We are 3 kilometers from Tyškov, all down hill, which is 25 kilometers from Brno."

He knew it had been foolish to hope that he'd gotten clear, but still the news of it left him wordless for a moment.

In the sudden seriousness of her expression, he realized she'd sensed the effect of her answer on him. "Is—is it that bad?"

"No! … No," he lied, shaking his head, forcing a smile. "Just a surprise. I had no idea I was so lost."

"Is there anyone you wish to notify?" She was sounding him out warily.

"You have a telephone here?"

"No, but I can ski down to Tyškov."

"Is it still snowing?" He was asking these questions while his mind ran around in circles, trying to arrive at a course of action.

"Yes, the first big one of the year." She said it as though she liked the idea.

"Do you have a car?"

"No, a bicycle ... But it will be of no use now until spring." She was studying him speculatively, waiting for an answer of her own.

"I'm very grateful to you for saving my life." He wanted to reach out and take her long, tapering fingers in his hand. "I got stupidly lost, and I was driving too fast ... I skidded off a bridge into a stream somewhere in the vicinity ... I guess I walked most of the night."

He didn't want to look at her. He felt she'd know he was lying, and though his life might depend on the lies he told, he didn't like lying to her. He had another coughing spell and then asked, "Is there just you and your father I have to thank? I seem to remember your father."

"Yes, there are only the two of us ... I don't think you'd better get up."

"I'd like to thank him, too. Do you suppose my clothes have dried?"

"Please, you should stay in bed, until tomorrow, anyway." She was asking him a favor, her eyes troubled.

"I'll see how it goes ... In the morning, perhaps you could show me how to get to Tyškov."

"If you feel up to skiing."

"And how do you get to Brno?"

"By bus ... on the Autobahn ... it's very quick."

Their eyes met again and held, and he wanted to say, "Let's stop all this careful obliqueness. I'll tell you everything," but he knew he couldn't, so he tried to smile reassuringly and changed the subject. "I think I recall your saying something about a Conservatory. Are you a student?"

She returned his smile, obviously pleased. "No, a teacher."

"In Tyškov?"

She laughed lightly. "No, I'm afraid Tyškov is not that much. In Brno."

"And what do you teach?"

"Piano and composition."

This next one was important, and he wondered how to word it so that it sounded casual. "The—ahh—doctor ... you didn't actually speak to him about me?"

"No ... Just that I would call later."

"And at the Conservatory ... did I make an interesting topic for discussion?" He smiled as he said it, trying to make a joke out of it.

The friendliness went out of her eyes. They became cool and speculative. "My father taught me to keep my own counsel at a very early age. I've never regretted it."

He had a coughing spell, partly because he wanted to steer away from the obvious, and partly because he couldn't help it. "Excuse me," he rasped.

"Would you like something to eat? I'm going to get dinner now." Some of the coolness was gone.

He didn't feel at all hungry, but he nodded, "Yes, and I don't want to appear in your father's bathrobe for the occasion, so would you bring me my clothes?"

He saw that she realized he meant it. "All right, but you're being foolish."

When she came back with his clothes, they included a worn, tweed suit-coat and a pair of heavy walking shoes, undoubtedly borrowed from her father. She was apologetic about his own shoes, telling him she was afraid they were no longer usable. He thanked her gravely, hoping that she would not question their supposed quick deterioration ...

In rising, he made two discoveries. He felt weak and unstable. She was right ... he should stay in bed. That was bad enough ... perhaps after a good night's sleep, he'd feel better. It was the other that really brought him up short. The gun was gone from his mackinaw pocket. The other equipment he'd known was lost in the crash, but not the gun. It had been with him, of that he was sure.

When he made his entrance into the main room of the house, she came from the dining area at the far end and formally introduced him to her father. It was then he was jarred by the realization that the man was not only confined to a wheel chair, but that he was also blind. The handclasp had been strong, though agitated; the voice matched it, pleasantly modulated but coming in quick bursts.

While he expressed his thanks for their having saved his life and offered their hospitality, he was able to fairly well establish the character of the house and sense the enigma of its furnishings. The long, heavily crossbeamed main room was centered by a massive stone fireplace, with doors to either side of it leading to respective bedrooms. Another door beyond her own entered onto a small pantry and kitchen. It faced onto the dining area at the far end of the room.

The furnishings did not match the rusticity of the dwelling. They told another story. The shelves of books, the piano, the few paintings, the chairs, though they were not out of joint in a caretaker's home, they had obviously not been built for it. And so, by the time Costain sat down to dine, he knew that his host and hostess were living amidst the relics of a nobler, more affluent past, but what was not obvious was why they were allowed the privilege, if they were the inheritors of die old castle and its holdings.

Although the food was plain and in keeping with the times, he was even more acutely aware that the setting was not. The beautifully hand-made cherry-wood dining table and chairs spoke of age and grace and a different mode of life. The candle-light delicately reaffirmed it and softly mirrored the patina of the polished wood, lending an aura to the surroundings, touching the faces of his host and hostess in its subdued glow.

Costain didn't think it was the shadowy half-light or his fever that made it difficult for him to keep his eyes from her face. An obscure line from somewhere kept going through his head— "And I shall spread green rushes at her feet so that she may walk softly."

Costain had to force himself to eat, had to concentrate grimly on everything he said and did, had to try to ignore the alternate spells of chill and heat that racked him. He was glad for the candlelight, not only for the spell it cast, but because it must also help to hide his condition.

The conversation, though not exactly stiff, was polite and innocuous. They did not ask him the questions that must be uppermost in their minds, and beyond giving them a false name and explaining he was on a short holiday, he did not enlighten them.

There were a few things he wanted to know himself, but he had to go slowly, and he had to keep his eyes from her face, because the look of her made it difficult to think straight. It was as crazy as all the rest of it, but that's the way it was, and if he never saw this woman again after tonight, never spoke to her, never told her what had happened to him the moment he set eyes on her, it was all right. All right! This stupid fever! … The trouble with having a normal conversation today, he lectured himself, was that seldom did such a conversation exist. It couldn't be normal, even if it sounded so, because you had to be terribly careful what you said to anyone, particularly to complete strangers. It meant there were few subjects on which you could converse without wondering if what you said could be sighted to your disadvantage. He could talk about wind tunnels and free flight ranges, and she could talk about Beethoven and Dvorak, and this sightless wreck of a man who was her father, what could he talk about? Pain? The glory of the State?

"Would you care for more?" She broke in on his feverish, almost drunken thoughts.

"No, no, thank you. I've had plenty … It was excellent."

"You're too kind. Father?"

"No … No." There was trouble and worry and annoyance in the reply. The blind man had also been deep in his own thoughts.

Costain wiped his mouth, choked back a cough and put down his napkin. Out of the corner of his eye, he saw the blind man's fingers start to tap gently on the arm of his wheel chair. The silence between them stretched out, and Costain could hear the faint whisper of the snow on the window pane close to his head. The window was already half buried in its white sheet. Good. The longer it snowed, the better.

"I'll clear the dishes, Father." It was as much a question as a statement.

"Yes … You and I will go in by the fire." Costain had the impression that the sightless eyes could look right through him.

There was no further conversation until he'd followed the crippled man's wheel chair down the room to the fireplace. There, he took the fire tongs from their incongruous brass stand and turned a log over in the grate. The flames shot up, smacking lust-ily. He added a smaller log to the fire and wondered, as he lifted it, who did the cutting and hauling for these two. He turned from his chore to see his host staring at the flames.

"I can't see it, and yet, I can see it all as clearly as you," the older man said. "Being blind, I can see certain other things, too … far more acutely than the normal person … like yourself."

"I shouldn't wonder." Let it come out as it would. The effort with the wood had left him dizzy and out of breath. There was a fire burning in his chest. He sat down heavily on the bench.

"I believe your arrival here, sir, was accidental."

"Yes … I—I can't thank you enough."

"Never mind that." It was punctuated with an impatient ges-ture. "The gun I removed from your jacket pocket tells me one of the two things. Since it is forbidden for anyone but police to carry such weapons, you are either a policeman or a fugitive. In either case, we have shown you our hospitality, meager as it may be. Since it is still snowing and will probably continue until daylight, I won't ask you to leave until then … But then, you must go—is that clear, sir?"

"Perfectly."

"You have nothing else to say?"

"Only that you needn't fear me. I'm an aeronautical engineer by profession."

"I don't fear you, sir! Or any man!" It came out fiercely, the hands like talons gripping the chair arms. "My only fear on this earth is for my daughter!" The mouth worked, chewing on bro-ken words. "Ph—physically help—helpless as—as I am, I—I tell you I have only one reason for remaining alive … To give her what little protection my name affords!" He raised one hand and beat it down on the chair arm with emphasis. "I assure you, it still affords some!"

"I'll leave tonight, if you wish, but—"

"That won't be necessary, but whoever and whatever you are … I want that you—I want it clear to you—so that you can tell your masters—or keep it in your mind, or—or—whatever you like!" The lines of the blind man's face were darkly etched in the firelight. His face, for the moment, reminded Costain of a tragic mask. Aware of the slightly incoherent sound of his outburst, he paused, wagging his head as though to clear it.

"Sir," Costain said firmly, "I'm indebted to you. You need not worry about me."

"Words!" The head went up angrily, the slightly aquiline nose fiercely arrogant. "Words! … Once they might have meant something to me … but I've learned—I've learned! … Sounds—all the sounds—that come in the night to rip and tear the bodies of the dying!"

Costain knew he must say something to quiet his apparently demented host. Before he could, the blind man went on, now in a calmer, more level tone. "With my acutely trained perception, you'd think I'd know … You'd think I could tell … I can tell much … but they not only blinded my eyes—they blinded my trust … Only Lisa, only Lisa and Otto I trust." This last was almost crooning.

"I'm here as a stranger," Costain said heavily, "I'll leave as one." It was repetition, of course, but if he could get it across, that would be enough. Right now, he didn't feel capable of getting anything else across.

The blind man gave no indication that he'd heard. He spoke now from the sight and memory of another time. "If you are of the police, you will find in the records that when Baron Stefan Hostelec was thirty years of age … he inherited the estates of his father … The castle … the acreage—all the great holdings that had been in the family for over three hundred years … even the village ... And you will find that before Hostelec had reached his fortieth year ... he had given most of his lands back to the peasants who farmed them ... Yes! A great humanitarian, who saw evil in one man owning more than his share ... A great liberal, who rejected his proprietory rights ... and was rejected in turn by his own caste ... who called him a mad fool ... helping to endanger a system that had gone on forever ... and so must continue forever!"

Despite his own discomfort, Costain found himself becoming absorbed. The rise and fall of the voice, the quick clenching and unclenching of hands, the play of shadowy light over the marked, sightless face, held him as did the words themselves.

"Even Hostelec's wife could not understand him ... snubbed socially ... But Don Quixote Hostelec was then a man of many windmills ... he'd knock them all over ... The peasants loved him ... He liked that ... good for his vanity ... Certain proletarian political parties wooed him ... the knight in shining armor gave them his benediction, his money, his active support ... All men must be brothers ... Such a noble idea ... Christ-like! ... But the good baron didn't know that noble ideals are slaughtered by wolves and jackals. The baron was both an egotist and a fool! ... He paid for his folly ... he paid ... and others!"

The blind man paused in his bitter reflections, breathing deeply, and a memory that had been tantalizing the circuits of Costain's brain sparked. Radek's voice, commenting from out of the past: "Stefan Hostelec, the best man we had in the south ... Betrayed to the Gestapo ... Made to watch while they shot down his wife and children ... tortured and killed him ... Pity, a good man."

Radek had been wrong on two counts. The baron still had one child, and he lived.

"Listen!" Hostelec's hand went up like a claw. "I am here now like this, because when Hitler's men came, I fought them."

"I know." It was out before Costain could stop himself.

The blind man sucked in his breath, stiffening. "You know! Then you are of the police!"

"No! I heard ... What you did is known!"

"What else do you know!" It was flung out with acid disbelief.

"Nothing ... Just that."

"Pahh! Then know this. We traded one form of slavery for another! ... Worse! ... Do you agree!"

"This isn't necessary. You don't have to say anything to me." A sudden chill shook him, and he tried to keep its effect out of his ambiguous reply.

"Ahh! You think I'm afraid to talk to you! ... You think—because I kept silent—because I said nothing while we ate—that I would not talk—would not say these things?" He dropped his voice, but the venom became only more concentrated. "I said nothing because of Lisa ... I am alive here now—will be alive because of Lisa!—If you know what the Nazis did to me—you know I am still a symbol to the people in this part of the country! ... Yes, I paid for my youthful folly, and I paid for my dedication—the ruined hulk that remains—shall remain!" He beat his palm on the chair arm. "Because out of my folly and dedication, I am a figure which your new order must accept ... and recognize ... and leave alone! Leave me alone! ... There is no more land, no more baron, only a broken, old man living amongst the few relics of a better world!"

In spite of his attempt to keep his voice down, it had risen sharply in this latest outburst, and Costain swung his gaze about to see if Lisa had overheard.

She had, and she came out of the pantry with a towel in her hands. The blind man's head pivoted around, as he detected her quick approach. A grimace imprinted his face. The look of concern and annoyance that reflected on her own remained.

"What's the trouble, Father?" Her eyes were on Costain.

"No trouble!" the blind man grated, and then sighed wearily.

Costain said, "I thought I should leave tonight. Your father wouldn't hear of it. I didn't mean to upset him."

"There's no need to get excited, darling." She stood behind her father's wheel chair, stroking his head gently. "Of course we won't let him go tonight." Her eyes said to Costain, either you're lying or you're a fool.

Costain started to speak and coughed instead, and then, for a long minute, he couldn't stop, and when he finally did, his body had broken out in a sweat, and he was shaking all over, and he knew he couldn't hide it from her. He saw a touch of fear in her stare.

"I'll fix you a place to sleep," she said, and then to her father, "You know what Otto said about getting excited."

"I'm all right." He reached up and patted the hand resting on his shoulder. "I'm all right, dear."

She left them, and Costain huddled his body forward toward the fire, wondering how it was possible to be hot and cold at the same time. "You can't get sick," he said firmly to himself, and he knew he was sick and getting sicker ... A good night's sleep, that's all he needed ... He hadn't had that since—since when?

He realized his host was speaking again. "I—I beg your pardon?" He turned from the fire and, in the grip of fever, had the quick impression that the blind man was either a ghost or a statue.

"—life has come to this ... so much—to be had, to be given ... Dead ... Other times, better times ... of hope." The finely shaped head quested, nostrils flaring, as though those times could be smelled as well as seen. It all came out in a sad, whispering litany of despair ... "Where did it go wrong? ... Each man pitted against the other—and no man knowing his friend ... She's all that's left. I'll not die until—" The words trailed away in a mumbling glissade.

And then another silence and the fire popping, the flames dancing, dancing as Costain felt himself dancing. He could hear the engine of the plane idling. The carburetor heat must be on. It was the carburetor heat that made all the difference.

When she rejoined them, he stood up and tried to tell her about it. He made no protest when she led him to a cot in a small alcove off the kitchen. He had nothing to say when she sat him down and helped him out of his borrowed coat and shoes, and then assisted him in getting his half-clothed body under the covers of the cot. He wanted to tell her so many things, all about himself, all about how long he'd been looking for her. He wanted to reach up and hold her face between his hands, and his last, knowing act that night was an unsuccessful attempt to do so.

CHAPTER FOURTEEN

Costain was flying. He was sitting in the left-hand cockpit seat of the B-25, observing oily, black puffs of flack walking in toward him, soiling the sky. The thing about it was he knew exactly what was going to happen. He couldn't stop it from happening … all very vivid and clear. Planned. The snug flight deck, the racketing snarl of the engines, the instruments trembling to the vibration, the plane jerking nervously under the impact of the seeking flack … there was the ever-present, permeating, sour stink of fear.

"Look," he said to Paul French, his co-pilot, speaking clearly and distinctly, despite the uncomfortable muzzling of the oxygen mask, "it's not so much the fear of death as the fear of not having a chance to live."

"There's something up there in the sun," the co-pilot said.

"I'm twenty-one years old, Paul. I've just begun to breathe. I don't know anything. I want to know something before I die. Even you know more about it than I do. You're married. What is it to love a woman? Be loved … I don't even know that."

"God, I hope they're ours! We can't get clobbered this soon." The co-pilot squinted upward against the sun's glare.

"It's all just getting started, and now—! I can't say this to anyone but you, Paul. Most of the time, I don't even dare say it to myself. It—it came in the night like some kind of slithering deformity. It climbed up on my chest and began lapping at my throat, and when I woke up and tried to strangle it, it disappeared inside me ... an obscene infection! And it's got me! Got me by the balls!"

"Jesus, they're coming down! On your toes, guys! Bogeys at three o'clock high!"

"I shouldn't be here! It's not right! If that stupid, drunken bastard hadn't fallen through that window! I tell you I'm not going to die until I know something more about living! And you can call it any thing you want!"

He never knew whether it was the fighters or flack that got them. Whatever it was, it prevented him from pulling out of formation and fleeing for safety.

Now the plane was cart-wheeling wildly down the sky, plunging earthward, the shattered stub of the left wing engulfed in flame. Fast-building pressure had him pinned to the seat. He was fighting against it! ... Fighting, and somewhere a voice screaming gibberish!

He was looking up at a graceful expanse of cloud. It was revolving slowly, and there were many lines running up to it. "My 'chute," he said, "my fine, uplifting 'chute." He could hear the air whispering through the vent, saying, "Shhhhhh, shhh-hhh." Such a peaceful sound ... like the river ... He'd like to lie on the river bank now and watch the quiet flow of water ... In his twenty-one short years of life, there were two particular rivers: the Susquehanna near Easton, and the Labe running through Melnik ... The Susquehanna of his Father and the Labe of his Mother ... He was of his Father and Mother, of two rivers, of two countries, of two languages, of two backgrounds ... the current of both rivers drew at him, and he knew he must not die until he'd found a river of his own ... Lisa.

He was going to hit the ground now, and his badly injured leg was going to break, and there would be no chance for escape ... He was going to be on a train in the night, the pain beating at him in smothering waves, and a soft, compassionate voice speaking to him in German. "Schlafe ... Schlafe."

"All right, I'll sleep, and then it will be later, hospitals and months later ... in the winter." The snow was clinging to the barbed wire strands, trying vainly to hide the static misery of the prison camp. And then, as there always was and probably always would be—Jan Radek!

"He's one of the top boys in the Czech underground. We're hiding him out here as an American in place of one of our boys who managed to get away. You're half Czech, Costain. You might want to get to know him."

Radek, with his very pale, laughing eyes, his wide, curving, almost girlish mouth, and something a lot tougher and harder in back of both ... Radek, with his dry, friendly manner, his great warmth ... It was always difficult to look at Radek and see him as a daring man, dangerous and ruthless ... behind the softness, steel.

Grinning, brushing the long, uncut, blond hair back, "Look ... I am not—how say—so hot on my speaking of English. Maybe you are not so hot on your Czech. We teach each other, hey?"

"One gets rusty," he had replied in Radek's tongue, "but 1 grew up speaking both."

"Ahh, you have lived in Czechoslovakia, hey?"

"Before the war ... in the summers. My mother's home in north of Prague ... Melnik."

"Wonderful! Wonderful!" ... the flashing grin ... "to find a countryman here amongst all these Americans. We shall become good friends, you and I."

Good friends ... good friends ... good friends must never part. Confession is good for the soul with good friends. "I was afraid. I turned yellow."

"We all experience that. No one is above it."

"Not you, Jan. If you felt it, you wouldn't show it."

"You didn't show it."

"I got shot down before I could."

"It does no good to beat yourself. It's silly. Come on, we'll play another game of chess."

"I could sign up for an escape try instead of rotting here, waiting for it to end."

The long-lidded lashes raising the eyes, joking—not joking ... "Would you like to go out with me? ... Go home for ahh—visit?"

"Humm? You mean when it's over?"

"Sooner than that," the grin mischievous.

"How can you get out of here?"

The soft, pleasant voice becoming softer, "I'd only planned to stay until I felt it wise to leave."

"You mean just like that? Walk right out the gate?"

"Oh, come now. I've been working on a plan with the Escape Committee. It's a very good one," a sly wink. "There would be room for you. You've flown for your father's country; now come be a partisan for your mother's."

"It's crazy!"

"Yes, of course. It's all crazy."

"You mean you'd take me with you? You'd trust me!"

The small, almost delicate hand patting his shoulder, "My dear fellow, I didn't consider the idea a moment ago."

"But now—after what I've told you ... You know what I'm like inside."

Smiling ... "Yes, I'm a very good judge of character. But you must stop thinking that you are the only man in the world who has given in to his fear. Most of us do, more than once. It's the true man who will still it and then face it down ... Will you join me?"

And of course he knew he would, knew he would make that incredible escape, he and Jan Radek precariously and painfully slung to the underbelly of the garbage truck. He did it, feeling at peace with his conscience, glad, and strongly exhilarated.

With Jan Radek, he became a partisan, a valued member of the underground.

Through Jan Radek, he learned to overcome fear, to face it down, to mature in the deadly game of hit and run.

Because of Jan Radek, he was now running for his life.

"Jan," he said, "you got me into this, but you can't get me out. It's not your fault really, just bad luck ... bad luck except for her ... except for her ... except for her."

Costain opened his eyes to bright daylight and shut them again quickly. It took several fumbling moments to orient himself. There was a violin quietly sobbing an unfamiliar melody. This was no dream. His head felt light and empty, his body weak. He was hungry. The pain in his chest had moderated. He thought his fever had gone. A good night's sleep was all he'd needed. He'd better get himself organized and see what was what.

He was surprised to find that throwing back the covers took considerable strength. He was dumbfounded when he tried to stand, and the room spun around, and he fell back on the bed, dizzily nauseated.

Costain kept his eyes closed, lying still. The sickness slowly receded but did not leave him altogether. He could feel perspiration on his forehead and neck.

The violin had broken off, replaced by a new sound he couldn't identify. He opened his eyes and raised his head onto the pillow and saw Stefan Hostelec sitting in his wheel chair in the doorway, staring past him with his sightless eyes. On his lap was the violin and bow. To Costain, he looked frail and ancient in the bright morning sunlight.

"Good morning," Costain said, amazed at the smallness of his own voice.

"You are better, sir." It was not a question, and there was no warmth in it. The hands that held the violin and bow were motionless.

Like a hooded old hawk, Costain thought, and replied, "Yes … I—I'm sorry I overslept."

"It was more than sleep, sir. You've been here a week." It was clear the blind man didn't like it a bit.

Costain said nothing for a moment, trying to assimilate the shocking information. A week! Seven days! His mind fumbled with the heavy stone of it. "A week!" and it was a bare whisper. "What—How!"

"You can thank my daughter that you're still alive. We were snowed in for nearly three days. It wasn't until Saturday that she could get to Otto—Doctor Gerlach."

"The doctor, he—he—"

"He had drugs. They seemed to have helped."

Costain began to shiver. He realized he was lying with the covers off. He managed to tug them up over his body. He felt numb all over. They had him now! Helpless. Couldn't run!

"Perhaps you would like to have your friend, Jan Radek, informed of your whereabouts!" The name was a filthy word in Hostelec's mouth, the statement flung out with something more deep-rooted than disgust.

It left Costain incapable of coherent reply. How in the name of Christ!—He closed his eyes, breathing deeply, fighting to keep calm.

"Well!"

"How do you know Radek?"

"Is he your brother, sir? In your delirium, you called upon him as though he might be your brother!"

Costain wondered how he could feel fear from the presence of a man both blind and crippled, with nothing more dangerous in his hands than a violin and a bow. He felt himself starting to slip down into darkness again. He gritted his teeth and shook his head, trying to shake it off. "I—I fought with Jan Radek in the underground ... years ago ..."

"Years ago, nothing! It's not what was years ago, it's what's today! Right now!" The blind man raised the violin as if he might throw it. His face had become an unhealthy, reddish color. "You and the Radeks, you have made it what it is today!"

"No! I have nothing to do with it! I told you my profession!"

"You lie! You lie! I heard what you said!"

"What!"

"Enough!"

"Not in years!" He could hear his voice rising shrilly in protest. He had to stop this! Had to stop arguing with this idiot! Had to get control!

"Jan Radek is a blot on our land! ... He fought the Nazis to betray us to the Communists! He sits in Prague on a throne of dead men ... who trusted in him! ... He and his fellow traitors! I know you are one of them! A kind fate delivered you into my hands! We know you came here by accident! You can't be traced here ... You won't be leaving, you filthy pig of a man!"

The rasping, furious lash of words were echoing hammer strokes in a tomb, and Costain lapsed into unconsciousness again, trying to protest their ironic falsity.

Twice more during the day, he awakened for brief intervals. Each time, he tried to summon his dangerously misled host without success. Somehow, he must convince him that he had not seen or spoken to Jan Radek in over ten years.

The third time Costain awoke, it was to look up into the face of a stranger, a bald man of indeterminate age, with a broad, high-domed forehead. He wore thick-lensed glasses, which magnified his eyes, making them appear slightly grotesque. His chubby, round face was clean-shaven, the mouth small and red. He was seated beside the cot, stethoscope plugged into his ears, the end of it on Costain's chest. He blinked at Costain but said nothing, listening. He wore a conservative black suit and a big imitation ruby on his pudgy ring finger.

The doctor finished his examination, plucked the instrument from his ears and Costain's chest. "Feeling better?" It was a light, colorless voice, brusque and business like.

"Yes. How am I?"

"Coming along nicely." The doctor looked down at Costain with his goggly eyes, weighing. "Stefan tells me you talked."

"He talked! Is he crazy?"

The small lips pursed, considering … "Humm, obsessive in some ways."

"I—I think he wants to kill me."

The doctor nodded, putting the stethoscope into the bag beside his chair. "I know. I shouldn't worry about it."

"Worry about it! You bet I'll worry about it until I'm able to move under my own power."

"Your power … or Jan Radek's?" the doctor asked quietly, calmly.

"Now don't you start this foolishness! I told him who I am and what happened to me. Because he found I had a gun in my pocket, he—"

"A regulation police weapon."

"Which I happened to still have since the end of the war!"

"Which is illegal and punishable by a severe jail sentence." The doctor picked his bag up and shut it with a "snap."

"And maybe that makes me foolhardy, but it doesn't make me any part of the present regime!"

"Shhh! Shhh! Quiet yourself, sir." The doctor looked toward the door. "Stefan doesn't believe you, and frankly, I don't myself." The soft, bulging eyes appraised him dispassionately.

Costain opened his mouth to protest and then shut it again, a voice of warning crying out, "Be careful! If he doesn't know who you are, he may find out! Don't tell him anything."

"All right," he said sullenly. "All right, have it your way."

The doctor held up his hands as though on the verge of performing a trick. Delicately and precisely, he ticked off each finger on his left hand with the forefinger of his right. "An engineer ... without papers of any sort ... possessing an illegal weapon ... not having wife or friends to notify of his accident ... allowing his subconscious to call out repeatedly to a man high in the Administration ..." The doctor lowered his hands. "What would you think, sir?"

Costain had hold of himself now, and he knew what he'd let them think, all depending on how this next question was answered. "I suppose you've made inquiries?"

The doctor didn't answer right away, gazing blankly in the direction of the bag which he had set on the bed. "Naturally, it is proscribed by law to report all cases," he said, as though feeling his way carefully over an icy spot ... "but I have not reported yours as yet."

"Why not!" He snapped it out as though angry.

The doctor shrugged imperceptibly, "I thought it best to find out who you are first."

"You seem to have made up your mind about that."

"Yes ... and you'll never be able to say you haven't received the best of care under the circumstances."

"What about that crazy old fool in there? Do you think I want to be left alone with him!"

"Are you afraid of a man who is both crippled and blind?"

"I might be, if he had a gun."

"I'll see that he doesn't harm you." The doctor stood up, unruffled, voice and manner proclaiming him beyond rude feelings, but Costain knew otherwise, knew that his loathing was simply veiled behind thick lenses and a bland look.

All right, he wasn't going to go on protesting. He couldn't. They'd cast him in this part. He'd have to play it. And then a new thought struck him. "I—I suppose the girl ... his daughter has me all figured out, too?"

"I have no idea what she thinks about you, sir. Stefan would not want to alarm her. She saved your life, and if she thought as Stefan and I ... Well—" He shrugged his shoulders, reached for his bag, and then said with a sigh, as though to himself, "You know, it's really almost too good an opportunity to lose."

"What are you talking about?"

"You, sir ... I owe the baron a great deal ... a very great deal."

Costain stared up at the doctor open-mouthed. He felt wrung out, used up. "You—you'd let him kill me! ... on such flimsy evidence!"

"Many good men I know have died on less."

"And to allow him to kill me is to solve what!"

"Nothing. Absolutely nothing."

"Then what are you talking about!"

"I said I owe Stefan that much."

"Well, goddam you, what was the point in saving my life in the first place!"

The doctor patted the top of his bag gently. "Perhaps to give you a chance to explain."

"Do you think you've given me that?"

The doctor was an owl, blinking his eyes in all-knowing wisdom and slowly shaking his head. "You haven't explained."

In that instant of physical weakness and mental confusion, Costain nearly did explain. There was something hypnotic and dreadful about the doctor's eyes. Was it better to be at his mercy as a supposed underling of Radek's, or was it better to tell them who he really was!

Suddenly, she was in the doorway, looking in at them. Her smile for him broke the nightmare web of it. The sight of her calmed him. The tray in her hands was such a homey, matter-of-fact thing. It made him realize that some of his weakness was hunger. He grinned back at her.

"Oh, I'm so glad you're feeling better," she said. It was full of genuine sincerity, as was the expression on her face. She didn't think him one of them. She didn't know. His spirits began to rise.

"I'll be back to see how you are on Friday ... in three days ... weather permitting." Although the inflection in the doctor's voice didn't change, the meaning was obvious.

"You're staying for dinner, Otto," she said to the physician, stepping to one side to let him past. Costain saw she was taller than the doctor, and her slim figure clothed in skirt and sweater made him appear dwarflike.

"I can't, thank you, Lisa. You know I'd like to but—" he shrugged.

"Father will be so disappointed."

"I'll explain to him. Perhaps when I come again." He glanced back at Costain. "Right now, I think you have enough on your hands ... On Friday, sir." Then he was gone.

She came slowly to the side of the cot, holding the tray carefully. "Are you hungry?"

"Ravenous. I'm also indebted to you in a way that I can never repay."

"I—I'm glad you're going to be all right," she said, setting the tray down on the chair. "I did nothing, really."

"Everything." He found it pleasantly impossible to take his eyes from her. "I don't know how you managed."

"There was nothing I could do, but keep you in bed … keep you cool."

"And listen to me babble?" He smiled.

"Oh, you did rather a lot of that," she said lightly, "and now I think you'd better stop talking and try to do some eating. There's broth, and tea and toast."

CHAPTER FIFTEEN

L isa Hostelec lay looking out through the opening of the snow-frosted window beside her bed at a bright star high in the cold, clear night. The star glittered and winked in its infinite setting, a golden focal point around which to weave her thoughts ...

She had tried not to think of her life as anything more than it was. There was her father to care for. There was her work at the Conservatory—her music. But of late, she found it becoming increasingly difficult to keep herself inside such a rigid framework ... a kind of day-to-day vacuum, a routine bordered by rising in the morning and going to bed at night. It was becoming unbearable. And yet, as long as her father should live, she could not deviate from it. There was no good in trying to look ahead or to either side. There was no one on earth more dear to her than the proud, tragic man for whom she cared, and there was no good in looking back, in remembering her mother—her brothers—what happened to them. This was the best life she could expect for now. One day it must end, of course. Regardless of what Otto Gerlach said, she could see that the poor, dear, suffering man was failing ... not just physically, either. "Dear God," she whispered, "hasn't he suffered enough? I don't want to lose him, ever! But he deserves peace ... peace!" She felt tears start to her eyes and blinked several times at the star, holding on to its distant light. And what happens then? ... There had been several at the Conservatory interested in her for more than her musical ability, but they'd known she was the daughter of Baron Hostelec. Although the title was no longer permissible, it was still used in her father's case as a sign that the regime recognized all he'd done ... all he'd given ... Peter Dubrek had been the only one foolish, or gallant enough to make definite overtures toward her ... And what had happened to Peter? They'd discouraged him quickly enough. Officially, such advances were not at all welcome. Oh no, they were saving her for better things. When her father died, they would confront her with a marriage for the convenience and prestige of the State. "Baron Hostelec's Daughter to Wed Minister of Food Supply for Hana Region—Love Match."

They saw no need in hurrying the matter. Everyone knew her father's condition, knew how much he needed her. To try and force the issue while he lived would only arouse bad feeling, and why should they do that? Of course, when it happened, she would simply refuse. What could they do about it? They might prevent her from marrying anyone else, but they certainly couldn't force her into such a marriage ... She wasn't being naive or childish about it. They must take her for a fool. Even poor Papa did that. No, not really. He just wanted to try and protect her ... to defend her from the harsh realities of all that was going on ... Right now, he was trying to hide the fact that he had taken a violent dislike to their unexpected guest. He was so terribly suspicious of everyone ... and everything ... This man who had come out of the storm ... like the Erl King, whitely frozen ... This man whose eyes were filled with something she had never seen ... never felt before. Even after the snow had stopped, she had been reluctant to leave him. Why? Because he was sick and helpless, and she had a special sympathy in her heart for the sick and the helpless

THE PURSUIT OF AGENT M

because of her father ... No ... No, it was more ... An engineer ...
from Ostrava. It seemed she had heard something about someone from Ostrava lately ... That violinist, what was his name? ...
No matter ... Who was it he called out to in his unknowing, over
and over? Radek ... Jan Radek. The name was not unfamiliar ...
someone high up in the government had that name, she thought.
Perhaps that had been what had upset her father. It took little
enough these days.

"A stranger has come into your life," she whispered to the
star. "A stranger to whom you have said little, a man whom you
know nothing about ... whom you have nursed ... a man who
fills you with a warmth ... and is no stranger ... no stranger at
all. It is so odd ... and I think now you are being childish ...
romantically childish."

She turned her body restlessly, her eyes still holding the star.
She felt the weight of her arm lying across her breasts. She was
aware of their contour and fullness. She ran her hand along her
side, flat over her stomach and down the curve of her thigh. She
was a woman, and for a moment in the silence and privacy of her
room, she allowed the star to overcome her strong-willed nature.
She gave way and let herself become engulfed in a great loneli-
ness. She knew the overwhelming need to be a woman, loved ...
not the paternal love of a crippled, half-demented father ... but
the love of a man, loving her as a man should ... needing her as
a man needs ... giving herself generously, and so having her own
need fulfilled.

Lisa closed her eyes, blotting out the star and shaking free
the forbidden desires that beset her. She was indeed a fool! She
must stop this and go to sleep now. She saw Costain's face smiling at her. She heard his voice, not words, just the sound, the
warm, strong sound.

"Good night," she whispered to it. "Good night, no matter who you are."

Baron Stefan Hostelec had come to know the time of day by smell, by feel, and by habit. Now he knew it was dawn because he could smell it and because it had ever been his habit to awake at this time. He was also able to judge the kind of day it would be.

It was going to snow again, and that was fine. It was going to be a fine day, for he was not going to wait any longer. He'd had enough of Otto's cautiousness. Always, Otto had been one to hesitate, to hold back. "Stefan, we must be careful. We must not take unnecessary chances! Let us be sure before we move." Pahh! What more surety was necessary! ... He might be blind, but not that blind.

The weapon spoke volumes in itself; nor did a man, out of his mind and babbling, call on someone out of his life for many years. This so-called engineer from Ostrava was one of Radek's own, dispatched on some errand of evil, and by his own misfortune, delivered into these hands.

He clasped his long, strong fingers together. The rest of his body might be little more than wreckage, but his hands still retained their power ... their strength. His ability to play the Brahms C Major attested the fact if nothing else did. "Tumtuhtah tum tum, tumtuhtah tum." He must work on the coda with Lisa. It wasn't quite right ... Lisa! Lisa mustn't know. Could he manage that? ... Otto was not coming back until Friday, but he was not going to wait until then. He would not wait! In the old days, he had not waited, not listened to Otto Gerlach then ... not now, not now. Otto was the one who always wanted to wait ... reason he was not Medical Director or even Assistant Director of the new Center. Oh, he was ambitious, all right, could even be ruthless in his desire to rise, but his timidity ... held him back, held him back. Failed to act, lost. Lost ... so much lost, ended ... He'd try to sleep. In sleep there was escape from this milky world of nothingness ... this gray, desolate nothing. Empty! Empty! ... And pain, physical helplessness. Why didn't he simply die and have done with it? He couldn't, not yet, not yet. For Lisa, not yet, until it was arranged, and she was safe from them ... No, and not until he'd had this last and final satisfaction. "The Lord God Jehovah hath delivered him into mine hands ..." One enemy had broken the body of Baron Stefan Hostelec ... This worse enemy had tried to break his spirit ... had nearly succeeded. Admit it, admit it ... Longer periods of shadows and darkness, not know- ing, not caring ... not able to make himself clear ... not until he heard her voice, her step, felt her touch, and knew why he must care ... Otto must hurry! Must! It couldn't go on with him much longer ... And now this small blow he could strike before the end—this death he could exact for the honor of a people betrayed and chained by the Radeks of the world ... There must be a way to do it without her finding out ... or maybe she'd have to know. He'd go back to sleep again, and when he awoke, he'd think about that, but one thing he knew. He wasn't waiting any longer ... for Otto ... for anyone. He would kill.

Doctor Otto Gerlach drove southward on the new Autobahn toward the city. From the look of the sky, he expected it would be snowing before he arrived. But it was neither the weather nor the medical conference he was to attend that occupied his thoughts on this gray November morning.

He had known who Costain was the moment he laid eyes on him, had known despite the stubble of beard—the gaunt, wasted face. Even if he had not recognized the man from the circular sent to all in the medical profession by the authorities, he would have known him from the newspaper photographs. There was little that happened around Otto Gerlach, significant or not, that he did not mark down in the copious catalogue of his mind.

That Lisa had not recognized the fugitive simply proved that her aversion to reading newspapers was unswerving. Of course, it was Stefan's fault, but in this case, it was something to be thankful for …

Stefan. He was fading fast … blood pressure alarmingly high … could have a stroke any moment … only his stubbornness had kept him alive these past months.

And now, into his hands—into the hands of Otto Gerlach—had come this opportunity which he had thought practically impossible … had scarcely dared to dream of … Stefan was his only worry now. Stefan, in his present state, might not wait … Lisa gone all day. As long as the man was rational, he'd do nothing to jeopardize his daughter's position. It was the last thing he'd do, but would he remain rational? Was he rational right now? He hadn't liked the look on his face or the things he'd said last night. Perhaps he should not wait until Friday. Perhaps it should be done today. But there must be no rush. It had to work … Lisa would become Mrs. Otto Gerlach, and her husband would get some of the notoriety and recognition which he had long deserved. He'd make a few eat humble pie yet.

Like all good plans, he told himself, its simplicity was its guiding force. Once he set it into action, little could go wrong … For months now, Stefan had been under the impression that he had been trying to arrange a way to get Lisa out of the country into Austria. Because of the extreme care and personal danger involved in attempting such a feat, Stefan had been patient and understanding until of late. But now that the old warrior knew he couldn't hold death off very much longer, he had grown impatient, insistent, even abusive. "Otto, you must act!"

Gerlach had to admit there were times when he felt a sense of guilt and disloyalty in leading Stefan on. But he was not about to risk his life, his career, to satisfy the unrealistic wish of this embittered old lion ... no matter how much he owed him for the past. More than that, he was not about to help Lisa remove herself from his life, not while there was the slightest chance for himself.

Thanks to Stefan's understandable desire to shield his daughter from anything unpleasant, he had quite naturally not told her of the supposed plans to get her out of the country. He'd do that when it was time for her to leave. He didn't realize that Lisa could be as stubborn as himself and would refuse to leave him under any circumstances. Stefan's answer to that was she would be taken away by force, if necessary.

But now there was a better plan, a real plan, all brought about by the presence of a fugitive too ill to run. He'd rather enjoyed trying to frighten the man into a confession. He thought he nearly had, but then it was just as well to let him stew in his own juice. He'd be that much easier—that much more grateful—when the time came. His capture was going to bring more than a handsome, monetary reward; it was going to bring a tremendous amount of prestige to his captor ... Dr. Otto Gerlach. The thought of it actually excited him.

When he returned—whatever day he decided on—he would tell Stefan the truth about the fugitive. Stefan would be overwhelmed, sick with remorse for misjudging the man. He would want to make restitution.

Then he would give Stefan a second piece of news.... The plan for Lisa's escape had suddenly reached fruition. He had made contact with a group in Znojmo who were in the business of smuggling people across the border. Why couldn't the fugitive go along? Excellent! Excellent! ... He would drive the two of them to the assigned spot himself.

The fugitive would be overjoyed. Stefan would be beside himself at the good news, and the only one left to convince would be Lisa. He had an idea how to do that, too ... When she arrived home from the Conservatory, she would find her father dying. Her leaving would be his final wish. It would all be staged. He would give Stefan morphine ... and if he made the dosage over-large, was he not being merciful?

When it was over, he would drive Lisa and the fugitive to Tyškov, where he would have the police waiting. He'd not tell them why they should be waiting. He'd simply say he had something to bring them. There'd be no chance of their taking any of the credit ... A medical doctor would bring in the man none of them had had any success in hunting.

Lisa would be in a state of shock at her father's death. She wouldn't really know what was going on. If later she protested his actions, he'd explain it had been all for her, the only way he knew how to protect her from a dangerous criminal. And he would be in a position to protect her from any questioning, from anything. He'd gain her sympathy and, with the blessings of the Administration, make her his wife.

It was really a plan of which to be proud. He'd thought it through carefully and clearly. He had not rushed into it. He'd considered all contingencies on the parts of everyone involved. He would know how to react. His name would become a byword overnight—Doctor Otto Gerlach. He would soar!

Costain had been awake off and on throughout the morning. He had awakened first to the light being turned up in the kitchen and the quiet sounds of her preparing breakfast. He had that false feeling of physical well-being one who has been ill often experiences upon awaking. He debated getting up and joining her, and when the smell of coffee came to him, he would have made the attempt, but she suddenly appeared in the doorway, looking into the half-darkened room.

"Good morning," he said.

"Good morning. I hope I didn't wake you." She kept her voice on a level with his own.

He saw she was wearing her ski clothes. "Getting ready to leave?"

"Yes. How are you feeling?"

"Almost as good as new."

"That's good, but you must take your time. Would you like some breakfast?"

"That coffee smells delicious."

"I'll take care of my father first. Then we'll have something to eat together."

"Fine."

It was fine. Though it was nearly light out, they used a lantern, and it felt more to him like evening than morning. He sat propped up in the cot, breakfast on a small table between them.

His appetite was somewhat stiffled by a fragile feeling of excitement … her closeness, the faint, subtle scent she wore, the quick, graceful gestures of her beautifully shaped hands, her face …

"I suppose this is a regular routine for you? I mean, getting up and—"

"Yes. Every day but Sunday."

"It must be difficult."

"No, not really. I'm used to it."

"How long does it take you to reach the village?"

"On skis, about fifteen minutes."

"Downhill all the way and uphill back, hey?"

She smiled. "Pretty much so, but it's good exercise."

"I shouldn't wonder. What about the weather?" He glanced toward the window.

"Well, sometimes it misbehaves, but not too often, thank goodness. My being caught here for three days was most unusual, particularly at this time of year."

"And what does your father do when you're not able to get home?"

"Up until now, he's been able to manage by himself. We make preparations. He's a very remarkable man."

Costain set his cup down on his leg. "Yes." He looked directly at her. "Only I wish it were possible to convince him that I'm no more than I seem."

"What do you mean?"

He held her gaze. "I mean, he thinks I'm some sort of police officer."

"You—you mustn't take it seriously," she said quietly, looking away from him. "You can see how he's suffered. He—he's terribly suspicious of everyone. I'm sorry."

For a moment, he could think of nothing to say, losing himself in her eyes.

"More coffee?" She focused her attention on his cup, seeming a bit flustered.

"No. No, thanks. I wish you'd call me Mark, Lisa. I'm not a police officer."

"It's none of my business, really."

"Yes ... I want you to know ... after all you've done."

"It was what anyone else would have done." She busied herself putting jam on a bun.

"I know it's been hard on you, but I'm glad I came here ... Sometimes ... you come to a place, a door opens, and everything changes. Do you know what I mean?"

She raised her head, looking at him intently. She gave a slight nod. "Yes ... I think so." It was little more than a whisper.

"Time," he said. "You can get lost in it. You can get so you don't know what time it really is."

"How do you mean?"

"Since the war and the finishing of my education, my world has been the future ... Five, ten years from now. When you design aircraft, you don't do it for today."

"No, nor for tomorrow either, I believe."

He had to think a moment before he realized what she meant. "You're referring to the purpose of what you design and build?"

"Yes ... to destroy. Kill."

"Not exactly, not in my line. We're working toward what's out beyond the earth. Space."

She sighed and gave a little shrug. "You foolish men. You poor, foolish men. You go find new worlds to conquer, and what a mess you've made of your own. With all your tinkering, you'll blow it up one day ... And what will you have proven? ... What did my father prove?"

"Still," he said, not wanting to get sidetracked into purposes, "it's what I've done, what I'm doing. There's beauty in flight—well, I mention it because of what I said about time."

"We all try to stick our heads in the sand and forget time," she said and then smiled. "Only you put yours in the clouds."

"You teach counterpoint, and I study the ionosphere, and time doesn't have any real meaning ... until you knock at a door and it's opened ... That's all I'm trying to say to you."

She shook her head. "I don't know. How can I know?"

"I can't answer that, and were there any time for us, I wouldn't be talking this way so quickly. But, as soon as I can get on my feet, I've got to leave."

"Is Ostrava so far, Mark?" It was the first time she'd used his name, and she asked the question with such a meaningful softness that he could only stare at her and feel a wrenching in his chest.

"Under the circumstances," he said flatly, "it's far beyond the moon for us, Lisa."

"Then why say anything?"

"Blame it on my weakened condition. I had to tell you, even if for only one day, or two, you've given time a meaning for me."

She shook her head. "It's useless."

"Yes, but small and useless as it may be, it's the only true value left; perhaps there never has been any other."

"We—we're talking in riddles, really."

"No, we're not. You know exactly what I'm saying. You know exactly what I mean. It may be presumptive of me, but you know what I feel because you feel it also."

"This is not right," she said firmly. "I don't know you. You—you come here—you're sick—I—I—just—"

"Just be honest, there's no time for anything else, believe me. If I'm being delirious, all right, tell me to be still. Tell me to apologize. I'm simply speaking frankly."

She smiled wanly. "Yes, my dear ... you certainly are."

He reached across the table and took her hand. He felt her fingers fasten strongly about his own, and the electricity of it was a current all through him.

She looked at him, shaking her head in a sad kind of wonder. "So sudden," she whispered, "so sudden! I—I feel like I might come apart." A rueful smile ... "I'm sure I'll take a spill going down to the village."

"It's going to snow. Do you have to leave?"

"A little snow isn't enough to stop me."

He grinned. "You've got a sick man on your hands."

She laughed lightly. "Who has made a remarkable recovery and is trying to be a very bad influence."

He didn't like thinking that if he could keep her here today, her father wouldn't be apt to try anything, and by tomorrow, he should be recovered enough to handle whatever move the old boy might make. "And suppose this turns into one of those days that you can't get home?"

"I'm sure it's not going to. I've become a rather expert weather reader, but I'll leave food for you both, and there's plenty of kerosene in the heaters."

He let her hand go reluctantly. "You can't stay, just today?"

"I can't, Mark. I have my job, too ... And if Ostrava is beyond the moon, what would be the point?"

"This isn't Ostrava."

"This isn't anywhere."

"It feels like home. Please stay, Lisa."

"No, don't ask me to do this."

"Why?"

"Because—because it's difficult enough to live as we must live from day to day, but it would be worse, longing for something that—that—" She broke off and stood up. "Please don't be angry with me. I'm not used to—to anything like this."

"I know. I'm not either. I was being selfish."

"If it starts to snow hard, I'll try to come back early."

"Will you do me a favor? Find me something to hack off this beard?" He rubbed the heavy stubble around his chin. "I'm not looking my best."

"Certainly," she chuckled. "You do look rather fierce."

"When you come home, we'll sit by the fire."

"I don't think you should get up yet. Otto wouldn't like it."

Mention of the doctor brought Costain down to earth. "The doctor is a good friend?"

"Oh, yes, for many years. Father helped him go to medical school."

"Good doctor, hey?"

"Why, don't you think so?"

"I never trust doctors," he smiled, "only nurses."

"I don't know what we'd have done without Otto," she said seriously. "He's got a large practice in Brno, and yet, he comes all the way out here every chance he gets, sometimes twice a week, mostly to give father some company."

"He must do a lot of traveling."

"Yes, a great deal. I don't envy him. And now I've got to travel, too, Mark, or I'm going to miss my bus and be late."

"I'll be waiting for you to come home."

"I—I'm glad we talked. I—I won't be able to keep my mind on my work all day … And I'll be wondering one thing."

"What's that?"

"Why Ostrava must be so far away."

He had shaved with a bowl of water in his lap, a small mirror in one hand, and a very dull, straight razor in the other. He did the best job of it that he could, painful as it was, and now he was half awake, his mind weaving an intricate mesh of thoughts and pictures … Lisa, her words, her looks … A doctor with a wide practice, much-traveled, willing to accept the suspicions of a half-crazed patient … And the patient—Stefan Hostelec in his wheel chair … Her father … threatening, dangerous … His own position more dangerous by the moment. He must try to get up, get his strength back, be ready when the doctor returned. When? Friday, he'd said. This was Wednesday … He'd be taking the doctor's car … to Mikulov or Znojmo? Mikulov meant flat country, the Marchfeld. West of Znojmo was the edge of the

Boehmer Wald. It would be better to try and reach the heavily wooded, higher ground. One thing he had to get back was the pistol. Had to convince her father that—

The sound shafted through his thoughts like an arrow, and he came fully awake as Stefan Hostelec wheeled his chair into the narrow doorway. There was a robe covering the lower half of his body. On his lap was the pistol. He picked it up, his head rigid, all available senses seeking. His face was fixed, molded in resolve, the hand clutching the weapon slightly palsied.

There was a water glass close to Costain. It was the only object within reach, beside the pillow under his head. Dammit, he'd known this was going to happen! Innocuously, he thought, "All he needs are two antennae, then he could pick me up on his radar."

He was like the man in the water with the shark approaching. One school of thought said, thrash about, the other said, lie still. Hell's bells, if this sweetheart once started pulling the trigger, he could pretty well spray the room. It was so still, he could hear the baron's breath puffing faintly. "Well!" he practically shouted it, covering the sound of his hand reaching to fasten around the glass.

"Don't move! Don't move!" The blind man thrust the pistol out, fanning it from side to side. He used his free hand to wheel the chair forward.

"You think this is going to help your daughter!" Costain kept his eyes riveted on the hand holding the gun, gathering himself. "Is this going to protect her?" Helplessly, he knew his own actions were going to be neither swift nor sure.

The edge of the wheel chair struck the foot of the cot and halted. "Now! Now!" It was a glad sigh. The pistol stopped weaving. It was pointed above Costain's head and slightly to the right.

Costain knew that, in speaking, he would perfect the blind man's aim. He took a breath, struggling to keep his voice normal. "You're all wrong about me, baron."

"No! I'm not wrong! I've got you!" The barrel lowered with a fierce jerk.

At the vehement reply, Costain hitched himself into more of a sitting position. "You haven't got anybody," he said. "I'm nothing more than I told you. Ask your daughter."

"Leave my daughter out of this!"

If he could only keep him talking! With each reply, he'd move himself up a little higher. "She can't be left out of it. If you kill me, what happens to her?"

"She'll be safe, no matter what I do. Otto will see to that." Now, there was a strained steadiness to the baron's voice that Costain liked less than the usual ranting. He'd managed to get himself into a half-sitting position. He was going to try and shift the water glass into his right hand, if there were time! If there were time! The barrel of the gun was no more than five feet from his chest! … Too far to reach out and grab.

The blind man drew himself up straight. "Nothing you can say will make any difference now, sir. I am your executioner. I'm the last remnant of conscience."

"You're a crazy, old bastard!" Costain snapped, cocking the glass to throw, some of the water spilling on the sheet. "Conscience! A fat lot of conscience you are!"

His rude outburst unsettled the baron, piqued him. "You can't lie to me!"

"Lie to you, hell! I can't even tell you the truth!" He saw this kind of rough frontal attack was having an effect.

The other's head shook angrily. He tried to lick the last vestiges of doubt from his thin, bloodless lips. "You can't explain a thing! Not a thing!"

"If you must know, it's none of your bloody business, Baron Hostelec, who I am, other than I'm not someone you think I am!"

The blind man's head shot up, his aristocratic nostrils distended by this latest effrontery. "It is if you value your life, sir!"

"What did you say about conscience!" Costain scoffed. "Because I refuse to go into my genealogy, you're going to kill me, is that it?"

"I know enough of your foul genealogy! You were sired by an obscenity named Radek!"

"Poppycock!" He knew if he threw the glass now, he could't miss. He hesitated. Did he dare one more try before getting violent? He wasn't in any condition to do battle, but he should have enough strength to disarm the man after he'd stunned him with the tumbler. Yet, all the fool had to do was pull the trigger … Just one, quick pull …

"All right, Baron Hostelec, Keeper of the Holy Grail, last of the great martyrs," he grated, "are you going to execute me? Are you going to wash your sensitive hands in the blood of an innocent stranger, whose only crime was to drive too fast on an icy road and put you and your daughter to some inconvenience because of it!"

"Be still! Be still!" The blind man shook his head as though to shake out the words in his ears.

"You want to know where I got that gun," Costain raced on. "I stole it! From whom and where is also none of your business, but if you'd like proof of my profession, ask me anything under the sun about aircraft and their design, and I'll confound you with my knowledge!" He took a deep breath. "Now put down that gun! Put it down for the sake of your daughter, if for nothing else!"

The last came out as a sharp order. It produced silence, the milky eyes staring past him, the awful largeness of the pistol's open end pointing right at him. Costain sighed and said evenly, "Baron, I've got a glass of water in my hand. I was going to bean you with it, but all this talking has made me thirsty. I'm going to drink what's left in it." He did so, noisily, feeling as if it would take gallons of water to fill the vast cavern in his stomach.

"Otto will find out." The baron said it more to himself than to Costain. "Otto will find out once and for all." And then to his intended victim, haughtily, still in command, "You can't get away. You will tell Doctor Gerlach where you work. He can check up. You won't trick me, sir! You—you can thank God that I'm a fair man, willing to give every benefit … I am honored here." He spun the wheel chair around with one hand, placed the pistol back in his lap and propelled himself carefully out of the room.

CHAPTER SIXTEEN

Costain lay with his eyes closed, wrung out, useless. That he'd managed to talk Lisa's father into a reprieve gave him no feeling of security. Let that last hold on sanity snap, and Hostelec would come free-wheeling through that doorway again, past all point of reason, beyind talk, beyond anything but a final, futile effort to repay. "Vengeance is mine, sayeth the Lord." Baron Stefan was Lord here, and there was no assurance he would wait on friend Otto's coming.

While Costain lectured himself about the precautions he must take, his system slowly settled down. Then sleep tried to take him, and he pushed it aside by throwing off the covers. The coldness of the room was an inspiration to move. The very snug-fitting, too-short, woolen pajamas did little to shield him … She had said something about kerosene heaters. Perhaps there was one in the kitchen.

None of his clothes were in evidence. He'd have to locate them. There was no closet in the tiny room. "Time to get up," he said, and rose in one, quick motion, steeling himself against what he knew must follow.

When some of the sickness had faded, he opened his eyes. He was looking out the window at a scene of falling snow. It was the same as it had been the morning he'd arrived, hardly any breeze, just sifting down thickly. If it kept up, would they be snowed in again? This seemed to be an unusually early season.

He shivered and knew he couldn't stand still debating the weather. He took a step beside the cot and then another. He was light in the head and weak in the knees with a whole display of white specks popping before his eyes, but he was going to walk into that kitchen, no matter what. "Come on, Lazarus," he said, "you don't need to pick up your bed, but walk."

He accomplished the trip three separate times. On his first venture, he brought back a handsome stag-handle carving knife. On the second, he sought out his clothes and found them in a small pantry closet. He returned wearing the sweater he'd commandeered so long ago, and his socks. On his final trip, he went out of the kitchen and into the main room to see what his host was up to. The large living room was empty. The fire in the fireplace was dying out. It was very still in the house.

Costain went back to his bed. He ate some of the food she had left for him and told himself he'd rest a moment. Instead, he fell into a deep, dreamless sleep. When he awoke a number of hours later, he was angry for having slept, but he felt much refreshed. The sound of the baron playing his violin was also reassuring. What was the melody? ... Something Slovakian ... or Hungarian perhaps. He didn't know that much about music ... It cried out ... so full . . a lament for whom? For what? For anything? ... For Lisa and himself. "So sudden," she'd said. Yes, so sudden, like an explosion. Getting into this mess had been just as sudden ... Hans Goltz—almost a stranger ... an ominous stranger in his ill-fitting uniform. How had the little ferret ever become suspicious? Once a Goltz got his hooks into you, you were done. Even if the timing had not been so critical, there would have been no chance to talk his way out of it. There had been no other recourse ... So the things that mattered, whether they centered on survival or falling in love, happened very suddenly for a man named Costain.

Costain got up and made his way out of the room and into the kitchen. There he rested, listening to the violin's piercing intricacies. He saw the snow had nearly stopped. What light there was, was fading fast. He was surprised to find it nearly four o'clock. Would she be returning soon? He had to get this over quickly. He'd have to watch his step. He couldn't stumble or bump against anything. Damn his legs, anyway! He'd needed a wheel chair himself. He'd have to watch his breathing, too.

Costain stepped into the living room, holding on to the door jamb for support. Her father was sitting at the far end of the room, close to the boxlike heater. He was facing on an angle toward the fireplace. The pistol was no longer in his lap. It was on the table beside his wheel chair.

It was going to be a very long, difficult walk. He would have to do it in stages … First to the couch with its back to him, then to the piano where it faced the windows on the far side of the front door, and then the chasmlike open space to the table itself. He wished the blind man would start playing something loud and long.

He was one step from the couch when the baron stopped playing altogether. In the middle of a phrase, he broke off; his violin remained tucked under his chin, the bow raised … the head cocked, listening … listening!

Costain thought, "Good Lord, he knows I'm here already!"

The blind man sat absolutely still. Costain could hear the clock ticking, the wind starting to rise. He heard an ember hiss faintly in the fireplace. His own weakness was growing, the lightheadedness coming back. He didn't have anything to lean on. He was going to have to lie down!

The Dresden clock saved him. He was completely unprepared for its pleasant chimes, but he recovered quickly enough to use its sound to cover whatever noise he made in gaining the couch. He sat down on it, the trembling in his legs frightening.

The baron had a faint smile on his lips, and when the chimes ceased, he gave a little nod of satisfaction and resumed his playing. Costain realized, with relief and admiration, that the blind man had known the clock was going to strike and had stopped playing so as not to have the two sounds clash.

He waited five minutes before he dared to rise and make the journey to the piano. He had to pass several chairs and a table, but he didn't stop to rest by them for fear they'd move against his weight. He didn't stop because he didn't know how much longer he could stand up.

By the time he reached the piano, his body to him had become a mass of wet, quivering clay. He knew he was going to pass out, and in gaining the piano, he laid the upper half of himself across its top. He heard the sound box echo with faint discordance to his clumsiness, but there was nothing he could do about it.

The violin broke off its flight. He'd given himself away! He didn't have the strength to lift his head to see what the blind man was doing. He lay still, wishing he could pull his entire body onto the piano cover. Then he heard the sound of a car shifting into a low gear and, like a puppet whose string had been pulled, he shot upright.

He saw the baron had heard it, too, that his attention was focused on the approaching sound. He took a breath and quickly crossed the remaining distance to the table. He had his hand on the gun before Hostelec was suddenly aware of him.

The blind man's head swiveled about, trying vainly to recognize an alien presence. "Who—who is it!"

"I came for my gun," Costain said. It was a whispered gasp.

The blind man dropped his bow, his hand shooting out to the table. Costain gritted his teeth and tried to shake his head clear. Now he had to have this man's help or he was done! "Listen! Listen!" he said. "I—!"

"It's Otto!" the Baron announced triumphantly. "You won't get away!" He clutched the violin to his chest.

"Otto!" The pistol was a great weight in his hand. "How do you know!"

"I know!" It was a cry of disdainful confidence. "He didn't wait until Friday! Your gun will do you no good!"

Costain heard the car door slam and took two hurried steps to the heavy, wooden chair beside the fireplace. He sat down. Everything in the room had turned a whitish gray. He was breathing through his mouth in labored gulps. He leaned his head forward. He couldn't collapse now!

The front door swung open, and Doctor Otto Gerlach came across the threshold, stamping the snow from his feet, slamming the door behind him. He wore a heavy, black coat with an astrakhan collar and hat to match. The hat gave him a taller, more powerful look. "Stefan!" he cried, and Costain was surprised to hear excitement in his voice. He came hurriedly toward the blind man, medical bag in gloved hand. Costain knew the doctor had not noticed him.

"Otto, be careful!"

Otto ignored the plea. "Stefan, it's all arranged for Lisa! Everything is ready!"

"Lisa! What! What! How!"

The doctor patted the older man on the shoulder. "I didn't want to say anything until I was sure. You've waited so long. I got word just a few hours ago. It's got to be tonight. I—"

"Otto!" It was a shout of warning. "He's here in this room! Be careful what you say!"

Costain saw the doctor catch himself in mid-cry, his mouth closing emptily. He thrust his head out, eyes blinking, his gaze sweeping the room.

"I'm right here," Costain said.

"What are you doing out of bed, sir?" The doctor was immediately full of professional annoyance. He came toward Costain.

Costain managed to raise the pistol. "I went for a walk to get something of mine."

"He's got the gun," the blind man cautioned unnecessarily.

Costain did not expect to see the doctor smile, but after several wide-eyed blinks, it was there. "It's all right, my friend, you can put it away. I learned all about you today. You're front page news." And then to the baron, "Stefan, we've been all wrong about our friend here. He's all he said he is and a great deal more. He's not one of them, Stefan; they're trying to catch him."

Costain listened to the doctor give a comprehensive account of his crime and his unusual ability in having evaded capture. He listened to Lisa's father pour out his dumbfounded apologies, pitiful in the recognition of his irrational judgment.

"Why didn't you tell us!"

"It isn't something you go around telling people, and if I had told you, would you have believed me?"

"But Radek!"

"You wouldn't believe that either."

"Forgive me! Forgive me!"

"I forgive you."

"I think we can make amends, Stefan," the doctor smiled benignly, polishing his glasses, "since everything is arranged for Lisa." And with that, he explained, and Costain seemed to hear it only in pieces. "Naturally had to be very careful ... didn't want to get your hopes up, Stefan ... very delicate matter ... Group in Znojmo that's actually in the business of smuggling all sorts of things in to and out of Austria … Your name did it, Stefan … I'll take her there myself tonight, soon as she gets home."

If a blind man's tragic mask can glow with joyful anticipation, if it can become sharp and aware despite its staring, sightless eyes, that is what happened to the face of Lisa's father. "You're sure, Otto! There can be no mistake!"

"None whatever. I've checked everything. Lisa will be safe by this time tomorrow, perhaps sooner."

"Oh, thank God! Otto, my dear man, my dear friend! I can never … never repay you!" The tears were unabashed.

"Now, Stefan, calm yourself. You mustn't get overexcited. I knew it was just a matter of time. I'm sorry it took so long." The doctor turned his attention to Costain. "And you, sir, I think perhaps we can help you, too. How would you like to get across the border?" He winked slyly. "I'll just bet you would."

"Yes, of course!" The baron jumped at it. "If they can take Lisa, they can take him!"

"Exactly." The doctor bobbed his head in agreement.

God, if this could only be true! "I—I'm sure they don't do this sort of thing for love," he said hesitantly, waiting for the doctor to reassure him.

"I've already seen to it. I hope I wasn't presuming. I was told for Baron Hostelec they would be glad to take an extra person. Naturally, I didn't mention your identity." The doctor rubbed his hands together, noticing that the fire in the fireplace was nearly out. "Here, we must fix this," he said. "It's cold in here. It's getting colder out. We're going to have a severe winter, you mark my words."

"It's wonderful! … Wonderful!" the baron said, oblivious to talk about the weather. "We shall repay you for our insulting behavior, and we shall repay the pig dogs by helping you to escape." It was settled.

Costain wondered if his sense of disbelief was due entirely to the fantastic opportunity. Lisa's father wanted to get her out of the country. Reasons were obvious enough. The good doctor had somehw arranged it, and because the baron bitterly hated the Administration, Costain was going along for the ride. The whole thing was difficult to assimilate.

The baron and the doctor prattled on, the doctor stoking up the fire, explaining details. When he paused to fan the incipient blaze with the bellows, Costain said, "Does your daughter know about these plans?"

"No. What would be the point in telling her until they were made?"

"She won't leave you alone. Why don't you go, too?"

"In my condition! Ridiculous ... Out of the question!"

"Stefan is right."

"Then she won't leave either."

"She'll do as I say!"

The doctor arose from a squatting position by the hearth with a grunt. "I think I've got that thought out, too." He put down the bellows and brushed off his hands. "Stefan, our friend is correct. Lisa would never consent to leave you under ordinary circumstances. That's why we've got to do a bit of play acting. When she comes home, she's got to find you in bed ... dying. It will be your final wish that she leave."

There was a pause in which Costain could hear the newly laid fire gaining strength, and then the blind man began to cackle merrily. "Excellent, Otto! Excellent! I'd never thought of it! Oh, most excellent! I shall be a proper-dying man!"

Good Christ! Costain thought, what next!

The doctor came toward him smiling faintly, the magnified eyes filled with what must be amusement. "We've got to get you back to bed, sir. You've got to get all the rest you can. It will be a long, cold ride. I'll give you some pills before we leave."

Costain had insisted upon getting dressed. More than giving him a feeling of preparedness, it helped his morale, put him past the invalid stage. False as it might be, he believed that, clothed, he was in a position to act. He had insisted also that the lamp be turned up in his room. He was not going to fall asleep. He had to think, and he had to wait for her arrival. He needed her help to straighten this thing out. Although his earlier efforts had tired him badly, he didn't think they'd brought back the fever. He was warm enough, lying under the quilt. It was past five. She should be coming soon ... soon.

"And what's she coming home to?"

"It'll be a helluva shock ... although I suppose it's not unexpected."

"Yes, but what an incredible trick to play on one's daughter."

"Look at it from his point of view. He knows he's dying ... his last chance to help her ... never leave him otherwise, God, what a break!"

"For you."

"Yes ... and if we go out together."

"You can't look at it in that light or that far ahead ... the doctor, look at him."

"He's going to risk his roly-poly neck for me."

"That's the way it looks."

"Does it? Can you believe it?"

"It's not easy, but that could be because it's too good to seem true."

"There's something a little too good to be true about big-eyed Otto."

"Can't judge him by appearance."

"Have had to judge on less than that ... good at it. Something too hard to take about him. He might risk it for Lisa or her father, but why for Costain?"

"Because he hates the regime as much as the old boy."

"Enough to endanger his life ... career? Don't you believe it."

"It could be that he's sure enough of himself ... his plan ... a doctor's car is not likely to be stopped. If it were, he could always say he and Lisa were the criminal's hostages."

"He's got it all figured out ... everything ... right down to the baron's death scene, and by tomorrow, you'll be in Austria with her, where you can live happily ever after. Hah!"

"So it sounds impossible. Getting this far was impossible ... What other reason—or reasons—could he have for doing this?"

His debate with self was cut off as he heard the front door open and close, heard her voice. He could picture her father and the doctor in the baron's room waiting their cues. The blind man was to get a shot of morphine to add to the realism, a cruel act to assure her safety. He could see the macabre logic of it, but he didn't like it a bit. He thought it stank.

He listened to the quick, shocked rise of her voice, playing counterpoint to the flat, monotone of the doctor's, waited until both had died away, before he arose. From now on, all that happened in this house was going to affect him. Weak as he was, he was going to be present. He'd watch this scene played out. He might even take part in it.

In the diffuse glow of a single lamp, Costain saw her kneeling by her father's bed. The doctor hovered like a hug moth opposite her, and between them the baron lay a frail, shriven figure, out of place in the rich, overlarge proportions of his princely couch. With his head thrown back upon the pillow, beard, chin, and nose arching starkly, he seemed already dead. Only the slow, rasping tide of breath, the one hand that clasped her own and its partner that clutched now and again at the coverlet, refuted the impression.

The light haloed the rim of her hair, and to Costain, it was almost as though she were kneeling before an altar. Neither she nor the doctor were aware of his entrance. He sat down in a chair by the door.

"Lisa?" It was a soft, questioning sigh.

"Yes, darling." The quiet reply was full of love, but firm. The firmness touched Costain.

"I want you to go. with Otto … tonight."

"Of course."

"Please!" The baron was not going to be humored. "This is my last wish! My only wish! … the only thing I ask of you! … All these months, Otto has worked … while I've waited. I—I can't wait any longer, Lisa. You must go with him tonight!"

"Papa, you're not going to die."

"I am! I am! … Can't you see I want to die! Must you torture me! I want peace; I can't have it if you won't obey me! I want you to get out of this accursed country!" It was more than play acting, and Costain thought that the drug might not have been necessary after all.

"Please, darling," she whispered. "Don't get yourself excited. I'll go with Otto."

"Tonight!"

"Must it be tonight?"

"Yes, it's got to be tonight," the doctor interjected quietly, but with a persuasive undertone.

"Why?" The very question Costain was asking himself.

"Because it's been arranged. It's a matter of timing."

"Can't it be another time?"

"The risk is too great, Lisa … for all of us." The moth seemed to flutter a bit.

"Lisa!" The cry came out full of impatience and anger. "Don't deny me this!"

She raised his hand in her own, pressing it to her lips, her head bowed.

Costain got up and left the room. He couldn't listen to any more of it. It was monstrous, yet it was right; yet there was something badly wrong about the rightness. He heard her whisper, "All right, darling … all right," and then a gasp, "Promise! Promise!"

He sat on the bench before the fireplace where he had sat that first night. "A matter of timing," the doctor had said.

"Why make it up? What could he gain?"

"He knows who you are, Costain."

"Odd he didn't know until today."

"A matter of timing."

"But if he were going to turn you in, he would have brought the police."

"It would have been a simple thing to do … But her father wouldn't have liked it."

"Still … still … If he'd known who you were before today, he could have turned you in anytime."

"Go back to the beginning. Go back over everything he's said and done since you opened your eyes and saw him hovering above you. You've got to be right about this."

When she came out of her father's room, he stood up, and she stared blankly at him for an instant. Then, she came to him with surprise, holding out her hands to his. "Mark, what are you doing up?"

He held her lightly. "Waiting for you."

"You shouldn't be up." He could feel her fingers on his shoulders.

He looked down at her. "Is he gone?"

She nodded shortly and laid her head on his chest. "I—I know I should weep and—and feel terribly sad ... I know I shall later ... but I know, I know, Mark, it's better—he—he—"

He stroked her hair, waiting for her to get control of herself. She'd just had one shock, and now it looked like he was going to give her another.

"Lisa, we've got to talk alone a moment. Can we go in your room?"

"What is it?" She raised her head, looking up at him.

"Come along." They went into her room, walking slowly, her arm around his back a helpful support. He sat down on her bed with an involuntary sigh.

"Oh Mark, why are you out of bed like this?"

"Because Doctor Gerlach has offered me the chance to go with you. I'm going with you, Lisa, because I would like to go anywhere with you but it's more than that." He reached out and took her hand. "I have to go with you."

She studied him silently, the softness in her eyes becoming reflective. "So sudden," she said. "I sensed there was something more to you ... I wondered what seemed familiar about you ... You remind me of my father long ago ... when I was just a little girl ... There is a sameness in the eyes ... a look ... a feeling of strength, or maybe stubbornness ... that won't give in ... Are you fighting them all by yourself, dear man?" She laid her hand on his cheek, and he felt it down to his toes.

"I'm running from them," he said, taking her hand away and holding it tightly. "Didn't you see the newspapers today?"

"I don't often read anything but the music and stage revues, but today I did." She smiled wanly. "I think I was looking for something about you. Was there something? What have you done?"

Costain stood up, jolted, yet not really surprised.

"How many newspapers in Brno?"

"Why quite a few, I suppose, but—"

"Lisa," he laid his hands on her shoulders, "my life depends on leaving here tonight."

"How lucky for you that Otto has made all the arrangements. Were you lying to me about being a designer of ships to the moon?"

"No, but you mustn't interrupt."

She couldn't stop now. "I don't want to leave him alone … not till he's decently buried … until there's been a Mass said for him. I—" And now the tears did come, and he held her while she wept and knew that right now she was in no condition to understand and act on what he had to tell her.

He looked up to see the doctor standing in the doorway. In that swift meeting of glances, Costain read surprise and outrage. It was quickly blinked away by the thickly lensed eyes that viewed them.

"I think we'd better make plans to leave."

Lisa turned at Otto Gerlach's voice, brushing the tears from her eyes. "Oh. Must we go so soon, Otto? Can't we wait until—?"

"He's at rest, Lisa. There's nothing more you can do for him," the doctor answered gently. "I'll take care of everything when I come back."

"It's not right."

"Believe me, Lisa, it must be now."

"Can I pack a bag?"

"Yes, a few things will be all right."

"Well, you're both going to have something to eat before we leave," she said firmly, looking at Costain.

The doctor checked his watch, "I'm really not very hungry."

"I insist. Mark, you should lie down until it's time ... Now—now leave me, please."

Costain followed the doctor out of her room. He wanted to take her advice, but he sat on the couch instead, and watched Gerlach warm himself at the fireplace. To get results he was going to have to make the doctor angry.

"Is he really gone?" He kept his voice down.

"Yes ... It's just as well."

"The morphine?"

The doctor placed his backside to the fire. "He would have gone anyway."

"You just helped him along."

"I've always done what I could to help him."

"Because he helped you." It was a statement, not a question.

"Because he was my friend."

"And risking your life for his daughter, that's part of it."

"I don't look at it quite so melodramatically."

"You could be caught."

"I don't expect to be."

"How far to Znojmo?"

"About 90 kilometers. We'll figure two hours to be safe."

"Do you know any of the details of how we go out?"

"No, just that you go out."

"Right across the Marchfeld?"

"I don't know. I should think west into higher country. You mustn't worry. I've some pills to give you."

"I can manage, thanks."

"You'd be wise to take them."

Costain didn't reply. He sat staring at the doctor. The doctor turned again to the fireplace and the silence between them began to make itself felt.

"You—ahhh—seem to have made friends with Lisa?"

"She's a very good nurse."

The doctor bent and picked up the fire tongs, "Have you told her about yourself?"

"I didn't have to." He'd been waiting for this.

"Oh? How so?" The log was resettled. The fire gathered new strength.

"She read all about me in today's papers ... like you."

The doctor set the tongs back in their holder and brushed off his hands. He faced Costain. "You don't trust me."

"That's right."

"Because you realize I've known about you for longer than today."

"Why lie about it?"

"I had my reasons. There was no need to upset you ... After all, couldn't I have notified the police at any time?"

"I'm deeply indebted to you," Costain laced it with sarcasm. "'I don't want to enlarge a debt I can never repay. You've risked enough for a wanted criminal to whom you owe nothing out of friendship, or gratitude, or anything ... except your devotion to the late baron."

"I'm not doing this for you. It's for Lisa and Stefan. It just happens to be your good luck." There was strong hint of irritation showing through.

"I don't want to press yours," Costain said, deciding to force the issue now. "Tell me where I must go in Znojmo, and I'll drive Lisa there."

"Out of the question!" It was snapped out, the blandness husked away.

"Why!"

"Why—why for a good many reasons, sir! What about my car? How would I get my car back?"

"I'm sure the people you've been in contact with, will be glad to return it."

"I can't count on anything of the sort. I'll have enough trouble when I report Stefan's death proving I know nothing about his daughter's disappearance."

"How will you prove it?"

"I've arranged that!" The doctor was growing upset. "I've arranged everything!"

"Even the baron's death."

"Now see here—!" The doctor caught hold of his rising blood pressure. He took off his glasses, and with a handkerchief from his lapel pocket began to polish them. "I don't blame you for being cautious—even distrustful, but—"

"I'm glad you don't blame me," Costain overrode the peace overture. "I am distrustful, Doctor Gerlach, about a lot of things. You could say my life depends on it. I ask myself why does a dear friend torment his dying mentor by encouraging a false impression about a stranger? ... Why does the dear friend also torment the stranger as to his identity ... when he knows it full well!"

"But I told you, sir—!"

"You've told me nothing that satisfies my distrust. You may be the original good Samaritan, Otto, but I don't trust you ... yet."

The doctor shrugged disgustedly. "You're a fool, sir."

"Possibly."

"To deserve distrust, the distrusted one must have a motive; what motive do I have?"

"I could guess, but I don't know. I'm just saying I can't take the chance to find out."

"You can't remain here now."

"You can tell me where to go in Znojmo."

"I have Lisa to think about! I'm not letting you take my car. If you were stopped her life would be in danger."

"And if you were stopped with the both of us?"

"You'll be lying in the back seat with your face bandaged, a blanket over you. You're being taken to the hospital."

"You've really got it all pegged, haven't you?"

"If you want to deny yourself the chance to get away, I can't do anything about it."

"No, you can't. All you have to do is to tell me where I can locate the people in Znojmo."

"I haven't the right to endanger those who are giving you this chance." The doctor dropped all attempt to hide his exasperation.

Costain took the pistol out of his pocket and rested it on his knee. "Do you know this morning the baron nearly killed me with this because of you?" He raised the weapon, sighting it at the floor. "As I see it, either you will tell me where I can find these dedicated border crossers, and Lisa and I shall go meet them, or you can refuse to tell me, and I'll borrow your car." He looked up at Gerlach and smiled.

The doctor started to speak and then he shut himself off. He stared coldly back at Costain. "All right," he said with a perfunctory nod, "I can see there's no point in argument, so let's compromise. I'll drive down to Tyškov and make a phone call; if the people on the other end agree, you can take my car ... and Lisa. Or you can steal my car without my calling, and go straight to the devil!" He turned calling sharply, "Lisa!"

She appeared so quickly Costain thought at first, she might have been standing in the doorway listening to them. "I'm sorry, Otto," she said, coming toward Gerlach, "I'm not going to leave now." Costain saw her mind was made up and she was in complete control of herself.

"Lisa, you promised your father," the doctor said softly.

"It was his wish, not mine."

"If you stay here, they'll—"

"I don't plan to stay here … for long." She glanced quickly at Costain and then back to the doctor. "After the funeral, if you can fix it so that I can get into Austria, all well and good, but not tonight, not now, no matter what I promised. I can't." This last she said for Costain alone.

The doctor threw up his hands with a sigh of resigned disgust, "I've done all I can do."

She came to him, "I know you have, Otto … and I can never thank you." She looked toward Costain, "Take Mark."

"He doesn't trust me, the idiot!" There seemed to be as much hurt in it as annoyance.

"Mark!" And then she saw the gun in his hand, "Mark, what on earth!—"

"Excuse me, Lisa." He set the pistol on the couch next to his leg. "The doctor and I have certain areas of disagreement on procedure."

"But you can trust Otto! I'd trust him with my life."

He stood up and rested his hands on her shoulders. "I don't want him taking any more chances. I just want to borrow his car. All he has to do is tell me where to drive it. I thought you and I could save him the long trip."

"I can't go now, Mark." He saw in her eyes that she wanted very much to go.

"It's not the same with you as it is with me," he said.

"No, you have to go quickly."

"Very quickly, now."

"But you do understand why I can't at this moment."

"I'll wait for you on the other side."

"I'll try to come soon."

"There's so much I want to say to you."

"And I, too … Oh, Mark."

"We'll go in your room for a moment." Costain put his arm around her shoulder and began to guide her in that direction. He seemed oblivious to the doctor.

They had nearly reached the bedroom door when Otto Gerlach reminded them of his presence. "Lisa, get away from him!" The order cracked.

They faced the doctor who was now standing beside the couch, Costain's pistol in his hand. Costain felt Lisa stiffen, heard her breath catch. "You might be able to trust your life to him," he said evenly, "but you see, it's not quite the same in my case, is it, Otto?"

"I'll shoot you if you don't obey me," the doctor said.

"Otto!" Lisa started forward.

"Get out of the way!" Gerlach took two quick strides, grabbed her wrist and spun her out of Costain's line. "This is for you, Lisa." The doctor spoke quickly, his attention unblinkingly glued to his victim. "This man is not only wanted for murder, he's a threat to the both of us. Turning him over to the police is the only thing we can do." It was more than an explanation, it was a plea for understanding.

"Well, now at least we've got it straightened out," Costain said, "but I'll be damned if I know why you waited so long. It nearly fooled me." He started toward the doctor.

"I said I'd shoot!" The warning was shrill with undeniable intent.

"Mark, wait!" Her cry was punctuated by the metallic click of the hammer, striking the firing pin. There were several more agitated clicks while Costain bent over as though to tie his shoe. Instead, he fastened his hands on the edge of the circular rug and straightened up with a vigorous yank.

Otto Gerlach, with the carpet literally pulled out from under him, described a short but definite hyperbolic arc, landing on his back with a room-shaking crash.

"I said I didn't trust you, Otto," Costain reiterated. "I'm really surprised you weren't more astute. You should have tried this when I was helpless."

He stopped and picked up the gun from the floor where it had come to rest. He smiled up at her ruefully. "Forgive me," he said, "I didn't want to frighten you, but this seemed one way of finding out."

Although she was reluctant to have him do so, Costain had put Otto Gerlach in the root cellar. Now it was time for them to say goodbye. She had fed him well. He was warmly and serviceably clothed, but he had decided against taking away any extra food or blankets. Such items could be traced back to her.

"Now you know what you're to do?" They were sitting on the couch, she curled sideways with her head against his chest.

"Yes." She lifted her head. "Mark, you look so pale. You're in no condition to travel."

"Tell me what you're going to do."

She swallowed and began to recite. "At five-thirty tomorrow morning I'll let Otto out—the poor man will be frozen. I'll ski down to the village and tell them about father. Then I'll report Otto's car as having been stolen. Oh, Mark, must I do that? Can't it come out later?"

"No, you tell them right then. You tell them Otto has been here since this afternoon with your father—with him all night. Neither of you know when the car disappeared."

"But suppose Otto says something else."

"I've instructed him as to what he'll say. He's in this up to his ears. This is his only way out. If they ever learn I was here, and he was taking care of me—. You be sure to get rid of all signs of my having been here, even though I'm sure they're not going to suspect I was in this house. The emphasis will be on your father's death."

"I know. I know ... I'll never get rid of you having been here ... not inside me." She raised his palm to her lips and kissed it.

He pulled her head roughly down against his chest again, holding it tightly there, "Lisa, my love ... my love ... so sudden, my love ... and so brief."

"I'll never see you again! They'll catch you." It was a choked whisper. "Oh, Mark, my dearest."

"No, you can't think that. Listen," he lifted her head so that they were looking into each other's eyes, "listen, there is so much we have to know about each other that we could not meet like this—could not know a love so swift, only to lose it before we've had a chance to live it."

"What chance have we?" she asked quietly, shaking her head. "You, a wanted enemy, and I, some kind of Vestal Virgin for the glory of the State. Even if you escape, what—?"

"While we live there's a chance!" He said it fiercely, knowing he was trying to convince himself as much as he was her. "I—I don't think a cruel fate brought me to your door, I think it was a kind God. I'll go away with your memory locked up in me, and that's more than I had when I arrived."

"What good is a memory, Mark?" She laid her head on his shoulder and he stroked her hair. "Can I touch a memory?" She put her hand on his chest over his heart, "Can I feel it? Can I talk to it ... live for it?"

"It's better than no memory," he said stubbornly, knowing the weakness he felt now was not from sickness, knowing he should try to keep his mind on his departure, no matter how difficult it was going to be for the both of them.

"Oh, you poor, dear man," she sighed, "can you be satisfied with so little?"

"Now listen a minute," he tried to sound business-like. "I'm going to give you an address in Vienna. When you get there, you go to it and say that you want to get in touch with me."

"Oh, Mark, how will I ever get there if Otto was lying?"

"I don't know. You'll have to try."

She studied him a moment, smiling wanly. "I'm not being very helpful, am I? But then, I've never been in love, so I'm not very good about it."

"'You're very good about it. You're wonderful, but it's no good to accept defeat … ever."

"You know that, don't you?"

"Yes, I know it."

"I want to know what you know. I want to know all about you. I want to know who you are—you realize I don't even know that?"

"One day, one day."

"One day, but not today, or tomorrow … no time, not to talk, not to be together … not to live properly. I'm in love with a stranger, a hunted man, but I—"

He stopped her outpouring with his lips, and when they drew back breathless, there was a new expression on her face, that seared through him. She said his name as he drank hungrily of her mouth again. His mind snarled at him with unyielding bitterness, that there was no time, no time for this either.

Costain drove the doctor's car down the narrow, snow-covered trail with great care. He must not skid, and he must not get stuck. The snow had stopped, but in the open spaces the wind was starting to herd it into drifts. It was going to be a cold night, a long night, but no colder than leaving her had left him, no longer than the distance growing between them.

"Lisa, Lisa," he said in the close empty darkness of the car, "be here with me now, ride with me."

And then the other voice, intruding rudely, but rightly, "Get your thoughts away from her, or it'll be a precious short ride."

The trees thinned out suddenly, and he saw where the road sloped down into the lights of Tyškov. A short distance ahead, there was a side track that cut away on a diagonal from the cluster of buildings and made its connection with the main road beyond. He saw this as another piece of luck. There could be police in the village who might recognize the doctor's car. Snow-blanketed as it was, he turned into the track, shifting into lowest gear, thankful that he could avoid possible trouble.

CHAPTER SEVENTEEN

The sun cleared the upland ridge behind the church and sent its rays down through the small sacristy window. Father Paul's strongly shaped hands and the paper they held were bathed in the golden glow. He looked up at the window and felt warmth drive the cold from his fingers. He sat staring at the suffused window for a long moment. Then he arose and went into the chancel where he knelt at the altar and prayed.

When he walked down the aisle between the orderly rows of silent pews, he saw that the interior of the little church was flooded in the new light of the early morning sun. Even the stone walls had taken on a softer hue. He went into the vestibule, and using both hands flung wide the church doors. He stood on the stoop, gazing down the gently sloping valley to the houses of Vilivesko. The neat carpet of snow between had been greatly thinned by two days of mild weather and a night of rain. This morning did not smell or feel of December. He inhaled deeply and then let the air go out with a rush as he caught sight of Costain.

He'd suddenly popped out from behind a clump of firs and was running, running in a staggering lope toward the chapel. Father Paul's eyes swept the ground behind down to the village. He saw no sign of pursuit, but as Costain fell to his knees and stumbled upright again, the priest heard it. Its thin, ominous wail came crying along the valley, cruelly knifing open the new-found day.

Now Father Paul could see Costain more distinctly; a big man, bearded ... bareheaded, shapeless clothing, mouth gaping. He stumbled and fell once more, and Father Paul ran down the chapel steps to aid him. Costain staggered to his feet, weaving, and the priest looked into glazed and frenzied eyes and saw the mindless expression of the animal run to earth. Out of the man's throat came one tortured word. "Sanctuary!"

It was a cry like a wolf howl, and it struck Father Paul to the heart. It was a supplication that even this poor wretch must know was useless in this time and place.

He got his shoulder under Costain's arm and supporting him as best he could, guided him the short distance to the chapel steps. He was aware of three sounds: the terrible broken whistling of Costain's breathing, the insistent and now sharper wail of the siren, and the echo of a great plea "Sanctuary!"

Inside the church, he helped Costain to sit down in the first pew. Costain promptly fell over. The priest debated whether to let him lie where he was until he was more fully recovered when he noticed the mud-caked, snow-soaked shoes. He hurried outside and tried to cover Costain's footsteps by walking up and down the trail, but he could only obliterate the tracks for a short distance. The siren had ceased its wailing. He could detect activity in the village square. He smiled tightly, knowing there was one sure way to do the job. Mass would be a half hour earlier this morning. He pulled the bell-rope and each time the bell rang, it sent its beckoning note across the valley. "Sanctuary! ... Sanctuary! ... Sanctuary!"

When he saw the first of his parishioners, leaving their homes and starting toward the chapel, he went back inside the church and found Costain where he had left him. His breathing had quieted somewhat, though he still lay sprawled along the pew, one arm flung across his eyes.

"Are you able to sit up?" Father Paul asked.

At the sound of the priest's voice, Costain pulled his arm away from his face and stared up at him. Then he pushed himself into a sitting position and shook his head vigorously as though to clear it.

Father Paul took Costain by the arm and got him on his feet. "I'm going to put you in the sacristy," he said. "Stay there until the Service is over. We'll talk then."

"Have to get out of here," Costain mumbled, "… get away."

"You need to rest first."

"No, catch me … bad for you." Costain tried to pull his arm away from the priest's hold.

"Don't worry about me. You'll be safe in here, just stay here." He held open the door.

Father Paul left Costain slumped in a chair and went to the church entrance to welcome those who had responded to the summons to Mass. He prayed they would arrive before the police, but only half his prayer was answered, for as the last of the score of villagers greeted him and filed into the chapel, he saw the police car come out from between the buildings and drive up the track, skidding and swerving in the soft mixture of mud and snow.

He knew a moment's fear. Had someone in the village seen him go to the aid of the hunted man? He gave the rope a last tug and the final bell note spoke its single word down the long valley, giving him back his strength. He was prepared for the occupants of the car as it came to a fast braking halt.

There were five of them, all in uniform, four carrying sub-machine guns and a thin-mustached officer to give them their orders. The four underlings fanned out in a line and began casting about for signs.

"Father," the officer snapped, full of authority and poorly suppressed excitement, "we're looking for a filthy criminal. He was known to have come this way, have you seen him?"

"Young man," Father Paul said, scowling down at the officer who was actually no younger than himself, "I am about to say Mass. Would you and your men care to come inside for the Service?"

The officer stared at the priest, slightly incredulous, and then recovering replied coldly, "I'm not interested in your Service. I'm looking for a rotten murderer." He swung his his attention to his men and called, "Have you found anything?"

The men moving in a line across the snow shouted negative replies, but helplessly Father Paul could see that their present course would take them to the clump of trees where he had first seen the hunted man.

"Well, what about it?" The officer was speaking to him again.

"I don't know of anyone in Vilivesko who is a murderer," he answered, knowing that he could not go into the church until he saw what was going to happen.

"We're not after anyone here!" the officer explained with annoyed impatience. "We chased him here! He's trying to get across the frontier. We've been after him all the way from Jennice."

"Oh," Father Paul said vaguely. "From Jennice. I know a good many people there. What's his name?"

"Look, Father, have you seen anyone who—!"

The shout of success from the trees spun the officer around. Three of his men were running to converge on the fourth who'd given the call. The officer tugged his pistol free of its holster and went galloping down to join them.

Father Paul waited until the group began to follow the new-found tracks. Then he went in and closed and barred the twin doors. The only other entrance was the side door leading out of the sacristy. He'd bar that, too. He would celebrate Mass without fear of intrusion.

When it was said and done, he asked his people to remain for a moment. He did not stand in the pulpit but under the vaulted chancel arch, almost in their midst. "Some of you probably know already that the police have come to Vilivesko, seeking a criminal." He raised his hand and quieted the stir. "There's no cause to be frightened. Have any of you seen the man they're after, a stranger?"

A general exchange of glances brought no information that anyone had seen the fugitive, and he gave an inward sigh of relief. Of course, these few didn't speak for the whole of Vilivesko, but then it seemed likely that the man in the sacristy had made a point of skirting the village.

"Some of the police are outside right now. When you leave do not appear fearful, do not be in a hurry. Answer their questions and go about your business … And now something a little more normal," he smiled, "Mrs. Dobec, would you have David or one of his friends get word to Peter that I would like to see him here right after his school. I've never known a more forgetful altar boy."

He blessed them and strode down the aisle to open the barred doors and face whatever was to come. He felt greatly refreshed, sure of himself.

The officer was waiting with two of his men. The other two were nowhere in sight. Each villager was closely scrutinized as they came down the steps. "None of my people have seen your man," Father Paul said in a loud clear voice.

"I'll tell you this," the officer replied with the same clarity, "the punishment is death for anyone foolish enough to try and help him! We've found his tracks!" He pointed. "We know he's hiding close by! You are to return to your homes and stay there until further notice!"

"Would such a person try to take refuge here with the frontier so close?" Father Paul asked.

"We've found no trail beyond this path, and unless he can fly he's hiding right around here somewhere. We'll have a look through your church now, Father."

The priest set himself. "This church is the house of God, sir," he said forcefully. "If you come to worship or to confess your sins, you will be welcome, but you will not desecrate my Father's house as long as I can prevent it!"

The words were flung down and their sudden impact left a heavy momentary silence. It was broken by a harsh belch of laughter from the officer. "Don't hand me any of your sermons!" he scoffed. "Just get out of the way." He started up the steps, and Father Paul, waiting, thrust out his hand. The officer flinched and threw up his arm, expecting a blow.

There was a golden crucifix in the priest's hand. "Touch me," he thundered, "and you profane His Holy Cross!"

The officer paled slightly. Though they had done a good flushing job on him, the residue of an earlier faith had not been entirely washed away. He was obviously thrown off balance, unsure of himself. "Now see here, Father," he said. "I'm not going to desecrate your church! We just want to see if the man we're after might be hiding somewhere in it."

"You think I'd hide such a person!" He continued to appear outraged, knowing he must hold his advantage.

"No, of course not, but he might be hiding, and—"

"There are but two rooms in my church," he flung his arm back. "Would I not know what was in those rooms!"

"Well, yes, I suppose so, but—"

"Then go hunt your tormented wretch on more fertile ground! This is a house of peace!" he shook the crucifix at the officer.

The officer was now even more unsure of himself. He glanced angrily at the set-faced group of men, women and children who stared blankly, silently at him. There was no telling what he might have done next, but the sound of distant sirens put an end to it for the time.

Father Paul raised his head, listening, realizing that reinforcements were arriving.

"You two go join the others," the officer gestured toward the land behind the church. "Cover all the ground to the first ridge! Go on home now!" he shouted at the tight-knit group of villagers. He flung a final hostile glance at the priest. "I'll be back!" he snapped and then hurried down the steps to get into the car.

From some far distant pinnacle Costain had heard the Mass being said, but he didn't know what it was ... someone calling his name ... the wind in the tree tops ... the water gurgling treacherously beneath the thin ice ... the hiss of snow under stolen skis ... car wheels spinning futilely in a snow choked lane ... village south of Brno ... Lisa? Lisa! ... That's how it had started, with Lisa. The loss of the car had been compensated by finding the deserted cabin in the hills west of somewhere. How many days spent there? Five? Seven? What difference? ... Strong enough to start moving again ... By night, only by night ... South and west. Find the high ground, the wooded high ground ... Only by night and the bitter cold to gnaw from without, while hunger gnawed from within ... Days and nights, and oh Lisa! ... River! River! ... How far? Skis! The wonderful clean swiftness of skis! Go on winged feet, fly, fly! Ah, but it must have been the stolen skis that put them on to you again. The patrol so suddenly there ... having come from the village ... Thank God for darkness! but not the rain, not ever the rain ... On foot, running through the rain, the muck. Run, Costain! Run! Lisa, help me to run!

Costain jerked upright in the chair and looked up into the steady gray eyes of the priest.

Father Paul held his finger to his lips and said very quietly, "You're feeling better?"

Costain stood up, taking in his surroundings. "How did I get here, Father?"

"You don't remember?" There was more than surprise in the priest's lean face.

"No. I—I don't."

"You came here, asking for help ... a short time ago."

"I see." Costain put his hand in his mackinaw and felt the hard reassurance of the pistol. "Thank you, I'd better leave."

"I'm afraid that wouldn't be wise." Costain listened to his explanation with a grim feeling of wonder.

"Why are you hiding me, Father?" He liked the look of this priest with his close-cropped blond hair, his resolute face with its prominent nose, hawking above a firm wide mouth.

Father Paul replied with his own question, "Are you fighting them?"

"I was ... now I'm running." He felt no reticence in answering. Perhaps he was too far gone to care.

"You killed one of them."

"Yes ... to escape."

"What do you think led you here?"

Costain realized the priest might even have been a younger man than himself, but suddenly he had the feeling of being many year's Father Paul's junior. "I don't know," he said. "Maybe it was God?"

Father Paul's smile revealed his own youth. "Yes, I think so ... Now listen to me, they'll come back here. I expect the whole countryside will be swarming with them soon. I may not be able to prevent them from searching."

"Then I'd better get going. Am I far from the border?"

"You can't go at this time. There are four of them on the ridge behind here right now. I have a place to hide you, although I'm afraid it will be quite uncomfortable."

Father Paul raised his hand. "We have no time to argue. Unknown to yourself, you came here asking for sanctuary. Once the Church was strong enough to grant it. For today I shall grant it as best I can. Come."

The hiding place was a narrow crypt-like hollowing behind the altar, and Costain found the priest had not exaggerated. It was thoroughly uncomfortable; cramped, hot, practically airless. Still, it was a good place to hide because, unless very closely examined, the altar appeared to be attached to the church wall. And so, despite his discomfit, Costain lay in the small, dark space filled with a gratitude he could never express and a sense of safety which he knew to be completely irrational. He blamed such indulgence on the worn, battered condition of body and nerves. He could not push what was left of himself much further without rest. So he was resting, but feeling safe about his position was the height of folly. He fell into a deep sleep, deploring his own attitude.

He slept through the search which came about noon, never aware that Father Paul, his feelings obviously shocked by such sacrilegious outrage, took the colonel now in charge of the hunt and two of his hunters on a thorough tour of inspection. He could not know that the colonel, though satisfied Costain was not hiding in the church, was not at all satisfied by the inability of his men, helicopters, and dog packs to unearth him.

Costain didn't know anything until a whispering voice, repeating the same words over and over dragged him back to wakefulness. "Wake up! ... Wake up!" It was the priest.

"I'm awake," he said groggily. He was slimy with sweat, half suffocated, his throat and chest burning.

"Shhh!"

"Sorry."

"I'm kneeling before the altar. Keep your voice at a whisper. Are you all right?"

"Yes ... What's happening?"

"They've brought many more men. The frontier is blocked east and west for twenty or thirty kilometers."

Costain grunted. "I should be flattered."

"Every house has been searched and will be again, no doubt."

"It sounds jolly. Where do they think I went?"

"From what the colonel said they think you have a confederate, that you've been hidden somewhere in the area."

"Well, he's right enough. Are you above suspicion?"

"They've been here, but their last contact with you was close enough, so it's likely they'll come again."

"And take your church apart stone by stone."

"There's that chance."

"What time is it, Father?"

"Past three."

"That late! Are they watching the church?"

"No one is directly outside, but they're all around."

"So any way I go out, they'll see me."

"Until after dark."

"Have I got that long?"

"I've been praying that you do."

"I'll pray for that, too."

"I have a plan of sorts."

"Oh? ... Is there a way?" Costain choked back a cough.

"You may not like the sound of it at first."

"You mean give myself up, Father?"

"Shhh! No, it involves a boy."

"You're right. I don't like it."

"Wait until you hear. He's a most unusual boy."

"I'm sure of it, but I involve no boys of any sort."

"I sent for him this morning. Whether they'll let him come or not, I don't know, but if they do he—"

"Father, I don't know what you have in mind, but forget it. You've done more than any man should already. When it's dark, I'll leave. I—" A muffled series of thumps stopped him.

"There's someone knocking!" He heard the priest's startled whisper, and then he lay still listening to the knocks repeated, thinking he heard a voice to go with the sound. He fished the automatic out of his pocket. What would he solve if he took one or two of them with him? Senseless killing. He flicked the safety back on. What better place to die than in a church? A modern Thomas à Becket without the stature, the meaning, or the popularity to be remembered ... except maybe in Vilivesko. Somehow he had gone past being frightened. He'd accept what came with one last prayer: "Please, don't let this wonderful man of God get into trouble over me." It was surprising how many of all kinds still fought—un-united, alone, not with a gun, but with a word, a thought, a faith ... the innate courage to try and help the man with the gun.

"It's all right," the priest's whisper came sighing through to him, and he was conscious of his body going slack.

"They brought Peter. I think it's safe for you to come out and get some air now. You can sit on the sacristy floor."

Costain had no chance to protest, for while Father Paul was speaking he was pushing the altar away from the wall. The unaccustomed light caused Costain to wince and cover his eyes with his hand.

"I hope it hasn't been too difficult. It was the only place I could think of." The priest was all concern, and when Costain lowered his hand, he saw Father Paul's outstretched one. He took it and came to his feet feeling cramped and clumsy. He glanced about quickly. It seemed dusk had already invaded the church. The altar and the chancel candles were bright islands of light.

"Where's the boy?" he asked, angered and confused that the priest would permit a child to become a party to this thing.

"He's my altar boy when the spirit moves him ... or I can catch him." It was all a mild joke.

"Look, how can you bring a boy into anything as dangerous as this, Father? Don't you know—!"

"Please keep your voice down! ... If Peter is brought into this, I don't think there'll be a great deal of danger."

"And if he goes out of here and talks?"

"Peter will never talk, my son ... he's a mute."

Costain thought he had never seen such blue eyes; full of brightness and light and merriment, full of understanding that transcends age or knowledge, and yet, overall, full of earthly innocence. A pixie with a snubbed nose and a much too large mouth. How old was he? Ten, eleven? Slight but wiry, his blond thatch close-cropped like the priest's.

It was Peter who extended his hand first. Costain took it and for an instant nearly knelt down and took the boy in his arms.

"Peter can't speak, but he can hear," Father Paul said. "I think he can almost hear what's going on on the other side of the world, can't you Peter?"

Peter nodded, still grinning at Costain, watching him sit down in the corner of the room.

"Peter lives on a farm with his mother and four older brothers," the priest explained. "It's roughly two kilometers from here beyond the ridge. In back of the farm the hills begin, some of them quite high. It's all forbidden ground because it's only another two or three kilometers from there to the frontier."

"Really?" Costain was beginning to wonder if the priest were out of his mind.

"If you can reach the escarpment in back of Peter's home, I think he can get you safely into Austria."

"Father, I beg your pardon, but this is absolutely insane!"

"No," the priest smiled and the boy shook his head vigorously in agreement. "Not as far as Peter is concerned … To you yes, it will be very dangerous, and you may not succeed in reaching the right place, but once you are in Peter's hands, the danger is over."

"Sure, and if I reach wherever I'm to reach, they won't have those hills full of trigger-happy police. They won't see the boy and shoot him down!"

"Please, keep your voice lower!" Father Paul admonished. "Just listen now, and I'll explain." Peter came and sat down on the floor beside Costain. He put his small hand comfortingly inside Costain's large begrimed one and grinned.

"Peter is as much at home in the hills and the woods as any animal, but you can be assured I would not throw him amongst the wolves." Father Paul crossed the room and peered cautiously out the window.

"Well, I'd like to know what else you call it?" He could feel the boy's eyes studying him with sympathetic curiosity.

"Peter will be in a place where he cannot be seen," the priest said. "Only he and I know of it, and I know because he confessed it to me. I think perhaps we've been saving it for just such a time as this. You'll be pleased to hear that Peter has crossed the frontier many times and no one on either side has ever been aware of it."

They were both smiling at him, and he shook his head and threw up his hands. "I'm through arguing," he said, "you tell me.

Father Paul told him, and then it was a matter of making sure he could identify the place, should he be able to reach it. They drew a rough map, and the boy, with the priest's help, instructed him on how he must travel. Between the church and his home there did not seem to be a blade of grass or a clump of snow with which he was not familiar. When Costain had it all committed to memory, there were still two points that troubled him.

"Suppose they go through another house search and find Peter gone?"

"They're bound to do that, and Peter won't leave until the search is over. If you arrive before he does, you'll simply have to wait for him."

Peter smiled at Costain, making signs with his fingers.

"He says not to worry. He'll come for you."

"That's another thing, how he's going to get from his house to where I have to meet him without being seen?"

"I can promise you he won't be seen. I'm sure of this, or I wouldn't allow it. In his games, he's made courses of travel even a rabbit couldn't follow."

"It's not right."

"What you've been doing, is that right?"

"I hope so."

"You believe so, or you don't."

"All right, I do, but it doesn't have anything to do with risking the lives of little boys!"

"It has everything to do with little boys. If it doesn't, you've been risking your life for nothing."

"All right, all right!" Costain said, sorry for his own abruptness, but unable to hide it. "I've got to move out of here as soon as I can after dark. Hadn't I better get back in my cubbyhole till then?"

With his laughing eyes on Costain, Peter began making swift gestures. "He says, you must be hungry," Father Paul translated. "He'll bring some food."

"Little man, little man," Costain said silently. "You're all the world, and I'll probably die tonight, trying to reach you and your unbelievable escape route, but I think it will have been worth it ... just to have met you."

CHAPTER EIGHTEEN

There was going to be a moon. The growing lightness of the sky proclaimed it, and Costain's memory recalled it. It was a growing moon, about a quarter full. It would set early, but early or late, it couldn't bring anything but bad luck.

He was lying in a slight depression no more than a hundred yards from the church. He had no idea how long it had taken him to reach this position, but with the heavily overcoated police guard marching his short post no more than thirty feet from him, he wondered how he was ever going to leave it.

There were three alternatives. He could lie here until the moon came up and revealed him to the hunters. He could lie here and freeze to death. Or he could move. If he moved and was seen, he was done. If he moved and could reach that big fir beyond the guard, he might be able to climb up into it and wait until the moon set before he moved again.

The priest had wanted to give him a white cassock to put over his clothes to blend in with the snow. He'd been adamant in his refusal. Once he left the church they were never going to know that he'd been there or Father Paul had ever set eyes on him. Now he wished he had such a cassock, but not at the priest's expense.

They had said goodbye simply, standng in the darkened sacristy and shaking hands in farewell. He had heard the whispered blessing and detected the hand moving in the sign of the cross. When the door had opened the priest had stepped out, making plenty of noise.

He'd announced who he was and asked whether it was safe for him to go to his home in the village. As he had strode into the night to meet the approaching guard. Costain crawled out behind him and was lying against the side of the building before the door closed shut.

From that starting point, he'd made his way on his stomach, bare inches at a time, to this. Now he'd run smack into the first cordon of hunters. If he got past this line, there would undoubtedly be another on the ridge, and if they had enough men, perhaps even another beyond that.

He could see that the guard walked his post more to keep the circulation moving than for any other reason. He did not link up with his fellow hunters on either side although they were close enough for Costain to detect the silhouetted movement of both.

"The only thing you can do," he told himself, "is to backtrack to that boulder and then try to crawl between the two of them." Much as he hated to give up such hard-won ground, he could see no other possible course.

By the time he'd wormed his way to the boulder he was horrified at how light it had grown. The moon was going to rise right off that ridge any minute and spot-light him like a prima ballerina. He'd have to stay where he was and take his extremely dubious chances against this shrinking hunk of rock.

The sound of gurgling water came faintly to him and he recalled what the boy had told the priest. There were several little brooks running down from the ridge. They were actually no more than nature's shallow drainage ditches, vanishing in dry weather. They did, however, furrow the ground and might possibly aid him. He hadn't thought much of the idea of crawling on his belly in icy water. Added to the discomfort, he felt it would be noisy.

Now the gurgling suggested that the brook might be free of ice. It had been mild lately, and although it didn't feel mild where he lay, the water could be running freely. Its sound would help cover any noise he made. He decided it was worth investigating.

The course of the brook ran no more than two yards from where he lay. He had missed it in his first approach because it angled away sharply in the opposite direction. He found that its drainage-ditch description was accurate, wide enough to take his body, deep enough to conceal it, but not much more. The water, though only an inch or two deep where he touched it, was flowing strongly over a muddy bottom. There did not seem to be any solid ice … just liquid ice. This was going to be a bitch-kitty of an experiment!

It was not the temperature of the water that bothered him most. It was the effect his body had on its flow. Had it been any deeper, he'd have had to give it up or drown. As it was, he had to keep his head cocked back toward his shoulder in order to breathe. And it seemed that every movement forward was accompanied by a horrendous amount of noise.

By the time he judged he'd passed between the two guards, the moon had risen. Its glow reflected serenely on the water, but did nothing to warm its frigid texture. The front of his body, plus arms, shoulders and head were completely soaked; and although his clothing deadened the chill and his concentration on avoiding both noise and drowning kept his mind off bodily discomfort, he knew that it would be foolhardy to continue in this manner if he could possibly find another. The cold was sapping his strength. It was making him clumsy and careless. It was high time to stop trying to simulate an out-of-season salmon!

Costain eased his head above the bank of the brook. God! The moon on the snow had everything looking like midday! He could see clearly the two guards between whom he'd passed, and he could see the two on either side of them. The tree he'd hoped to reach was now too great a distance to attempt. Instead, he chose a tangled clump of gorse to outwait the moon. It was the only hiding place available to him unless he wanted to water-crawl his way another fifty yards to a thin screen of larches. The larches would have to come later.

He had just settled himself in amongst the field growth when he heard the dogs and a second later spotted the patrol as it crossed the ridge-line. There were a half dozen men in it, one of them holding in three leashed bloodhounds. He knew they were bloodhounds by their call. A roving patrol! If they went down by the church they'd pick up his trail. There was no telling how many of these groups were out hunting him. If they kept on their present course they'd go right past the tree where he'd planned to hide. Costain was aware of holding his breath, but it was impossible to still the trembling of his body.

The patrol and the guards exchanged a flurry of remarks about their lack of success. From the exchange, Costain learned that the patrol was returning to the village to take part in the next house-search. He wondered if this meant the outlying farms had already been searched, that the boy Peter would be free to head for the assigned meeting place. No matter how skillful a rabbit he was, he wouldn't be able to move far in this light without being observed. "Lisa," he said to himself, "maybe someday we'll have a little boy like that one ... Yes, and maybe nothing at all!"

It was a short while later that the fickle weather, which had appeared bent on exposing him, turned suddenly to his aid. Clouds moved in. First a few scattered patches to filter the moon. Then, the main body, a thick-meshed blanket to blot it out. It was raining steadily when he arose from the thicket. He voiced a silent prayer of thanks, and walking up the brook, so as to leave no trail, he made his way to the larches. He was positive they had no one positioned amongst the trees. The moon had helped him there, and now, though it was all covered up, enough of its light filtered through so as not to leave the night impenetrable.

Costain had his first encounter on the reverse side of the ridge. He'd crawled on his belly past a point where he thought the next line of SSB police would be patrolling. The land was much the same as the other side of the slope: open and rolling with scattered clumps of trees. He'd used one of these clumps to conceal himself as he went over the ridge. He lay listening ... heard nothing ... got to his feet cautiously ... saw movement! heard footsteps! knew he'd risen almost in the face of an approaching guard! He lashed out fiercely with instinctive reaction, slamming the butt of his pistol into the approacher's face. There was both the feel and sound of sickening impact. The policeman crashed to the ground and Costain went down on his knees following up his attack with a series of vicious, chopping blows. The guard's body jerked several times and went limp. His hands on the man, Costain felt the strap and stock of the light submachine gun. He had just started to disengage it from its unconscious owner when the deadly beam of a flash-light began to probe above his head. He froze.

"Felix, are you all right?" a harsh voice called.

"Of course, I'm all right!" Costain growled the words, muffling them in his hand. "Turn off that bloody light! Can't a man do his business!"

The light went out and the voice receded with a chuckle, "Better not let the lieutenant catch you with your pants down."

Costain lowered the pistol, exhaling a long trembling sigh. When he stood again, he was holding the sub-machine gun.

Peter had said there was a track of sorts with a ditch on either side, cutting across the field in the direction of the hills and the particular cliff area he must reach. Now he had to find that track.

He went on foot, slowly, pausing frequently, trying to peer through the darkness, trying to detect sound over the steady hissing of the rain.

He found the track, but the ditches—the boy and the priest had suggested he follow to where the track crossed the stream—were too muddy and water-filled for anything but quick cover. He'd move off a few yards and try to follow a parallel course. He had to force himself to go slowly. He was expecting any minute to hear the alarm signify the finding of the guard he'd struck down. When they found him, they'd know for sure the direction his assailant had headed. They'd close in fast, but he could not run! … not run! Step, and a step! … not run! … not yet, not until he came to the stream that would guide him to the cliffs. "There were cliffs when you first escaped," he reminded himself, "now there are cliffs at the end."

Off to his left he heard the barking of dogs. He stood still, waiting to see if he could determine the direction in which they were headed. And then another sound stopped his breathing. Someone close ahead sneezed … and then sneezed again.

There was no place to take cover, no trees, no brooks, no field growth, not even a good size rock; only a downward sloping field with its threadbare blanket of slushy snow to clearly mark the way he'd come. "It is like playing the children's game of 'Red Light,'" he thought crazily … "Take a step, wait … take another, wait … The dogs are coming closer … Slowly. Slowly, you bastard! … Oh, to be able to spot the sneezer. The sneezer was catching cold standing out in the wet night. Didn't he know enough to go in where it was warm and dry? … Warm and dry. Would he ever be warm and dry again? Certainly … when he was dead … The rain, the rain, was it trying to tell him something or was it mocking … The dogs were telling him something. They were coming right at him!"

He detected movement in the murk ahead. He took another two steps before he lay down. On the ground he could see the bulky silhouette of the guard, moving back and forth.

Cradling the submachine gun in his arms, Costain wiggled off on an angle, hoping to locate where the next man in line was stationed. Again he'd have to try and crawl between the two. The patrol with the dogs was going to pass in back of him, but if the dogs were any good, if they had anything to scent by, they'd pick up his trail as soon as they hit it. Now a new sound came to him, and it wasn't until he'd traveled another two yards that he was able to identify it. It was the stream he must intersect and follow.

When he reached its edge, he saw that it was a good ten feet wide; a healthy vigorous stream, coming down from the hills, they had said, snaking across the fields to join the river that divided the valley. They had thought he might consider wading up it. It appeared too deep for wading, and the two guards whose posts terminated on the opposite banks told him it was out of the question.

Suddenly over the stream's sound, and the falling rain's sound, down the breeze over all sound, Costain heard the hue and cry that meant the hunters had found their fallen comrade or picked up the quarry's trail. There were whistles, shouts, the accelerated yapping of dogs. There were powerful fingers of light, jabbing at the darkness.

"Sounds like they've got him!" Costain heard it said distinctly.

"Or that he's headed this way," came the thoughtful reply, accompanied by the soft "snick" of a weapon's safety being slipped off.

"Either way, I hope to hell so. All I want to do is get dry."

"Stand alert!" The repeated order came down the line.

There was only one thing he could do now, and there was no time to consider all the things against trying to do it. He pulled off his mackinaw, gulped several deep breaths in preparation, held the last, and steeled himself for the shock. He went slithering over the bank of the stream head first. Despite the insulating shielding of his clothing, and the fact that he was already wet, the water's coldness was so great and shocking, it nearly drove the air out of his lungs. He knew he had to swim at least 30 feet, and beneath its surface all the way. He let go of the gun and began to swim against the current. The weight of his water-logged clothing would help keep him down, but it also made it more difficult to swim. Jesus God, he couldn't fight this cold! ... He had to come up! ... Had to! ... Had to! ... Blackness and rocks! ... Damn the current! The calf of his right leg was beginning to cramp! He couldn't hold his breath another second!

Costain surfaced, sucked in a mouthful of air, and submerged again. He'd come up no more than a foot past the two guards. Had their attention not been centered toward the sound of pursuit, they would have seen him. He managed a half a dozen more strokes before he came up again. Numbly he hauled himself on to the bank. At once he felt amazingly warm. On hands and knees he covered another dozen yards. Then he stood up and ran.

The sounds of the hunt were swelling. There was an array of bobbing lights behind him. If there were lights ahead of him—He kept the stream on his right ... Must it always be like this! Was there never an end to running! Could it be that he was already dead and that this was his fate to run, and run, and run, until he lost track of even his own ability to comprehend! Like this morning ... Sanctuary! There was no one here to give him that. Lisa, you are my sanctuary, give me your hand.

He had gained the trees, fronting the escarpment when the frontier patrol, stationed on its top, heard him and gave the signal. No doubt, they had been waiting for just such a possibility.

Two broad-beamed searchlights cut down through the naked trees, their deadly swath seeking him out.

He ran in a crouch, trying to dodge the beams. Time and again he avoided them by flinging himself flat behind tree or boulder, but dimly he knew it couldn't go on. They were closing in fast from all sides, coming down the cliffs ahead.

He came up against a sharp projection in the cliff wall and stopped running. There was nowhere left to run, and now he stood at bay. The rays of the search lights raked the ground before him. "Why not step out into it? Give it up, Costain! Enough! ... Thou shalt not be afraid for the terror by night; nor the arrow that flieth by day ... a thousand shall fall at thy side, and ten thousand at thy right hand; but it shall not come nigh thee ..."

Costain took a step toward the light and felt something strike his leg. He turned and another object hit him in the side. It was a stone. He saw the blur of a small face and an arm waving. It seemed to be coming right out of the foot of the cliff only a few feet away. He plunged toward it, hearing the priest say, "Where the cliff juts out like the prow of a ship." This was the place!

He hit the ground, rolled over, and the boy's hands were on him, pulling him into what appeared to be a shallow overhang. As Costain squeezed and pushed himself inward, conglomerate sounds of the hunt, rushing in for the kill, echoed in his ears. Dumbly he realized the opening was too narrow for a man his size, and then all at once everything gave, and he fell through the cave entrance right on top of the boy.

Not really sure of what he was doing, Costain helped the boy get the rock slab into place to cover the deceptive entrance. Anyone viewing it from without would see an overhanging indentation at the bottom of the cliff and nothing more.

Costain fell down and lay in the pitch darkness and heard the muffled sounds of pursuit pass by. He thanked God and the boy in incoherent whispers.

Later, on hands and knees, he followed his rescuer down a corridor that emptied into a large high-vaulted stalagmited cavern. The boy had built a fire earlier and now he added wood to it from a neatly stacked supply.

"Peter," Costain said, laying his hands on the small shoulders, "I thank you for my life."

Peter nodded, his face serious in the dancing firelight. He touched the wet shirt and pointed at the fire.

"Right," Costain said, and began to strip off his clothes. The miracle of his still being alive overcame his physical condition. He felt buoyed up and excited. The priest had not been exaggerating. This was an escape route right under their noses, discovered by an amazing little explorer.

It was daybreak when Peter parted the heavy jumble of brush and Costain looked down on the Austrian countryside. Their arrival at this hour was not due to distance traveled. His small guide had insisted he stay by the fire and get some of his strength back before taking the underground trek. More than that, Peter preferred to arrive home by daylight.

Costain had wondered what the boy's mother and brothers would say if they knew what he was about—what he had risked this night—what might happen to him if he were picked up on his return. There was wisdom in not wanting to make that return before it was light. The hunters would be chasing themselves in circles, and even if they caught Peter on his return it was unlikely they would either molest or suspect a child of this size, supposedly prowling around for curiosity's sake.

The journey from the main cavern had been through a maze of tunnels and lesser caverns. Often they had to crawl, an electric torch lighting the way. Once they had to wade across a subterranean stream and he'd carried the boy piggyback.

"Peter, how is it possible to find your way?" he'd asked, and Peter had shown him the blaze marks he'd made at intervals.

"Son, the only thing you didn't think of was a magic carpet for us to ride on."

Now they had emerged from the darkness into the daylight, and it was over. The land rolled down through the thin line of trees to the valley, and there was a village nestled there. It might have been Vilivesko, but it wasn't. Costain stood with his arm around the boy's shoulder, drinking it in. The day would be clear and mild like yesterday, but not like yesterday, never again like yesterday, and all the yesterdays from Ostrava.

He knelt down and looked into the boy's marvelous eyes. The grin of mischief was there, the grin of life, of the spirit, of tomorrow. He took the boy into his arms, and the tears ran down his cheeks. He had no words. He held the boy, and the boy held him in return.

When he rose, the boy quickly brushed the tears from his own eyes and thrust out his hand, trying hard to grin. Costain took it and they shook hands like men, and then Costain turned away and started walking slowly down the hillside toward the little Austrian village.

CHAPTER NINETEEN

Costain stood by the window that looked out on the long lines of traffic moving homeward through the early evening. It was not yet dusk, yet the day's work was done and the workers were scurrying toward their leisure. Beyond, above the trees, he could see Washington's Monument shafting cleanly. Somehow, at this moment, he thought of it as a knife. There was a hint of spring in the air, but there was no such hint in himself, only a leaden wintry sense of defeat with the knife piercing right through him.

"You saved this for last," he said.

"I thought it best." The voice was gentle, calm, knowing.

Costain turned and took in the tired-eyed man seated behind the desk. He was a small man with a handsome thatch of white hair and a strong straight mouth.

"You wanted to soften the blow, is that it?"

"If you like, Mark. I wanted you to have nothing else on your mind when you talked to the people here and out at Wright-Patterson and Edwards."

"And what good did all the talking do?" He made no attempt to hide the bitterness. "I couldn't tell them anything they didn't already know ... the Aero-Morava design was nothing new to anyone here."

"Much of what you told them was of great importance, of great help. Everyone you talked to was most impressed with you.

In fact, I've had a number of queries as to whether you'd be able to accept a job."

Costain hardly heard him. "I ran for nothing … only to save my neck. I brought nothing new back to you … and I killed Jan Radek doing it."

"Nonsense!" the little man snapped with asperity. "I told you Radek had been under suspicion. He knew it. We knew it. No matter what you did, they would have gotten him."

"If I'd have stayed put—"

"They'd have gotten you, too."

"And then Jan wouldn't have gone and stuck his neck out in Olomouc."

The tired-eyed man made an impatient gesture. "He created the diversion to help you, yes. He knew that if he could get Krupina ousted, it would put things in a turmoil, and that would give you a better chance but, Mark, he also did it because he saw it as a chance to get rid of Krupina."

"I know! I know!" Costain said heatedly, "and all he did was to expose himself. If he knew they suspected him, why didn't he get out while the getting was good! I'll tell you why, because he knew I was in trouble and he stayed to try and help me!"

"That is absolutely one hundred percent untrue! He would never have left … He knew he had to find the traitor in his group … Besides, though you were never aware of it, between the two of you, you did get rid of Krupina."

"You think that's worth the exchange, Radek for Krupina?"

"Sit down and stop talking like a fool!" The little man's voice was scathingly incisive, the tired eyes glinted. He paused a moment, gazing at his hands spread on the desk in front of him. When he spoke again, his calmness had returned. "I know your ordeal has been a severe and taxing one … not just the running, but the living there for ten years. I know you're bitterly disappointed that the news you brought out is not of the magnitude you judged. But, Mark, the information you've been sending back over the years has been of great value. We'd never have left you there if we hadn't felt it so ... You've lost an old friend, and we have not only lost an old friend, but also an irreplaceable part of our apparatus ... Jan Radek knew what he was doing—just as you have known what you've been doing. You reacted in the only way you could. You couldn't have known what he was up to ... Need I remind you, Mark, that in a war you must expect casualties, and usually it's no one's fault, it's just damn bad luck."

Costain sighed. He knew the words made sense, yet they did nothing to sooth the sickness the news had brought. "You're sure they got him?"

"Yes ... Last communication we received was that you'd stolen the plane. He suggested that if you weren't caught, we let it be known you had escaped. They might call off the search, and if you were still alive, it would give you a better chance of getting out."

"He thought of everything, didn't he?"

"Pretty near."

"And how did they kill him?"

"It was quite a devastating stroke, typical Radek." The little man said it with a grim touch of a smile. "He knew they were going to arrest him on a Tuesday morning. They didn't know he knew. Monday evening he called a special meeting of all the Group Heads. He'd placed a time bomb under the conference table."

Costain stared at the floor, digesting the information. "For Godsake," he flared angrily, repeating the question, "if he knew and you knew, why didn't you get him out!"

"I said he wouldn't come ..."

Costain got up and walked restlessly to the window again. "Do you know he was probably the most hated man in the whole country?"

"He played the part well."

"What are you going to do about it?"

"Who and what he was, will become common knowledge ... everywhere. It was a terrible blow to them to learn that their Minister of Security was actually a key agent on our side."

"Epitaph for a hero," Costain indulged himself bitterly. "He was not a traitor, friends, but a poor foolish hero in an age where heroes have become passé ... We must keep the western star burning. He didn't know it had become a big glittering neon light ... soft, fat, rotten-ripe for the taking!"

There was no immediate reply while the little man busied himself filling his pipe. "In the time you've been gone," he said finally, "you think we've changed that much here?"

"I'm not a good person to ask that. My perspective is slightly warped, but my impression is, yes ... It was more than luck that got me here."

"I know, but what's that got to do with it?"

"I was thinking of all the help I had. People who live without freedom know a great deal more about what it is to be free than those who live with it ... and abuse it."

"Perhaps its one reason why the Soviets are so frightened ..."

The little man puffed his pipe thoughtfully, and changed the subject. "What are your plans now? Will you take a position with our aeronautical people?"

"I'll think about it ... First, I'm going to take a rest."

"Good. Any place in particular?"

"Europe."

"Tired of being home already?"

"Just tired."

"Mark, you wouldn't do anything foolhardy," the older man's eyes probed unblinkingly into his own.

Costain shook his head. "No ... I wouldn't do anything foolhardy."

On a starlit night near the end of March, Costain crossed the border and returned to the vicinity of Vilivesko. He took the same route by which he had escaped, thankful to Peter for the cavern's well defined blaze marks.

In the heavy darkness before dawn he passed the farmhouse where the boy lived and sent him a silent greeting, thinking it was a sound even his little friend's ears would not detect. He gave Vilivesko a wide berth, sorry he could not stop and pay his respects to Father Paul. He traveled in a careful though relaxed manner, properly dressed and outfitted for what lay ahead. He was going all the way on foot, keeping away from populated places, holing up during the day. He estimated his time of arrival as sometime on the third night.

It was near nine o'clock of a clear, sharp evening that he crested the hill, passed the line of firs, and saw the house with the ruined manor like a cliff-block towering behind. He knew his heart was pounding from far more than exertion.

There were lights in the windows and as he approached at a fast walk, the breeze brought him the delicate, lovely notes of the piano. She was playing. He had never heard her play before. He moved to the window and looked in at her where she sat, his fists clenched with excitement. He did not know the piece she was playing ... plaintive, lonely. The sight of her was a different kind of music. He'd change that sad melody. He'd make it sing!

Costain went to the door and raised the knocker, whispering her name.